THE BLUEST SKY

ALSO BY CHRISTINA DIAZ GONZALEZ

THE BLUEST SKY

CHRISTINA DIAZ GONZALEZ

ALFRED A. KNOPF
NEW YORK

THIS IS A BORZOI BOOK PUBLISHED BY ALFRED A. KNOPF

This is a work of fiction. Names, characters, places, and incidents either are the product of the author's imagination or are used fictitiously. Any resemblance to actual persons, living or dead, events, or locales is entirely coincidental.

Text copyright © 2022 by Christina Diaz Gonzalez
Jacket art copyright © 2022 by Edel Rodriguez

All rights reserved. Published in the United States by Alfred A. Knopf, an imprint of Random House Children's Books, a division of Penguin Random House LLC, New York.

Visit us on the Web! rhcbooks.com

Educators and librarians, for a variety of teaching tools, visit us at RHTeachersLibrarians.com

Library of Congress Cataloging-in-Publication Data is available upon request.
ISBN 978-0-593-37279-1 (trade) — ISBN 978-0-593-37280-7 (lib. bdg.) — ISBN 978-0-593-37281-4 (ebook)

The text of this book is set in 11.5-point Sabon MT Pro.
Interior design by Cathy Bobak

Printed in the United States of America
10 9 8 7 6 5 4 3 2 1
First Edition

For Papi . . . and his friends who were like brothers

THE PALM FRONDS rustled in the warm tropical breeze as I hunched down to take a sprinter's stance. My best friends lined up next to me. Our daily race was about to begin.

"Ready?" Teo asked, adjusting his grip on the schoolbooks nestled under his arm.

I nodded and looked over at Isabel, who was poised to take off as soon as I counted to three.

Ahead of us the cracks in the sidewalk fanned out like an intricate spiderweb, providing an extra challenge to our competition. We had to reach the lamppost at the end of the street without stepping on any of the jagged lines that crisscrossed our path.

I untucked my shirt, pushed up my eyeglasses, and waited for a few people to get out of the way.

Maybe this would be the day that I'd finally win, although I wasn't too optimistic. My wins were usually in math competitions. I'd never been fast like Teo or agile like Isabel, but that didn't stop me from trying to beat them . . . even if the statistical probability was extremely low.

"¡Uno . . . dos . . . y TRES!" I shouted, hopping over the first crack and sidestepping another. I ran as fast as I could, but was quickly left behind.

"I win!" Isabel announced, prancing around the lamppost with one arm in the air and the other still holding her books. "And I saw you both step on a bunch of the cracks." Her ponytail bounced around as she taunted us. "I should really try out for the Cuban track team because . . . ¡Soy la campeona!"

"Ooh, you better write down the date," Teo scoffed. "April 16, 1980 . . . the *one* day you win. But we all know who the overall champion is." His smile showed off his chipped front tooth. "Me. Your older and wiser brother. The one who beat you from day one."

"Here we go," I muttered.

"Ugh." Isabel rolled her eyes and held up two fingers. "Dos minutos. You were born two minutes before me and I have to hear about it for the rest of my life. And you are definitely not the wiser one." She paused to look at me. "Right, Héctor?"

I laughed. It was the same back-and-forth almost every day. For twins, the two of them couldn't be more different. Isabel was short, fair-skinned with dark curly hair, and her personality was like a stick of dynamite . . . explosive at any moment. Teo, on the other hand, was the biggest kid in the entire sixth grade, but he hated fighting or any type of confrontation . . . except with his sister. And he didn't look much like Isabel either. In fact, some people thought Teo and I were the twins because we were always together and we both had tan skin, wavy brown hair, and similar noses. The only huge difference between us was our size.

"Héctor," Isabel prodded. "Back me up."

I shook my head. "No me meto." She wasn't going to get me involved in their pretend fight. I'd seen this play out several times where it was all a joke until someone took the teasing too far and then it became a real argument.

"Boys, ugh!" Isabel threw her hands up in mock disgust. "Why do I hang out with the two of you?"

"Because you have good taste!" I flashed her my biggest grin. "And we all know who the wisest is. . . ."

"ME!" the three of us shouted at the same time, then doubled over laughing. That settled, we continued our trek home.

As we rounded the corner, Isabel kept on about her victory. She figured that Teo's bigger size was slowing him down and that she would soon be the overall champ. I was about to suggest creating an equation that might calculate the size-to-velocity ratio when Teo reached his breaking point.

"All right, that's it." Teo dropped his books onto the sidewalk in front of a yellow-colored house that had patches of peeling paint. "I'll race you around the block, right now. First one to come back and tag Héctor wins."

"Nah." She smiled, knowing she'd finally gotten under his skin. "One win per day is enough for me."

"Chicken?" Teo challenged.

I leaned against the short white wall that bordered the house's front yard. There was no way Isabel was going to back down from her brother calling her out.

"¡Vamos!" Isabel spun around and thrust her books into my chest. "Héctor, hold my stuff and count us off."

I gave Teo a slight nod and he understood what I was about to do.

"¡Uno, dos y tres!" I said quickly, not giving Isabel any prep time while Teo took off running.

"¡Tramposos!" Isabel yelled as she chased after her brother, and I laughed at them as they headed down the street. "You're both cheaters!"

As they disappeared around the corner, I took a deep breath. I could almost catch a hint of salt air in the wind, even though we were miles from the coast. I wished it were already summer so we could ride our bikes down to the beach to go for a swim. Technically, we could go now, but every Cuban knew the water was best in months that didn't have an *r*, no matter how nice the weather was.

That meant there were only a few weeks left until my skinny, count-all-my-ribs body would be seen next to Teo's gargantuan frame.

I glanced over at my shadow on the stretch of white wall.

The dark silhouette made me look even longer and skinnier than I already was.

"Kleto," I mumbled to myself. It was the nickname my older brother, Rodrigo, had taken to calling me lately. It was his own slang, which was supposed to be short for *skeleton*. I pretended it didn't bother me, but it did. I wanted to have muscles, even tiny ones, and not just be skin and bones.

The elongated shadow on the wall seemed to taunt me. I narrowed my eyes and stuck out my tongue.

"¿Qué tú haces?" a voice called out.

I glanced over at a boy standing in the house's doorway. He wasn't very tall, but he was stocky, and as he stepped into the sunlight, I recognized him as one of the older kids from my school. People called him Tincho, and it was rumored that he had failed eighth grade twice because of cheating and fighting. He was someone I knew to steer clear of.

"Me? I'm not doing anything, just waiting for my friends," I explained, adjusting my eyeglasses.

"I saw you sticking your tongue out at my house. . . . You think you're better than us or something?" Tincho took a few more steps onto his front porch as a mangy-looking dog snuck out from behind his legs and growled at me.

"No, that was just me goofing around with my shadow." I sounded like an idiot, but this was not the time to be cool. Besides, his house didn't look bad. It was like most buildings . . . patched up with whatever people could find.

Tincho squinted as he studied me. "Wait . . . I know you. You're Rodrigo's little brother." He headed toward me. "Which means I know who your father is."

My pulse quickened. He seemed bigger than when I saw him from far away in school and had a hardened expression, like he was looking for trouble.

"Tu papá es un gusano," Tincho declared, pushing open the small front gate and walking out into the street.

Gusano. Worm. It was a word charged with meaning. It was an insult reserved for those who opposed the government. And opposing the government, or even expressing anti-revolutionary ideas, could mean losing everything. Your home, friends, job, and even your freedom could all disappear.

"Isn't that true?" Tincho persisted, getting closer to me. "He's a traitor, which probably makes you one, too."

"No, you've got it wrong," I said, backing away and getting ready to run. "You have me confused with someone else."

I wanted to defend my father, but I had to play it smart. It was something my mother had taught my brother and me from the very beginning. There was what we believed in private and what we said in public. Two versions of who we were.

"Liar." Tincho poked me in the chest. "I'm not confused."

"What's . . . going . . . on?" Teo said, pulling up to the scene a little short of breath, with Isabel only a few feet behind him.

"Nothing," I said, trying to defuse the situation. I had wanted to run away, but now I didn't want to seem like a coward in front of my friends. "Everything's fine."

"You know this gusano?" Tincho asked as he sized up Teo.

"Who are you calling a gusano?" Isabel pushed her way in between me and Tincho, standing right under Tincho's nose.

Tincho chuckled. "Tranquila, compañera." He sidestepped Isabel and kept an eye on Teo. "But you should know who you're hanging out with."

"I know who he is," Teo replied, his voice flat. "But you must not."

"Yeah," I added, trying to make my presence felt. "We've been friends since . . ."

Teo shot me a look that said it all. I needed to shut up.

"Well, do you know that his father is a traitor? My parents told me about him. He's just like those scumbags hiding out in the Peruvian embassy . . . trash-talking our country and trying to leave Cuba." Tincho turned to glare at me. "I heard your father was in prison for spreading lies about the revolution, until a few months ago when they kicked him out to go be with the rest of the escoria in the U.S." Tincho spit at my feet, barely missing my shoes. "That's what I think of you and your family, gusano."

I froze for a moment, not sure how to react. My father hadn't been spreading lies about the revolution, but he had been saying something much worse . . . the truth.

Mamá told us he just wanted more freedom. Freedom to voice his opinion, freedom to go where he wanted, freedom to choose what kind of life his family should have. But it was the truth about this lack of freedoms that got him into so much trouble that he did end up in prison.

"No, you don't understand." I took a deep breath and tried to push aside the feeling of disgust for what I was about to do. This was simply part of surviving, I told myself. "You're right that my father is a filthy gusano, but *I* don't agree with anything he's done. I love Cuba. I believe in the revolution . . . in Fidel." I raised my fist in the air to add more significance. "¡Que viva la revolución!"

Tincho scoffed. "I don't believe you. Like father, like son." He stepped closer, so that I could now smell his rancid breath as he breathed down on me. "Your brother is scum, too."

"No, i-i-it's true," I stammered, inching back until I was up against the short wall. "I'm nothing like my father. He's—"

"¡Basta! ¡Vete de aquí!" Isabel shoved Tincho as hard as she could, causing him to stumble sideways. She looked defiant standing between the two of us again. "I said GO!"

"Why, you little—" Tincho said through clenched teeth.

"Isabel!" Teo scolded his sister.

I pulled Isabel away. Things had gone from bad to worse. I had to fix it.

"Listen, Tincho," I said in the most soothing voice I could muster. "I'm not—"

I couldn't even finish my thought.

Tincho had already cocked his arm back and his fist was flying through the air. I swerved backward trying to avoid it, but I wasn't fast enough. The edge of his balled-up hand caught me on the mouth and the impact dropped me to my knees, my glasses flying off my face.

"¡Idiota!" Teo yelled at Tincho. "Don't you know who you just hit?"

"A traitor?" Tincho scoffed.

Teo pointed to me on the floor. "He's Marcela Fulgeira's grandson. Recognize the name?"

"Huh?" Tincho looked confused.

"She's the delegate to the National Assembly!"

"¿La Asamblea Nacional?" Tincho repeated, beginning to understand my family connections.

"Hey, Tincho!" A couple of girls from across the street had come outside to see what was happening. "¿Todo bien?"

Teo ignored them and continued directing all his attention at Tincho. "Do you know what kind of trouble his grandmother can bring on you and your family?"

"I . . . um . . ." Tincho shifted his weight from one leg to another.

All I could do was stare at Tincho's hairy knees, the metallic taste of blood in my mouth. I hated hiding behind my grandmother's name. It usually offset my father's legacy and kept our family safe, but suddenly I wasn't thinking about keeping up appearances anymore. I didn't care about being seen as a loyal Communist. I wanted revenge.

I wrapped my arms around Tincho's legs and knocked him to the ground. Before I could land a punch, Teo yanked me up by my collar and pulled me away.

"Enough!" Teo stretched out his arms to prevent anyone from moving as the girls across the street laughed. "Tincho . . .

go home. I know you don't want problems with Delegada Fulgeira . . . Héctor's grandmother . . . *right*?" He stared at Tincho, who had stood up again.

Tincho glanced over at the girls, then back at me. He slowly nodded, but his eyes were full of hate.

"All right, then, this is over. No one mentions anything about this . . . to anyone." He stared at me and Tincho. "Now, shake hands and no more talk about anyone being a gusano."

I wiped my mouth with the back of my hand and saw a smear of blood. My lip was busted. I'd have to come up with a story to explain this to my mom.

"You okay?" Isabel asked, handing me my glasses.

"Yeah," I muttered as Tincho extended his hand.

I went to shake it when he pulled me closer. He lowered his head so that I could feel his putrid breath blow past my ear. "Watch your back, gusano," he whispered. "There won't always be people to protect you."

A shiver ran down my spine.

Life in Cuba hadn't been easy before, but I had a feeling it was about to get a whole lot harder. The odds of avoiding Tincho in the future were not in my favor.

2

"**STICK TO THE STORY,**" Isabel warned as we walked down our street on the outskirts of Havana. "If my mother asks, you say that you tripped and fell while we raced. Keep it simple."

I nodded, pressing my school uniform's red kerchief against my lip to stop any further bleeding. We'd decided I should take refuge at their house until the swelling of my lip went down. I'd lived across the street from them all my life, and their house felt as much like home as my own.

"And don't bother explaining anything to Nani if she asks about it," Teo added as we walked up to the front porch, where their great-grandmother was sitting in her rocking chair looking up at the sky.

I had already figured as much. Nani spent most of her days confused as to who we were or even what year it was. She often thought Teo was her son, Teo's grandfather, who had moved to the countryside several years ago.

"Oh, and watch out for the new loose brick on the steps."
Teo pointed down while hopping over it. "The porch is falling apart like everything else." He walked over to Nani. "Hola, Nani," he said, giving the old woman a quick kiss on her wrinkled cheek.

"¡Pablo! Estás tarde," she said, looking at Teo but calling him by his grandfather's name.

"No, Nani. I'm Teo. Abuelo Pablo moved away a few years ago," Teo explained.

"Ah, sí. I remember. He's living with Charo." She smiled and pointed to Isabel. "And who is she again?" she whispered.

"Soy Isabel, Nani." Isabel gave her a quick peck on the forehead, pushing away the wisps of short white hair. "Your great-granddaughter."

"¡Claro!" Nani proclaimed. "I know that!" She then stretched open her arms while looking at me. "You come here, too."

I dutifully bent down and gave her a kiss on the cheek. "Buenas, Nani."

"Watch out for the dragons!" she said, resuming her patrol of the sky. "They've been all around here today."

I tried to hold back a laugh as Teo shook his head. It was such a Nani thing to say.

"Let me make sure that the coast is clear." Isabel opened the front door and peered inside. "Okay, let's go."

The three of us rushed straight to the kitchen in the back of the house.

"I'll get you some ice," Isabel said, opening the freezer door while Teo ushered me over to the sink.

"Is it bad?" I asked, pulling my bottom lip out with my hands.

"Nah." Teo took a quick look at it. "It's not even bleeding anymore. But it's pretty swollen. You need to put some ice on it."

"You guys know that back there, with Tincho . . . what I said about my dad . . ." I grimaced, replaying the whole episode in my head as Isabel wrapped an ice cube in a checkered dish towel. "I don't think he's—"

"We know," Teo interrupted. "You can't afford to be lumped in with your dad . . . especially with the Math Olympiad around the corner." He put a hand on my shoulder. "We get it."

"Here!" Isabel handed me the dish towel with the ice cube. "Put this—"

We all grew quiet as the sound of heels clicking against the tiled floor outside the kitchen grew louder. Teo and Isabel's mom was coming in. I quickly turned around and pretended to look out the window over the sink.

"Qué silencio," she said as she came into the room. "It feels like a funeral in here."

I gave a fake laugh but kept my back to her as if I were engrossed by something outside.

"It's been a long day, Mami," Isabel replied, giving her mother a light kiss. "You know what would help? Something sweet to eat. Do we have any of that mamey left over from last night?"

"Oh, I think I ate the last of it this morning," Teo answered, walking over to give his mother a quick peck on the cheek.

"Not quite," their mother replied in an upbeat tone.

That was one thing you could always rely on—their mother was a naturally cheerful person. I'd never seen her in a bad mood, though Teo and Isabel swore she got mad at them sometimes. I still couldn't imagine her losing her temper.

"I saved some for the three of you to eat as a snack," she continued. "Héctor, I keep meaning to tell your mother that one of Evelio's students has a family farm out in the countryside. The parents traded fresh fruit and vegetables with us for a little extra tutoring, and they'll likely trade for other things, too. It's a good resource to have. We just have to be discreet about it."

"Mm-hmm," I said, peering over my shoulder as she pulled a plate out of the refrigerator. My family was lucky because my grandmother could usually get us a bunch of extra stuff outside of our government rations, but most people had to either buy things on the black market for ridiculously high prices or trade for them, even for something as simple as fruit. It was all against the law, but everyone secretly did it.

"Ven, Héctor." Teo's mother motioned for me to follow her to the table. "There can't be anything that interesting outside. Have some mamey. I already have it cut up."

I glanced over at the dish towel that I'd left next to the sink. There was no blood on it, so maybe she wouldn't notice anything if I kept my head low.

"Um . . . gracias." I approached the table and sat down, staring at the placemat with the embroidered lemons along the edge.

"I'm just surprised one of you scavengers didn't find the plate when you first came—" She gasped as she finally looked over at me. "Héctor! Your lip!"

Without thinking, I touched my mouth as if I'd been unaware that anything was wrong.

"It's not too bad," Teo explained. "Just a little cut."

"Teo's right," I added as his mother rushed over to inspect me. "It doesn't really hurt."

"Uh-huh." She was now holding my chin and tilting my head up. "And how did this happen?"

"He fell," Isabel stated matter-of-factly while sucking some of the mamey's juice from her fingertips. "No big deal."

"¿Te caíste?" their mother repeated while looking straight into my eyes. "And exactly *how* did you fall?"

I squirmed a little under her stare. Isabel was right. Her mother would have made a great interrogator for the Cuban government.

"We were racing," Isabel said as she reached for another chunk of the cut-up mamey. "Next thing you know . . . boom! Héctor was on the ground."

"Is that so?" She kept a watchful eye on all of us.

"Yep." I nodded.

Technically, Isabel hadn't lied. We were just omitting a few facts.

"Well, keep some ice on it and when you're done eating, dab a little bit of honey on the cut. It'll help it heal quicker."

"Um, if I do all that . . . how long before my lip goes back to normal?" I asked her.

"Probably a day or two." She gave me the side-eye as she pushed open the kitchen door. "Your mother will definitely notice."

"Oh." I took a deep breath. My mother was even better at interrogating me. I'd have to be more convincing. Or avoid seeing her.

"You think Héctor can have dinner with us tonight?" Teo asked as if reading my mind. "He's going to help me with some math homework."

"Héctor is always welcome here." She gave me a little wink. "You know this is your second home."

"Gracias," I said as she left the kitchen.

None of us spoke for about a minute . . . just to make sure she was gone.

Finally, Isabel threw her head back and smiled. "Well, that went better than expected."

"I'm not so sure," I countered. "She knows something is up."

"But she doesn't care enough to really question you," Teo said, taking the biggest piece of mamey and popping it into his mouth. "*That's* what counts," he continued, a little bit of the fruit dripping out of the corner of his mouth before he pushed it back in with his fingers. "And now you can stay here and avoid having your mom see your fat lip."

"I guess." I was starting to feel a little better. "I'll run over and tell Rodrigo that I'm eating here. He can tell my mom when she gets home from work."

"I can do that for you," Isabel offered.

Teo raised his eyebrows and smirked. "Oh, really? Is it because you want to be helpful or"—he batted his eyelashes and cupped his hands under his chin—"because you want an excuse to see Rodrigo?" He gave me a wink.

"You're an idiot, Teo." Isabel pushed the chair back and stood up. "Now I won't help at all. Hopefully, Rodrigo doesn't see Héctor's lip and go squeal to his mother. But if he does, it'll be your fault."

She stormed out of the kitchen as I tried not to laugh.

"She definitely likes Rodrigo," Teo snickered.

"Oh yeah." I smiled. "But *why* she likes him . . . *that* is a mystery."

"Speaking of mysteries, I'm still trying to figure out how Havana's baseball team made those plays Saturday. They've got one of the worst records in the league and yet Jorge Beltrán *and* Rey Vicente Anglada hit grand slams *in the same inning*." Teo pushed the plate, with the last two pieces of mamey, toward me. "What are the chances?"

I gingerly placed a piece in my mouth, letting the sweetness overpower my taste buds. It was like a little slice of heaven. I quickly grabbed the last piece before Teo changed his mind and ate it.

"Actually," I answered with my mouth full, "it's a statistical anomaly. That's why it's never happened before. I was trying to calculate the odds and there's an equation—"

"Por favor." Teo covered his ears. "We're not in school."

"Fine," I relented, going back to a subject he did like. "Did you see how the Santiago de Cuba team is doing? I think they're going to take it all this year. They're on fire."

"No way!" Teo shook his head. "My boys on Villa Clara will make a run for the championship."

"Estás loco." I rolled my eyes at the suggestion.

"Really? Want to make a bet?" Teo's eyes twinkled. "Put up that 1953 Miñoso card if you believe in your team so much."

"Ha!" I laughed at such a feeble attempt to get me to put my favorite baseball card at risk. It was a relic, like so many things left over from the time before the revolution. "Nice try. You should know by now that I'm never giving up that card. Unless you want to offer that Mickey Mantle card of yours—"

"Hey, nothing left for me?" Teo's dad sauntered into the kitchen. "¿Se lo comieron todo?" He sounded shocked that we'd eaten the whole plate of fruit.

I shrugged, knowing that he was only teasing us.

"Guess my two growing boys need it more than I do." He smiled, put his hands on Teo's shoulders, and gave him a kiss on the top of his head. He looked across the table at me with my fat lip, but didn't say anything about it. "Héctor, how about I challenge you to a chess match tonight . . . after you help Teo with his math."

Obviously, Teo's mother had already given her husband the lowdown. "I'll definitely accept that challenge," I said, knowing that even though Teo's father had taught me how to play, I was the one winning more games lately. "And his math homework isn't too difficult," I explained. "It won't take long."

"Might be easy for you, Mr. Math Wizard," Teo teased as his dad walked over to get a glass from the cupboard. "But at least I can say that Cuba's next Math Olympiad legend is my homework buddy."

"Um . . . I haven't even made the team," I reminded him. "I'm far from being a legend."

"And how are things going in the International Math Olympiad world?" Teo's dad asked, taking out the pitcher of water from the refrigerator. "I heard that with Russia pulling out this year, the competition might get canceled."

"Yeah, looks that way. But that gives me another year to get even better. My teachers think I have a really good chance to make the team and represent Cuba." I sighed. "We'll see."

"Well, in my experience, teachers are usually pretty smart

and astute at recognizing talent." Teo's dad smiled as he poured himself some water. "I'd listen to them."

Teo rolled his eyes. "Yeah, you *would* say that."

I grinned. Teo's dad was a high school literature and music teacher . . . a fact that Teo hated. He dreaded the day that his father might become his teacher.

"How do you put up with someone that is so malcriado?" Teo's father asked me with a big grin on his face. "He must be spoiled to the core by overindulging parents."

"Yeah, sometimes I wonder how I do it, too," I said. "I must have the patience of a saint."

"HEY!" Teo threw his hands up in the air. "Why are you two ganging up on me? You'd think I was one of those guys in the embassy that everyone hates."

"Ay, los pobres." Teo's dad shook his head and pulled up a chair. I could tell that we were about to have one of our kitchen-table chats. "I heard they were starving over there. Can you imagine ten thousand people crammed into that small area with no food and no bathrooms . . . all wanting asylum to get out of Cuba? It's a disaster." He shook his head. "I'm pretty sure Fidel hasn't faced anything like this from his own people in the twenty years since the revolution."

I loved when Teo's dad talked to us like adults. He was one of the smartest people I knew, and he always encouraged me to ask questions. No subject was off-limits, even topics surrounding Fidel Castro and the Communist revolution.

"Well . . ." I leaned across the table. "I overheard one of our teachers say that a lot of the women and families who were hiding out in the embassy were choosing to go home again," I said, offering up some possibly new information. "She said that Fidel was going to give them exit visas if some country would take them. Do you think that's true?"

Teo's dad shrugged. "Maybe." He took a sip of water. "The powers that be may be thinking that's a quick way to get rid of the problem with those people, but think of the Pandora's box they'd be opening. Other people might think that they can actually voice their opinions without fear of being tossed in jail. And when the government clamps down on them, like they always do, more people might demand to leave, and then what happens? The government could lose all control. There could be hundreds of thousands wanting to go." Teo's dad pursed his lips. "Fidel won't risk that, so I have a feeling it won't happen."

"Yeah . . ." Teo had a faraway look in his eyes. "But imagine if we could go anywhere we wanted . . . wouldn't that be amazing?"

Teo's dad smiled. "Mi hijo, the dreamer."

Teo crossed his arms across his chest. "It could happen. Right, Héctor?"

"Um, I have to agree with your dad, Teo." I sighed. "Just look what they did to my father when he tried to leave. I mean, they labeled him an anti-revolutionary and sentenced him to nine years in prison . . . all for trying to escape on a raft."

Teo's dad gave me a sympathetic look. He knew the story as well as I did . . . maybe even better than me, considering I was only five when it happened and he had a ringside seat to it all. But he had always confirmed most of what my mother had told me . . . that it was much more complicated than Papá just wanting to go to the U.S. The short version was that Papá was too outspoken about the lack of freedoms in Cuba and had paid the consequences for it. In fact, he'd still be in prison if the Cuban government hadn't sent him to the U.S. a few months ago as part of some political exchange.

"And speaking of your father, have you heard if he's doing all right now that he's in Miami?" Teo's dad asked.

I shrugged. "I guess he's fine. Working in a factory or something." I thought about the one brief conversation I'd had with him a few months back when he first arrived in Miami. Mamá had taken us to someone's house to place the call because she didn't want any government officials to listen to our phone line at home. "I haven't really talked to him much," I added, staring down at my hands.

"I see." Teo's dad reached across the table and rested his hand on my arm. "You know, even though I'm sure that he's glad to be out of prison, I bet he wishes he could've seen you before leaving. Probably misses you now more than ever."

"Uh-huh," I muttered. Mamá insisted that Papá still wanted us to be together, but I had my doubts. Then again, I didn't really know him. I hadn't seen him in years, since he wasn't allowed visitors in jail, and my only real memory was of him giving me piggyback rides when I was about four. The rest were shards of memories, spliced together by whatever Mamá told me. But still, I wondered about him and what he was really like. I was torn between being curious, resenting him for making our lives more difficult, and wishing I could have a father like Teo's, who I could see every day.

"Living in the U.S.," Teo said wistfully. "Can you imagine how cool that would be?"

"*Teo.*" Teo's dad had a stern tone in his voice as he leaned back in his chair. "Living somewhere 'cool' has nothing to do with why Héctor's father wanted to leave. He wanted freedom. Which is a reminder—we speak freely here, around this table, but nowhere else. Our conversations could be . . . misconstrued." He shifted his gaze to me, then back to Teo. "Not a word to anyone else of what is said. No one. Understood?"

"I know, I know." Teo didn't look happy at being scolded. "But I can still dream, right? Wouldn't it be amazing to live somewhere else," he mused. "A big city, like New York or Chicago, maybe."

"Meh." I shrugged. "Bigger isn't better. Personally, I like it here. Plus, they don't have palm trees or beaches. The pictures I've seen make it look really cold, with gray skies."

"Well, what about Miami? It has beaches like us," Teo countered. "And I bet it's as nice as it is here. Maybe even nicer."

"No way," I argued. "Cuba has the best beaches with the

clearest water and the bluest sky. Everyone knows that." I looked at Teo's dad to back me up. "Isn't that right?"

Teo's dad shrugged. "Oh, I don't know. I'd have to see it for myself to decide, because when it comes to love . . . the eyes only see what the heart reveals." He began to chuckle. "Which explains why Sara still thinks I'm handsome."

"Huh?"

Teo rolled his eyes. "That's just his fancy way of saying that love is blind."

"And that choosing which place is best can be a matter of perspective," he elaborated. "It depends on what it is that your heart desires."

"Isabel would agree with that." Teo snickered and gave me a little nudge. "We know what, or who, her heart desires."

"¿Qué?" Teo's father widened his eyes.

"Teo!" I slapped him on the arm.

"What?" Teo chuckled. "It's obvious to everyone that she likes Rodrigo."

Teo's dad's face grew more serious.

"Teo is just teasing Isabel about it. There's nothing there," I said, trying to clear things up. "Rodrigo thinks we're *all* annoying pests."

"I see." Teo's father didn't seem convinced as he stood up and put his glass in the sink. "It may be time to have a little talk with Isabel. Set some rules about boys."

Teo's jaw dropped as he suddenly realized what he'd done.

"No, Papi. Por favor," Teo pleaded. "Don't do that. I was just kidding around."

"Uh-huh," Teo's dad mumbled as he left the room.

Teo had a panicked look on his face.

This was not going to go well. He had crossed a line and Isabel was going to explode.

One hundred percent probability.

3

THE NEXT DAY no one at school seemed to notice my slightly swollen lip. I had already managed to convince my mom that I'd simply tripped while racing Teo, and I was prepared to keep up the lie if anyone asked. Given my history of being clumsy and uncoordinated, it was certainly plausible enough. The only one who I had to be on the lookout for was Tincho, but our paths rarely crossed . . . lucky for me.

I glanced at the clock on the wall over the chalkboard.

Señora Andrade was rarely late for our after-school tutoring sessions. She was the eighth-grade algebra teacher who had "discovered" my talent for numbers a couple of years ago. She introduced me to the world of advanced math, where things seemed to just make sense for me. I loved that every problem had a solution, but that there was creativity with how to solve it. Señora Andrade had encouraged me to enter youth math competitions, and when I missed making the cut for the province's math team last year by only a few points, she offered to help me better prepare this year. That was how our weekly tutoring sessions had begun and how the dream of going to the International Math Olympiad started to seem like a real possibility.

I took out several pencils and walked over to the sharpener by the door. Turning the metal crank, I could smell the woody scent of the shavings as I made sure each pencil had as sharp a point as possible.

"Perdona la demora, Héctor," Señora Andrade said, rushing in from the hallway. "We had a teacher's meeting with the principal that took much longer than I expected." She walked over to her desk and dropped her purse inside one of the drawers. "I came as quickly as I could to make sure you didn't leave." She fanned herself with one of the empty folders on her desk. Her dark skin glistened, and I could see little beads of sweat along her hairline.

"Oh, I wouldn't leave," I said, taking a seat in front of her desk. "I appreciate everything you're doing. I'd wait an hour or more if I had to."

She smiled, her eyes lighting up. "I also brought you these. . . ." She tapped a stack of math books on the corner of her desk. "They're from my personal collection. I want you to have them."

"Gracias," I said, not having expected to get a gift. "But I can just borrow and—"

"No." She raised a finger to cut me off. "They're yours. It's not every day that one of our students has the chance to make the national math team. In fact, I think you might be the school's first."

I nodded. I'd looked this up months ago. No one from our town had ever qualified. I'd be making history.

She looked down at the papers on her desk. "So, now on to business. I graded the practice tests you did over the weekend and it seems like you were struggling with decomposing the polynomials with real coefficients." She grabbed a piece of chalk and began writing an equation on the blackboard. "Cuba presented a similar problem in 1973 as its submission for the Olympiad, so it'll likely be on any qualifying test."

I began to copy the equation from the board, my mind focused on spotting the best way to get to the right answer. Señora Andrade always said the key was in finding the simplest, most straightforward path.

We were both completely immersed in a discussion on coefficients when the school secretary, Señora Salazar, poked her head into the room and cleared her throat to get our attention.

"Disculpa la interrupción"—she walked toward Señora Andrade with a paper in her hand—"but you left the meeting without signing the declaration."

"Oh, I must've forgotten." Señora Andrade quickly took out a pen from her desk.

"Mm-hmm." Señora Salazar eyed me suspiciously while Señora Andrade signed the document. "Just remember to keep your eyes and ears open as Señor Linares instructed. It's the responsibility of all teachers."

"Claro." Señora Andrade handed back the paper. "We have a duty to our country." She had a tight smile as she pointed over at me. "Speaking of which, Héctor here is a very gifted math student and could represent our country in competitions worldwide. He'll make all of Cuba proud."

"Hmph." Señora Salazar didn't seem very impressed as she stared at the blackboard with all the algebraic expressions. "Cada loco con su tema. All that high-level math just seems like a bunch of gibberish." She scrunched her nose as if disgusted by the sight of it. "It doesn't help the average person."

Señora Andrade and I exchanged glances. "All that high-level math" was the key to coming up with new inventions and solving economic problems . . . even if a lot of people didn't understand it.

"It's actually much more beneficial than you can imagine, in science and engineering, so many things," Señora Andrade replied, picking up the chalk and going back to the blackboard. "You're welcome to stay and listen for a while."

I looked away to hide the grin on my face. There was no way Señora Salazar would want to stay. It was just an effective ploy to get her to leave.

"No thank you," Señora Salazar huffed, walking out of the room. "I have my own work to do in the office."

Once we were alone again, Señora Andrade's face immediately transformed into one of concern.

"Is everything okay?" I asked.

"Yes, of course." She smiled, but I could tell it wasn't sincere. "It's just . . ." Her eyes went to the window and she gazed out at the school courtyard before turning her attention back to me. "You're a gifted student, Héctor, but there is more to making the team than just passing the test." She pursed her lips. "Members need to epitomize the ideals of the revolution. Any type of stain on a student's record could disqualify them."

"Oh," I replied quietly. My father was gone and yet his actions were always haunting me.

"Your grandmother will carry a lot of weight, though. You should speak to her about the Olympiad. She may be able to smooth things over with the selection committee if there ever were to be an issue. . . ."

"Uh-huh," I muttered, staring at all the equations I'd written down in my notebook. There wasn't a solution to being labeled a traitor.

"I'm not saying that you *will* have issues. I just want you to be protected in case there are any concerns in the future." She paused and I looked up at her, our eyes locking. "Héctor, everything is becoming more scrutinized nowadays. The government doesn't want to be humiliated with a defection from any national team." She looked at me intently. "You have to be careful. We all do. No one can afford to have anything . . . misconstrued."

Misconstrued. It was the same thing Teo's dad had said. I nodded silently.

"You know why I'm telling you all this?" Her voice got quieter as she came closer to me. "Because I believe that you're going to pass the tests with flying colors." Her face perked up and she flashed me a big, genuine smile. "You're going to be Cuba's next math star! Right?"

"Sí, señora," I answered, rolling back my shoulders as if I were a soldier accepting my orders. "I'm going to follow my dreams."

"No," she countered. "Make your dreams follow you."

By the time I was done with my session with Señora Andrade, the sun was already setting and there were pink and purple streaks in the sky. I had the reassuring weight of my new math books in my arms, and I was determined that nothing would derail my plans for the math team. I'd decided to devote at least two hours every day to improving my math skills . . . maybe more on the weekends.

As soon as I walked into my house, I could smell that Mamá was cooking something good. The aroma of garlic and onions was enough to make my mouth water, so I dropped my books on the dining room table and headed straight for the kitchen.

"Hola, Mamá," I said, giving her a quick kiss on the cheek. "What's for dinner?"

"Picadillo," she answered, turning down the heat on the stove. "I'll make the rice in a little bit unless you're hungry now."

"Nah." I sat down on one of the vinyl chairs by the small kitchen table. "How was work?

"Lo mismo que siempre," she answered. "The life of a bookkeeper doesn't change much." She glanced over her shoulder at me. "How was school?"

"Fine," I said, watching as she opened a jar of olives and tossed a few into the ground beef that was cooking. "Señora Andrade thinks I'm making good progress," I said. "She even gave me some of her books."

"That's nice of her," Mamá murmured, placing the skillet on a different burner and shutting off the heat. She turned to face me, wiping her hands on her apron. "Can you have your brother come in here? I want to talk to the two of you about some things."

"RODRIGO!" I yelled at the top of my lungs. "MAMÁ WANTS YOU IN THE KITCHEN!"

Mamá put her hands on her hips and shot me a look. "I could have done that," she said.

I shrugged as Rodrigo walked in.

"¿Qué pasa?" he asked. "Is dinner ready?"

"Not yet," Mamá answered. "I just wanted to talk to you two about something."

"Can it wait? 'Cause if dinner isn't ready, I was just about to go to Rafael's house and drop off some stuff for tomorrow night's party."

"No, this is important." She twirled the gold wedding band around her finger.

A knot formed in my throat. I recognized that tone. This wasn't going to be a casual conversation.

"What is it?" I asked, unsure if I wanted to find out.

Mamá shifted her weight from one foot to another. "You both know that Rodrigo is getting close to being of military age. . . ."

Rodrigo leaned against the doorframe. "So?"

Mamá continued. "And of course, you know how Cuba keeps sending troops to that war in Angola that never seems to end." She sighed and shook her head. "We shouldn't even be there and I'm afraid that . . . that . . ."

Mamá seemed to be at a loss for words.

"Afraid of what?" I asked, expecting her to say something horrible.

She looked at Rodrigo, her eyes a little misty. "That I won't be able to protect you and your brother."

I sighed, relieved that this wasn't anything too serious. Mamá was just being a little dramatic.

"Oh, Mamá, you don't have to worry." Rodrigo wrapped his arms around her. "I'll go do my training and come back home. I won't get sent to Angola."

"Well, that's the thing," she said, breaking free of his hug.

"I don't want you to do the military training at all." Mamá took a deep breath. "I don't want to take any chances. I want us to go be with your father."

"What?" My relief turned to panic and I could feel my heartbeat begin to pound against my eardrums. "Leave Cuba? That's crazy. What about the Math Olympiad? I—"

"They have competitions everywhere, Héctor. And the idea of leaving isn't anything new. I may not have talked about it, but your father requested our exit visas soon after you were born. They've never been approved, of course. I haven't even dared to think about them for years . . . especially with your father being in prison. But now . . ." She paused for a moment. "Everything is different. You boys can sense that things are changing, right? All those people storming into the Peruvian embassy wanting to leave. It's the start of something. People may get to leave. I can feel it."

"No. That's just talk," I said, thinking back to my conversation with Teo's dad. "Nothing will change because it'd be like opening Pandora's box."

"Pandora's box . . . ," Mamá repeated, thinking about my comparison. "Yeah, that's exactly what I'm counting on. Things won't be able to be contained anymore." Mamá sighed. "People want a better life . . . even if they're afraid to admit it in public. So many of us are living double lives."

"I think you're hoping for something that isn't going to happen," Rodrigo replied, checking the clock. "But I guess it doesn't hurt to dream."

"Plus, things aren't so bad," I said. "We have friends and family here. Why would you want to leave . . . other than to be with Papá?"

"Isn't that reason enough?" Mamá shook her head. "Have I done such a bad job at reminding you of your father?" She began to pace around the kitchen. "Sometimes pretending to be someone else can make you forget who you really are." She ran her fingers through her dark curly hair. "And as for things not being so bad . . . what do you think would happen to you if you disagreed with the government . . . even just a little? If you voiced an opinion that didn't fit with what they wanted? You know that'd never be tolerated."

"Yeah, but that's because the government needs to keep order," I countered, repeating what I'd always been taught in school. "It would be chaos if everyone did whatever they wanted."

"Not chaos," Mamá corrected me. "Freedom."

"I guess," I said, glancing over at Rodrigo, who was fidgeting and looking at the door.

"Well, I think you two are old enough to know what's going on. I went by and asked about the status of our visas earlier today. I was told they're still pending . . . but I need you both to be prepared."

"Wait. You asked about them *today*?" I felt the panic rising again in my chest. "Why would you . . . Señora Andrade just warned me about how they'll be looking at all my associations and that I should get Abuela to help. I'll never make the team now!" I dropped my head into my hands as my brain began to spin with all sorts of worst-case scenarios. I had to fix this, but how?

"What do you mean we have to be prepared?" Rodrigo asked, his voice full of worry. "Do you think someone will come after us? Are we in danger?"

"No, no. We're fine. Asking about old visa applications won't do anything. . . . We could even say that we're preparing for Héctor's worldwide competitions." She gave us both a slight smile. "But I want you both to be ready to go if they *do* get approved."

"This isn't fair!" I exclaimed. "I've worked so hard—"

"Héctor, tranquilo, mijo." Mamá tried to reassure me. "For now you can still try out for the math team, and if we do leave, I'm sure you can do math competitions in the U.S." She glanced at Rodrigo. "And you can play baseball for whatever school you go to in the U.S. just like you do here."

"It's not the same," I argued. "Being here is my only chance to go to the IMO."

"Ugh!" Rodrigo threw his hands up in the air. "Enough about the stupid Math Olympiad! You'd think that's the only thing that matters."

"It's what matters to me!" I shouted.

"*Shhhhh!*" Mamá scolded us. "You need to keep your voices down." She took a long, deep breath. "I shouldn't have to tell you this, but we have to be careful. The only way we'll really be safe is if no one knows about our plans. We can't tell anyone. Not family, best friends, or girlfriends. ¿Entienden? Nadie."

Neither Rodrigo nor I said a word.

"Understood?" Mamá repeated more forcefully. "I want to hear you both promise not to say anything."

I still couldn't believe Mamá was doing this, but I slowly nodded. "Promise," I mumbled, knowing that if anyone found out about this, my chances to make the team would completely disappear.

"We won't say anything to anyone," Rodrigo said. "But you do realize that, after all these years, nothing is going to happen. We aren't going to go anywhere."

"Maybe." She turned around and picked up the spatula. "But I just have a feeling. Las cosas están cambiando."

I scoffed under my breath. Even if she thought things were changing, that didn't mean we had to change with them.

4

BE READY TO go.

Mamá's words haunted me in everything I did the next day. While I brushed my teeth, while I had breakfast, on the walk to school, even during class . . . it was all I could think about. It had only been two days since my fight with Tincho, and he was no longer my biggest concern. Instead, I feared that a government agent would one day knock on our door with visas in hand.

But it was what would happen *after* that knock that worried me even more. It wasn't just the Math Olympiad. Could I really leave everything and everyone I knew behind? And what would we be heading into? Some strange place where I didn't know anyone . . . not even my own father.

Plus, it all seemed so . . . so . . . traitorous. I loved my country. Leaving went against everything we'd been taught about being loyal and patriotic.

It felt wrong.

Maybe the person I was pretending to be in public was who I really was.

During recess I didn't say much. I sat next to Teo and a few other friends at the table we had claimed since the beginning of the school year. The courtyard was loud and rowdy as usual, and our conversation, like most days, was about baseball and girls . . . but I could barely pay attention.

"Oye, what's going on with you?" Teo asked as soon as the other boys got up from the table. "You're so quiet today."

I shrugged, afraid to say anything . . . even to my best friend.

"Listen, don't worry about Tincho. He's a bully, but he's not stupid. He won't mess with you now that he knows your grandmother can make his life miserable. And I didn't mention it to the other guys."

Of course! My grandmother was the key with Tincho, the math team, *and* my mother. She could calm Mamá down the next time she came over. Get rid of all her worries about Rodrigo being sent to Angola. Abuela was good at taking care of things. If anyone could convince Mamá that things didn't have to change, it would be Abuela.

"You know what, Teo, sometimes you're really smart." I smiled, feeling like a large weight had been lifted off my shoulders.

"Not *that* smart." He motioned over to Isabel, who was sitting with a group of girls. "I really messed up telling Papi about her crush. I've never seen Isabel so mad at me."

"She'll get over it," I offered, trying to make him feel better. "Just give her some time. Did you apologize?"

"Like a hundred times. She doesn't care." He sighed. "She won't even look at me. It's been two days and I think—"

"¡Atención! ¡Atención!" Our principal, Señor Linares, was standing in the middle of the courtyard, speaking into a bullhorn. "I have an announcement."

Everyone stopped what they were doing and an uncomfortable quiet filled the air. This was not normal. Señor Linares rarely spoke to any of us unless we were in trouble.

"After your next class, you will all be released early from school—"

Cheers erupted until he raised his arms demanding silence.

"As I was saying, you will be released early so that you can all participate in a civic duty this afternoon." He made eye contact with several people, making sure he had their full attention. No one uttered a sound, and he continued. "We have been notified that a former teacher from the primary school was one of the gusanos who invaded the Peruvian embassy and that she and her husband will be returning home to wait for their exit visas. We, along with many others in the community, will be there to greet them and let them know what we think of traitors."

"Un acto de repudio," Teo whispered to me as a few students clapped.

I nodded. Acts of repudiation were well-known in Cuba. If someone was perceived to be against the government or opposed to its revolutionary ideals, the neighborhood watch, or Committee for the Defense of the Revolution, would assemble a small mob to protest against them. It was something I had heard about, but never participated in.

Señor Linares then pointed to everyone in the courtyard. "I expect everyone to be there. Your teachers will be taking attendance."

A few students around us shouted, "¡Saca los gusanos! Get rid of the worms!"

Teo must have seen the concern on my face. "Don't worry, we'll stay in the back of the crowd. Tincho won't be a problem."

"No, that's not it," I said, although now I was worried about that, too. "I was just wondering who tried to leave. Can you imagine if it's someone we know?" I thought about the homes I'd seen with broken eggs and rotten food splattered against the walls.

"Does it matter?" Teo asked as Señor Linares left and the courtyard buzzed with students talking. "We have to go no matter who it is." He got closer to me. "We already have one person calling you names. . . . We don't need any more."

A lump formed in my throat.

More people targeting me. Was that my future if people discovered that my mom wanted to leave? Abuela could protect us only so much. Would Teo have to protest against me? Or worse . . . would I be expected to denounce Mamá like I did with my father?

I could feel my insides shake, but I tried to remain calm on the outside. There were two of me, like always.

"Hey, relax." Teo smiled, able to see through my mask. "We all know how things work. We do what it takes to get by. But the two of us, we always look out for each other, right?" His words felt loaded with honesty and loyalty, but also yearned for reassurance. "Brothers to the end."

"Right," I said, giving him a lopsided grin.

"Plus, like you said the other night," he added. "Nothing ever really changes in Cuba."

I didn't reply, but my facial muscles tightened as I fought to keep the grin from slipping off my face. I couldn't reveal myself or my family's secret . . . not even to Teo.

Things had already started to change. He just didn't know it.

5

BEADS OF SWEAT rolled down my back as I stood under the hot April sun, shoulder to shoulder with my classmates. We'd been standing in front of a small apartment building with peeling green paint and broken balconies for over an hour, shouting insults into the air. Eggs had been thrown by a few of the adults at the beginning, but now things seemed to be winding down. The teacher who wanted to leave Cuba had managed to get inside before any of us arrived, so none of us had seen her or her husband. They were hiding out behind the shuttered windows on the second floor as we continued making noise.

"How much longer do you think we'll be here?" Teo asked, his fist raised as the crowd chanted new insults.

I shrugged and yelled, "¡Gusanos!" along with the rest of the students.

Neither of us really wanted to be there, but we were going

through the motions so as to not stand out. The rest of our friends had somehow disappeared into the large crowd.

"Here." An older student handed me a small rock. "Follow my lead. This'll get their attention." He ran forward and hurled his own rock against the wooden shutters that covered the windows.

The hollow thud silenced the crowd for a moment, but then a cheer erupted as others began to do the same with smaller pebbles or pieces of concrete. More people pushed forward.

I spun around looking for Teo, but he had disappeared into the sea of older students.

That's when I felt the hairs on the back of my neck prickle. I slowly looked over my shoulder and saw Tincho. He was giving me the evil eye, and I could tell he was waiting for me to make a move.

I looked down at the rock in my hand. The shutters would prevent it from breaking the glass, so there wouldn't be much harm if I just threw it. And Tincho would certainly notice if I didn't. This was my chance to prove I wasn't a traitor without anyone getting hurt.

I cocked my arm back, ready to fling the stone, when an old woman banging a pot with a wooden spoon opened the front door and began to yell at the crowd. "¡PAREN! STOP!"

Everyone froze and focused on her.

"I live here, too!" she cried out, having captured everyone's attention. "Those gusanos who live upstairs need to be thrown out of our country, but you're going to break one of my windows with all that rock throwing." She shook her head in disgust as she surveyed all the students in the street. She pointed to a few of the boys with the wooden spoon in her hand. "And some of you have worse aim than the pitchers who play for Las Tunas." She paused to laugh at her own joke and a few in the crowd joined her. Everyone knew Las Tunas was one of the worst teams in the league. "And I can say that 'cause I'm a fan of those lovable losers. What about you?" She signaled to a tall kid in front, pointing the wooden spoon at him. "Let me guess . . . you like Cienfuegos?"

The kid scoffed and answered that he was a fan of Industriales.

More people were now smiling along with the old woman as she continued talking to the crowd. The mood had shifted.

I stuffed the rock in my pocket.

Our teachers soon began telling everyone that we had performed our patriotic duty and could go home to enjoy the weekend. Monday would be a regular school day.

"Nothing like baseball talk to defuse a crowd of hotheads, huh?" Teo said, sauntering over to where I was standing. "Some of those boys were getting a little out of control."

Instinctively, I touched the rock in my pocket. I was glad I hadn't thrown it, even though Teo would've understood.

"Yeah," I said, nodding. "But it wasn't too bad. I mean, it could've been worse."

"I guess." Teo pursed his lips. "But I feel gross just having been here."

"Why?" I chided. "You said it yourself earlier. It's just the way things are. Plus, I'm sure they know that not everyone here is really against them. We're here because we have to be."

"But now that I've actually been a part of one . . ." Teo paused, gathering his thoughts. "I mean, she's a teacher like my dad. I can't imagine how he'd feel if all his students did this to him."

I'd been imagining how it'd feel all day—I wanted to change the subject. "Have you seen the rest of the guys? Where'd they all go?"

"Nelson wanted to go hang out with Gloria, and the other guys followed along." Teo pointed to Isabel, who was walking toward us. "Help me out, will you? Tell her to stop being so mad. She listens to you."

"Yeah, right!" I laughed. "Have you met your sister? She doesn't listen to anyone."

Isabel marched right up to us, her arms crossed. "Well, are you two going home or what?"

"How about we go to the park for a while." I looked up at the sky, which was peppered with white puffy clouds. "It's a nice day."

"Meh." Teo shrugged. "Not in the mood."

"Okay," I said, trying to keep my voice upbeat. "Well, what about we race?"

"No," Isabel snapped.

Teo shot me a look, but Isabel caught him, which made things worse.

"What?" she challenged. "You want me to be nice in front of Héctor and act like your little joke was funny the other night? . . . Because it wasn't."

"I already told you I was sorry," Teo replied. "I don't know what else you want from me."

"I want you to not be such a jerk." She spun around and stormed down the sidewalk.

"You see?" Teo said. "This is what I've been dealing with. Help."

I could tell Teo was genuinely sorry for having told their father about Isabel's crush. "I'll do what I can," I said, and chased after Isabel while Teo hung back.

She slowed down as I approached.

"Don't start with me, Héctor," she warned as we got to the corner of a busy intersection. "And you better not be taking his side. You're supposed to be my friend, too."

"I know," I said, carefully measuring my words. "I'm completely neutral. Always have been."

"Good." Her shoulders seemed to relax a bit while we crossed the street and walked past a line of people waiting outside one of the government-run stores.

"You have every right to be mad," I added for good measure, glancing back at Teo, who was about half a block behind us.

"You better believe it," she huffed. "I had to hear my father lecture me about boys, and then my mother came to talk to me about feelings and a whole lot of other garbage. All because Teo thought it'd be funny to say I liked Rodrigo." Her eyes darted toward me. "Which I don't. You know that, right?"

"Uh-huh," I said, choosing not to say anything else. Instead I focused on a couple of stray dogs darting between the crumbling arches of a large two-story pink building. I'd learned a while back that sometimes the best thing to do was not give a fire any more fuel to burn.

About a minute later Isabel stopped and glanced behind us as Teo kept his distance.

"Did he tell you to tell me anything?" she asked.

This was my opening. A crack in her armor. "Just that he feels really bad about everything."

"And?" she asked.

"That he wouldn't do anything like that again," I offered, trying to smooth things over. "Can't you just forgive him? He's lost without you." I gave her a nudge. "Must be some sort of twin dependency thing."

She rolled her eyes. "Fine," she muttered, and waved him over.

When he got closer, she pointed her finger at him. "Más nunca," she threatened. "Never again," she repeated.

A huge smile spread over Teo's face as he lifted his hand in the air. "Promise." He gave her a little wink. "At least, not in front of Mami or Papi."

"Hmph." She nodded, seeming somewhat satisfied with his declaration.

Teo looked over at me and silently mouthed, "Gracias."

I gave him a little wink. "So, what are the plans for the rest of the day?" I asked, looking both ways as we continued our trek home past the rows of pastel-colored buildings and flat-roofed houses.

"We can play checkers," Isabel suggested. "We haven't done that in a while."

"Or how about chess?" I said, preferring it to a quick game of checkers.

"Ugh! No." Isabel quickly shot down the idea. "Papi and you are the only ones who actually like that game. It's your thing with him . . . not with us."

I smiled. It was true. Their father had taught the three of us, but I was the only one who really enjoyed playing. I liked that every time we had a chess match, he taught me a new strategy or sequence of moves. It had gotten to the point that whenever I beat him, he'd laugh and say that the student was soon going to become the master.

"How about we make it a checkers tournament with the ultimate winner getting . . . hmm . . . What does the winner get?" Teo asked.

"Winner gets to sit back and watch the other two do the dishes all weekend," Isabel announced.

"That sounds fair," Teo agreed. "I like the idea of watching you two work while I sit at the table relaxing."

"You're assuming you're going to win . . . which is highly unlikely," Isabel teased.

"Um, and if I win, are you two coming to my house to do my dishes?" I asked, unsure if this bet was really going to work out.

"Looks like our tournament may have to wait," Teo said, pointing down the road at his porch.

My grandmother was sitting in a rocking chair next to Nani. It was such a sharp contrast between Nani, with her wispy white hair and floral housecoat, and Abuela, with her business suit and perfectly groomed hair. I wasn't sure why they were both out on the porch together, but I was happy to see my grandmother. I wanted to talk to her about the Math Olympiad, and about Rodrigo serving in the military.

"Maybe she wants to stay for a while and visit with Nani," Isabel mused. "Don't give up on our checkers game just yet."

"Nani doesn't seem very talkative right now," I said, pointing to Nani, asleep in her rocker.

As we stepped up to the porch, Abuela put a finger to her lips. I chuckled silently, thinking of the conversation the two of them might have had before Nani drifted off. My grandmother didn't stand for nonsense, and Nani's views of the world rarely made sense to anyone but her.

Abuela quietly got up from her rocking chair, greeted Teo and Isabel with a quick peck on the cheek, then silently waved goodbye to them as she interlocked her arm with mine.

"Cuidado," she warned as she pointed to the loose brick on

the step as we headed home. "Qué abandono," she whispered. "Such a shame to let things fall apart."

I was about to tell her that Teo's family did the best they could maintaining the house under the circumstances, but I stayed quiet.

She was being overly critical.

Abuela, like everyone else, knew that most Cubans had little or no access to supplies. The American embargo had made getting things difficult, so what we did have usually came from the Soviet Union . . . and they didn't send a lot of construction materials. Plus, even when they did, no one could get them except for the ritzy tourist hotels that regular Cubans couldn't visit. Those places were reserved only for foreigners. There were two Cubas. The one that the tourists saw and the one we lived in. I guess it was the same way Mamá had taught us to lead our lives . . . always pretending for others.

I let out a small sigh.

"Bueno, Héctor." She gave my arm a little squeeze as we got to my door. "Dime . . . ¿cómo te fue el día hoy?" she asked, wanting to know about my day.

"Fine," I answered, choosing not to mention the acto de repudio. "Happy that it's Friday."

"I bet." She bent down to pick up a small bag that she had left outside on our porch. "I brought you and your brother a little treat that I picked up at work along with some olive oil and tomatoes."

"What is it?" I asked. Abuela's treats were always exciting, especially since she was privy to things that most Cubans couldn't get.

"Ah, you'll have to wait for your brother to get home," she said, pushing me away from sneaking a peek as we walked inside the house. "When do you think he'll get here?"

"Who knows?" I plopped on our sofa with the faded blue flowers. "I think he might have a girlfriend, so he may not get here until dinnertime."

"In that case . . ." She gave me a slightly devious smile as she took off her suit jacket and draped it over the edge of the couch. "If you go get your abuelita a cold glass of water, I'll let you see what I brought."

I jumped up and ran to the kitchen. Within seconds I was back with two glasses.

Abuela had already taken off her heels and was now lounging back on the sofa in her red blouse and khaki skirt. She was fanning herself with a magazine that Mamá had left on the table, but she quickly put it down to take the glass. "Ay, qué sed tenía," she said after taking a big sip of water. Then she smiled. "Bueno. Dale, mijo." She motioned for me to look inside the bag.

She didn't have to tell me twice. I opened up the brown bag and saw a triangular yellow box with the word TOBLERONE written on the side.

"It was left over from a meeting we had earlier today with some foreign officials," she explained. The box had already been opened, and I carefully pulled out the foil-wrapped bar. "It's chocolate from Switzerland."

My fingers got melted chocolate on them and I licked the delicious gooeyness.

"Ah, the heat," Abuela said. "Put the whole thing in the re-frigerator for a little while so the chocolate gets hard again. There are six little triangles . . . three for you and three for your brother."

I closed up the foil and slid the bar back in the box. I'd share my pieces with Isabel and Teo. It had been a long time since any of us had eaten chocolate and never any from Switzerland.

"Gracias, Abuela." I reached over and gave her a big hug. "You're the best!"

"Anything for my two handsome boys," she called out as I took the chocolate into the kitchen.

When I came back to the living room, Abuela started dig-ging. "So, tell me about Rodrigo's girlfriend. Who is she? Is she pretty? Is her family involved with el partido?"

El partido. Abuela loved to evaluate people based on their involvement with the Communist Party and was always disap-pointed when I had no idea. "I don't know much about her. She's pretty, I guess. I've seen Rodrigo talking to her a couple of times and I think her name is Marta . . . but it could be María."

Abuela chuckled. "Well, you aren't a very good source of information. Almost as bad as Nani." She tapped her chin with her index finger. "So, tell me about you."

"Well . . ." I sat down across from her on the wingback chair that matched the couch. "School is good, but more importantly . . ." I paused for emphasis. "Señora Andrade's been coaching me for the International Math Olympiad. She thinks I have a decent shot at qualifying for the national team next year and that I could even go to East Germany in '82."

"Representando la patria . . . ¡Qué honor!" Abuela exclaimed. "I love hearing this!"

"Yeah, I'd be the first student from my school to qualify." I sighed. "But there might be a problem."

"Oh?" Abuela took another sip from her glass, her eyebrows scrunched together. "Something I can help you with?"

"I don't know. Maybe." I flopped against the back of the chair. "It's about Papá."

"Mm-hmm." Abuela pursed her lips.

"Señora Andrade is afraid that the committee might reject my application even if I do well on the tests. She said they'd be looking at everyone I'm associated with. She thought you might be able to help, though."

Abuela leaned over and patted my knee. "No te preocupes," she said, smiling warmly at me. "I'll let the committee know that you're a true patriot . . . despite your father's actions." She gave me a wink. "I'll make sure they know that you take after me."

"Do you think that will work? I mean, if my scores are high enough." I could feel a sense of hope filling me up.

"Of course! But . . ." Abuela had a twinkle in her eye.

"School isn't everything. Now, tell me, is there someone you like? I noticed that Isabel is getting very pretty. She's got that dark curly hair like her mother and—"

"Ugh, Abuela! Gross!" I grimaced. "She's like my sister. We've grown up together."

Abuela shrugged off my comment. "But she's not your sister. Feelings change."

I thought about how Isabel had been acting around Rodrigo lately and how it was obvious to Teo and me that she had a crush on him. Abuela was right that feelings could change, but not mine. Isabel was my friend and nothing more. That was certain.

"Nope." I shook my head. "She and Teo are the same to me. Both are my best friends."

"They're a decent family," she said. "You could do worse."

"¡Ay, Abuela!" I pretended to gag. "¡Por favor! I'm eleven. . . ."

"Time goes by fast." She wagged her finger at me. "Look at your brother. Just yesterday I was bouncing him on my lap and now he's almost a man."

"Ha!" I laughed. "Rodrigo? A man? I don't think so."

"You might not see it, but . . . trust me . . . your mother and I certainly do. El tiempo se va volando."

I thought about Mamá worrying that Rodrigo could be sent to Angola to fight. Maybe Abuela was worried about it, too. Maybe she *couldn't* fix that? Abuela had always been able to fix everything else, though. Should I even mention it to her?

"What's got you thinking so hard?" she asked, noticing how quiet I'd become.

"Nada."

"Nothing?" She inched closer. "I'm your abuela, I know when something is wrong." She gazed at me with loving eyes. "Héctor, you can tell me anything."

I took a deep breath. This was my grandmother, the one who always did everything she could to help us. Of course I should tell her. "Well, it's about Rodrigo and the required military service."

"Ah, yes." Abuela nodded. "He is approaching that age."

"Yeah." I bit my lip, still unsure if I should keep talking. "And there aren't any loopholes to serving. . . . Everyone has to do it, right?"

"Claro. And I'm sure you and your brother will do so with pride when the time comes."

"Right." I stared down at my hands. I couldn't imagine holding a weapon or going into battle. "But there's all the fighting in Angola and stuff. . . ."

"Is this what's worrying you?" Abuela asked gently. "That one of you will be sent to fight in a war somewhere?"

"Sort of. It's just that Mamá mentioned . . ." I lowered my voice even though we were the only two people in the house. "I know she doesn't like asking you for favors, but maybe you can make sure Rodrigo doesn't go so that Mamá doesn't do something drastic to try to deal with it on her own."

"What do you mean *drastic*?" Abuela's voice was filled with concern.

I swallowed the lump that had formed in my throat. I hadn't meant to say that part. I couldn't betray Mamá . . . not even to her own mother.

"No sé." I shrugged as my stomach tightened into knots. "I guess I don't mean anything really."

But it was too late. Abuela could read between the lines.

"It's all the talk about those people in the Peruvian embassy," Abuela said, shaking her head. "It's got her thinking about your father, right? She's talking about going to be with him, and it's got you nervous." Her jaw tightened.

"No," I answered quickly . . . probably too quickly. "That's not it. I'm just overthinking things. You know me . . . always worried about something." I tried smiling and making it look genuine, but I was a horrible liar. "I shouldn't have said anything. Mamá would never do anything really crazy and she'd probably get angry if she knew that I asked you to get involved."

"No." Abuela's face softened again. "You did the right thing. Your mother is the one who is always worrying needlessly, and, unlike you, she's sometimes too proud to ask for my help."

Abuela stood up and reached for her suit jacket.

I sat still, frozen in place.

"You don't have to be concerned, Héctor." Abuela cupped my face in the palm of her hand. "You and your brother mean the world to me and I'd never let anything happen to either of you. There are other ways to serve the military right here in Cuba and I won't let you be sent far away. You'll see, I'll take care of things."

My shoulders relaxed a little. "You will?" I asked, still unsure if I had done the right thing in telling her.

"Of course, mi amor." She picked up her purse and headed to the door. "And now I have to get going, but I'll come over for dinner tomorrow and talk to your mother. Everything will be fine." She gave me a little wink. "Trust your abuelita."

6

A MOSQUITO BUZZED around my head as I dove under the sheet for the tenth time. The tiny bloodsucker had chosen me for its next feast and it was impossible to sleep. Streaks of morning sunlight were already filtering into the bedroom that I shared with Rodrigo when, unable to take any more torture, I grabbed my pillow and went to sleep on the sofa in the living room.

I woke up to my legs being swept off the couch. "Get up, dormilón," Rodrigo ordered. "Mamá wants the house clean before Abuela comes over tonight."

"Huh?" I rubbed my eyes, trying to get my bearings.

"You slept through breakfast," he said. "Mamá is hanging the laundry outside and she wants you to finish cleaning the house. I already cleaned the bathroom. You mop the floors."

"I'll do it later," I muttered, getting comfortable again with the hope of getting a little more sleep.

"¡Levántate!" Rodrigo yanked the pillow away and flicked me in the head.

He was more annoying than the stupid mosquito.

"What's your problem?" I sat up. "Why do I have to do it now?"

"Because my friends might come over, and I don't want them seeing you lying on the sofa like the sloth that you are." He tried to nudge me with his foot, but I grabbed his leg and pushed him back.

"Héctor . . ." The way he said my name was a warning shot. Rodrigo was a lot bigger and stronger than I was. Even when we goofed around wrestling in our room, he almost always pinned me down within seconds.

"I'm up," I relented, raising my hands in surrender. "Did you leave me any breakfast?"

"No, and it's almost lunchtime, Kleto," he said, looking out the front window. "You keep missing meals and you'll never gain weight."

I followed his gaze and saw Teo sweeping his porch. It seemed like everybody was doing spring cleaning on Saturday morning.

"You're finally up." Mamá entered the room carrying a stack of folded clothes. She set them on the chair and gave me a kiss. "I tried waking you up earlier, but it seemed like you needed to rest."

"Yeah." I trudged over to the bathroom. "I'll make myself something to eat in a few minutes."

"Oye, Kleto . . . catch!" Rodrigo flung my pillow at me from where he stood by the front door. "Don't leave your stuff out here."

"How about I make you some fried eggs, white rice, and platanitos for lunch before I leave?" Mamá offered.

"Where are you going?" I asked, trying to ignore Rodrigo's smug look.

"Running a few errands," Mamá answered vaguely. "I'm also going to stop by and see Cuqui. She told me yesterday that her son was going fishing and that if he caught enough, she'd trade my ration of flour for them. I thought your abuela might like it for dinner tonight."

A knock on the front door startled Rodrigo and he quickly tucked in his shirt.

"Go!" Rodrigo ordered, which of course made me stay.

He rolled his eyes, turned, and opened the door. I saw his shoulders drop as he greeted whoever was at the door. "Oh, hi," he said.

I took a few steps to see who was there.

It was Isabel, standing there with a sheepish smile. "Hi, Rodrigo." She twirled a strand of her curly hair while holding an empty mug with flowers painted on it. "My mom wants to know if we can borrow half a cup of oil. She says she'll replace it next time there's some at the store."

Rodrigo nodded as he looked past her to the street. "Yeah, sure." He stepped aside to let Isabel in without taking much notice of her. "You know where things are."

"Tell your mother not to worry about replacing the oil," Mamá said as Isabel came inside. "I have enough." She took the mug from Isabel's hand. "I'll get it for you."

"So, Rodrigo—" Isabel began as Rodrigo grabbed a pair of sunglasses from the table and raced to the door.

"I see my friends," Rodrigo called. "We'll hang out at Rafael's place instead of here. I'll be home later."

"Don't forget about dinner with Abuela!" Mom reminded him as she headed to the kitchen and Rodrigo left.

"Give me a couple of minutes," I said to Isabel, still holding my pillow. "Don't leave."

I quickly changed clothes and washed the sleep out of my eyes. By the time I rejoined Isabel in the living room, she was sitting on the couch watching Rodrigo and his friends through the front window. The mug with oil was on the coffee table.

"So, what's up?" I asked, taking a seat next to her. "Any plans for today?"

She shrugged. "Papi and Teo are going to try to fix the TV antenna and I got stuck helping Mami with the cooking." Her eyes were glued on Rodrigo, who had his arm draped over a girl's shoulder. "Is that his girlfriend?"

"Who?"

Isabel glared at me. I knew it was a stupid question to ask. It was obvious who she was talking about.

"The one in the white short shorts and red halter top," she

said, turning away from the window. "You can't miss her. She's the one with the big . . . everything." She sighed.

"Um . . . yeah, I think so." I noticed that Isabel was wearing her favorite pink blouse and her hair looked nicer than usual. "Did you dress up just to come over here?"

"No!" she answered sharply. She glanced back at Rodrigo and his friends again. "You should've mentioned that he had a girlfriend."

I didn't know how to respond. She got mad when we suggested she had a crush. I needed to change the subject.

Then it hit me.

"Hey, I've got something for you." I jumped off the couch. "Wait here."

I ran to the kitchen and brought back my share of the Toblerone chocolate. "Look what my grandmother brought. There's a piece here for me, Teo, and you. It's chocolate from Switzerland. You can have yours now if you want."

Isabel smiled, but shook her head. "Keep it until the three of us are together. Teo would kill me if I ate it without him."

"True." I pointed out the window. "But he's walking over now."

"In that case—" She snatched the chocolate from my hand, broke off a triangle, and took the smallest little nibble. "Mmmm." She closed her eyes and savored the morsel. "¡Qué rico!"

I motioned for Teo to come inside as he stepped up to our porch.

"Isa," Teo said as he came into the house. "Mami needs the oil if you have it and . . ." He paused, noticing Isabel's devilish smile. "Wait. What's going on? You two are up to something."

"Oh, Teo," she said. "Come here. You are going to love this. I already feel fancy and sophisticated."

"Huh?" Teo looked at me for answers.

I snapped off a chocolate triangle and held it out. "A gift from my grandmother. Real Swiss chocolate."

Teo's eyes grew wide as he sat down next to us. "Seriously?" he asked as he tentatively took it from my hand.

Isabel and I both nodded as we each took a bite of our own pieces.

Teo stared at the chocolate in his hand, studying it from every angle.

"It's going to melt if you don't hurry up and eat it," Isabel chided. "And it's not like you've never had a piece of chocolate before."

"But never from Switzerland. That makes it special." He held up the piece to eye level and inspected it a little more. "That's another place I want to go someday."

I focused on my little bit of chocolate. "Well, when you go, be sure to bring back a lot more of this. It's delicious."

"Teo, if you need help eating it," Isabel volunteered while licking her fingertips, "I can split it with you."

"Nope." In one quick move Teo popped the whole thing in his mouth. "By the way, do you want to play ball with the guys at two?" he asked, and as he spoke, I could see the melted chocolate swirling around in his mouth.

"And you want to travel the world?" Isabel shook her head in disgust.

Teo shrugged, ignoring his sister. "You don't have to go if you don't want to, Héctor. It's just a last-minute game."

"I'll go, but I said it last time. . . . I don't want to be in right field anymore. I want to play second base."

"Yeah, about that." Teo squirmed a little. I knew him too well. He was trying to come up with an excuse.

"What?" I asked. "Go ahead. Spit it out."

"I just don't think it's a good idea, that's all."

I glanced over at Isabel to see her reaction, but she was staring out the window at Rodrigo and his friends again. Her obsession with them was beginning to get annoying.

"And why not?" I pressed on. "Everyone switches positions except me."

"I know." Teo rubbed his hands on his lap. "It's just that . . ."

"You don't think I'm good enough to play infield?" I challenged. "Is that it?" I looked at Isabel again. "Isabel, would you please pay attention to us and not them?"

"It's not me," Teo insisted. "The other guys think that—"

"¡Alabao!" Isabel turned around to face us, clearly irritated. "Don't keep beating around the bush, Teo." Isabel stared straight into my eyes. "Héctor, you suck at baseball," she said without even hesitating. "You're smart enough to know that by now. I mean, you're lucky that they even put you in right field."

Her words hurt. Probably because they rang true. For some reason, all my friends seemed to have become better and stronger players, while I . . . hadn't. Still, I knew that I'd improve if they gave me a chance. Isabel was just being spiteful.

"What do you know about baseball?" I lashed out. "You're just a girl."

"Just a girl?" she said, her voice seething. "I don't play anymore, and I'd still be a better second baseman than you. *You're* just a math nerd."

I clenched my jaw. "Better a nerd than a dumb girl playing dress-up."

"Really? ¿Una niña tonta?" she repeated, standing up so she could hover over me. "That's what you think of me?"

It was the wrong thing to say to Isabel. I knew it the moment I said it, but I refused to back down. She had started this by saying I sucked at baseball. Why was she the only one who could toss insults around? She could dish it out, but she couldn't take it.

I folded my arms across my chest, raised my eyebrows, and waited for her next move.

"Ooooooh." Teo raised his hands, not wanting to have any part of what was about to happen.

Isabel turned on her brother. "Don't even pretend you

aren't involved. You know what I said is the truth, but you're too much of a wimp to tell him."

"You don't need to be so mean," Teo replied in his calmest voice. "And Héctor brings . . . um . . . untapped potential to our games. He's a good right fielder. You haven't seen him play in a while."

"Sure," Isabel scoffed. She grabbed the cup of oil and marched toward the door. "Eventually you'll admit I'm right." She turned back to glare at me. "Even if I am *just a dumb girl*."

Isabel stormed out of the house, slamming the door behind her.

"You got off easy," Teo said. "I thought for sure she'd punch you." He shook his head. "One big trompazo and you'd hit the floor."

I rolled my eyes. "As my mother says, perro que ladra no muerde."

"Well, I don't think that applies to Isa," Teo replied. "Her bite is much worse than her bark . . . except when it comes to you. She holds back with you . . . most of the time."

"Holds back?" I raised a single eyebrow. "She said I sucked and called me a math nerd."

"Sucked *in baseball* and you do love math," he clarified. "Not that I'm defending her."

"Am I that bad of a player?" I asked, not sure if I wanted an honest answer.

"No." He shook his head vehemently. "You aren't great, but you aren't horrible either."

I sighed. Teo was a good friend, but a terrible liar.

"Well, I'm going to skip the game today. I should stay and help my mother around the house."

"Aw, come on, Héctor." He gave me a nudge. "Don't be mad."

"I'm not," I insisted. "Abuela is coming over for dinner and you know that my mom likes to have things in perfect order when she visits. I'll go next time."

Teo side-eyed me.

"Really." I stood and fluffed up the sofa cushion, a clear signal to Teo that it was time to go. "I'll play another day . . . even if it means that I'm still in the outfield."

"Promise?" Teo asked.

"Yes, now calabaza, calabaza . . ." I gave him a little kick to get him to go. "Unless you want to stick around to help clean the house."

"Um, not really." Teo stood up and headed toward the door. "But I'll thank you for the chocolate by smoothing things over with Isabel."

I shrugged. "It'll blow over."

"You underestimate how long my sister can hold a grudge," Teo teased. "Trust me . . . you need my help."

"For calling her dumb?" I answered.

"You don't get it, do you?" Teo shook his head. "For someone so smart, you sure are stupid sometimes, Héctor."

"Hey!" I protested. "I don't need to be told that I suck and I'm stupid by my best friends."

"Not what I meant," Teo said, walking out. "And you know that. I'll see you later when you're in a better mood."

I sank back down onto the couch. So far my Saturday had gotten off to a horrible start.

SATURDAY AFTERNOON WASN'T much better than the morning. As soon as Teo left, I had the lunch Mamá had made for me and spent the rest of the day cleaning. At least, as much as I could in between reading some old comic books, reviewing some math problems, and taking a short afternoon nap.

Maybe the afternoon hadn't been altogether bad.

It just felt bad knowing there was a rift between me and my friends.

Before I knew it, Mamá was ordering me to shower and change because Abuela would be arriving soon. I could never understand why Mamá made such a fuss with her own mother. I knew Abuela could be a little opinionated, but she meant well. We were her only family and she showered us with gifts all the time. We didn't depend on the government rations in the libreta for our allotment of food, shoes, clothes, or anything. She was always able to get us whatever we needed.

Rodrigo pounded on the bathroom door. "¡Apúrate!" he ordered. "I need to wash up before dinner, too."

"All yours," I declared as I walked out.

"Just a warning . . ." Rodrigo glanced back at Mamá setting the table. "She's more stressed than usual."

"You're telling me?" I replied. "I've been here all day."

"¡Niños!" Mamá called out. "Your grandmother's here. Come say hello and—"

"I'm already here," I said, walking over to give Abuela a kiss on the cheek.

"Mmm." Abuela took a deep breath. "Qué olor tan sabroso."

"That's the fish I got for dinner," Mamá proudly explained as she finished setting the glasses on the dining room table. "Está en el horno."

"In the oven?" Abuela sighed. "Oh well, I guess that's fine. It's just that fried fish is usually so much tastier." Abuela turned her attention back to me. "And anyway, I was actually talking about Héctor. He smells wonderful. Are you using that nice soap that I brought by a few weeks ago?"

I shrugged. "I just use whatever soap Mamá leaves in the shower."

Mamá grimaced as she walked back to the kitchen.

Abuela got closer to me. "Don't think I've forgotten what you told me," she whispered. "I'm going to talk to your mother about this whole silly idea of you all leaving."

"Abuela, no. That's not what I said." She was definitely not remembering our conversation correctly. "I told you she wasn't thinking about that. Maybe you can just say that Rodrigo won't be going to Angola?"

"Uh-huh. Well, leave it to me, Héctor. I know how to deal with your mother and I won't even mention our little talk." She took a seat at the head of the table. "But the sooner we clear things up the better."

"What things do we need to clear up?" Mamá asked, walking back to the dining room table with a plate of sliced avocados.

"Nothing," I answered quickly. Mamá raised an eyebrow and hovered by the table waiting for an explanation.

"Nada, mija." Abuela patted Mamá's hand. "You always get so worked up about things. You need to relax." She peered over Mamá's shoulder toward the kitchen. "Can I help you with the food?"

"No." Mamá had a tight smile on her face. "You sit and . . . relax. I'll bring it all out." She turned and hurried back to the kitchen.

Abuela shook her head. "She is so difficult sometimes."

I gave her a little nod in agreement.

"Hola, Abuela." Rodrigo bounded into the room, giving our grandmother a quick kiss before taking a seat at the table. "Gracias for the chocolate. It was delicious."

"Did your noviecita like it?" Abuela had a slight smile on

her face. "And don't try denying that you have a girlfriend because you know I keep tabs on things. I have my sources . . . even if they don't know what her name is."

"No. I mean sí. I mean no. . . . I'm not denying having a girlfriend." Rodrigo shot me a look. "And yes, she liked it."

"Well, I'm glad you were enough of a gentleman to share it with her," Abuela replied as Mamá placed the filets of baked fish covered with chopped tomatoes and garlic on the table next to the bowl of white rice.

It all smelled delicious.

"And have you met Rodrigo's young lady?" Abuela asked Mamá.

"Um . . . no." Mamá began serving Abuela a plate of food. "Not formally."

"I see." Abuela took her plate and gave it a quick sniff before setting it down. "I'm sure Rodrigo will bring her around soon enough for all of us to meet her. Isn't that so, Rodrigo?"

"Sure," he said, reaching for his own plate of food before Mamá was barely done serving. "One of these days."

"Well, why don't you tell us a little bit about her?" Abuela suggested.

I could see how uncomfortable this was making Rodrigo, and part of me was enjoying watching him squirm.

"Not much to tell." Rodrigo stuffed his mouth with a huge piece of fish. "She goes to my school. I'd rather not say too much. I'd rather keep it all private for now."

"Well, I hope her family is active with el partido." Abuela paused for a moment. "Lately, there seem to be gusanos hiding everywhere."

Mamá tried to move the topic to something Abuela always loved to discuss . . . her work for the Communist Party. "So, how have things been going with the delegation?"

"Busy. I have to go to Camagüey for about a week . . . what with all of this nonsense about gusanos wanting to leave." Abuela rolled her eyes and sighed. "I don't even understand them." She shrugged. "I say let them go. We don't need traitors living in our midst. Leave Cuba for those of us who love it. Don't you think?"

I nodded and took a bite of the plátano.

"Mmm," Mamá said noncommittally. "Do you like the fish? It may have needed a little more salt."

"No, I think it's fine." Abuela took another small bite as if to confirm her opinion. "Well, perhaps a little more salt would have been better, but it still has buen sabor."

Mamá smiled and then we all ate in silence for about a minute.

"Rodrigo," Abuela said, having left most of the fish on her plate. "I've been meaning to talk to you about your military service. You're almost at that age now."

Rodrigo glanced over at Mamá.

Abuela continued. "I don't want you to worry. Not about Angola or anything like that. As long as I'm alive, I'll look out for you." She gave him a wink. "Your abuelita knows how to make things happen."

"Okay," Rodrigo responded, concentrating on the food and not the conversation.

I held my breath; so far this was exactly what I'd wanted. Abuela could make it so Rodrigo would be safe and then Mamá wouldn't need to worry.

"But you will have to get more involved in the party," Abuela stated. "I have some ideas for you and Héctor."

"No." Mamá shook her head. "You know I don't like getting involved in politics."

"But this isn't about you . . . it's about the boys. They're getting old enough to make their own decisions." Abuela looked over at me. "The party will take care of you just like it did with me after the car accident that took your grandfather and uncle." She placed a hand over her heart. "May they rest in peace."

"I don't want to talk about this," Mamá insisted. "When will you leave for Camagüey?"

"Sometime next week," Abuela answered, but she wasn't ready to drop the subject. "I just want the boys to understand that they are safe here because they are proud children of the revolution. That there is nothing to fear."

Rodrigo perked up. "Abuela . . . I just had a thought. Would you be able to use your influence to help my girlfriend's brother? Her family is worried that *he* might be sent to Angola. He's a little older than me."

"La noviecita has you hooked, eh?" Abuela chuckled. "Well, I'd love to help them, but . . ."

"But what?" Rodrigo's eyebrows scrunched up.

"But," Abuela continued, "I have to reserve my influence to help the two of you. And we do need strong young men to go help our brothers in Africa."

Rodrigo's face was full of disappointment.

"But you two can be tranquilo about your futures." Abuela reached across the table to hold Rodrigo's hand. "My connections can guarantee that."

"Yeah, sure." Rodrigo pulled away and scoffed. "Unless we don't measure up to the party standards because we disagree with the war."

"Rodrigo . . ." Mamá's voice had a warning tone. "That's enough."

Abuela pursed her lips and turned her attention to Mamá. "You see? This is why they need to become involved with the party, to see how things work from the inside. It would even help Héctor with the national team." She shook her head. "Subversive ideas can ruin their futures without them even realizing it."

"They don't have any subversive ideas and we don't need to become overly political," Mamá said. "That's why we have you."

"But, Mamá," I said, "if it helps me with the math team, then maybe I can—"

"It won't come to that," Mamá broke in, not making eye contact with me or Abuela.

Abuela scoffed. "Because you're taking care of things?"

Mamá slowly put her fork down on her plate, which was still half-full. "You know I've been doing a *good* job raising them—"

"Thanks to my assistance with your job . . . this house," Abuela interrupted.

"I have plans," Mamá said, carefully folding her napkin.

"What? Let me guess. To reunite with that traitorous husband of yours in Miami?" Abuela's voice had a hard edge to it.

For a moment it seemed like Mamá was about to explode, but then she took a slow, deep breath.

"I don't want to talk about him with you," Mamá said, her jaw clenched tight.

"You never learn," Abuela said, shaking her head. "You haven't seen the man in years and by now he's probably started a new life in the U.S. Your place is here with me and your children."

"That's not the way he is," Mamá replied. "And I didn't say I was leaving."

Rodrigo and I exchanged glances. The conversation was headed in a really bad direction and I needed to do something to stop it.

"You know that the International Math Olympiad was going to be in Mongolia this year but—"

"Don't deny what I already know to be true," Abuela interrupted, completely ignoring me and keeping her focus on Mamá. "Like I told the boys, I have my sources." She narrowed her eyes. "It was foolish to inquire about your visas and think I wouldn't hear about it."

Mamá quietly wiped her mouth and began to pick up the plates.

"Mija," Abuela continued, changing her tone to something a little softer. "If you're worried about the boys, I can promise you that they won't be sent anywhere. You know how much I love them. When the time comes, I'll make sure that they get good jobs with the government. Things that neither you nor that gusano father of theirs could ever provide for them."

Mamá spun around and I could see the flash of rage in her eyes.

"¡Basta!" Mamá threw the plate on the table, the silverware flying into the air. "I've had enough of your criticisms. I won't have you continue to insult Raúl in front of his sons."

"Have I said anything that is untrue?" Abuela raised her hands and glanced at me and Rodrigo. She then pointed an accusatory finger at Mamá. "Y cuidado con cómo me hablas. I do a lot for you and you don't want that to stop."

"I have to be careful how I speak to you?" Mamá shook her head. "No, no more. I won't surrender to your bribes or threats anymore."

"Threats? Me?" Abuela feigned ignorance. "Yo no te estoy amenazando, querida."

"Por favor. There's always an unspoken threat with you. We have to do what you say or else. Live up to your ideals or face the consequences." Mamá paused. "The boys know this, too. Your love comes with a price."

The walls of our small house felt like they were closing in around us. I didn't want to be here, but if I got up from the table, things might get worse.

"It comes with a price? Ha!" Abuela scoffed. "You have *never* had to pay the price for your actions. I've always protected you from the consequences of your tonterías. Your little rebellious tantrums to get attention. Thanks to me, you still have a job . . . a house . . . your children. You could easily have been in jail like that descarado piece of garbage you married. Maybe I should have let that happen to teach you a lesson."

"GET OUT!" Mamá shouted. "¡VETE! I don't want you in my house and I don't want you in my life."

No one moved. Silence enveloped the room as if a bomb had been dropped and we were now in the eerie, quiet aftermath.

Abuela stood and calmly picked up her purse from the chair by the sofa. "Be careful in rejecting me and my help, mi amor," she said in a cold, calculating voice. "I will not lose my grandchildren to Yankee imperialism and all of its lies."

Mamá marched to the front door and swung it open. "And I will not lose my sons to you or the Communist Party. We'll make it on our own and neither you nor this government will stop us."

I couldn't believe Mamá had just said that. She had rejected Abuela and the government—out loud.

"We'll see about that," Abuela sneered, stepping outside. "And we'll see how much you like living without my protection."

"It already feels better," Mamá declared, slamming the door after her.

I sat frozen, unsure of what to do next.

I suddenly felt like we were on a small boat that had been set adrift with nothing to guide us.

Mamá stared at her trembling hands, then looked at us. "I'm sorry you saw that," she said, clenching her fists. "Or maybe I'm not. That's not what family should be. *Our* family . . . the four of us will be together again. That's all that matters."

Neither Rodrigo nor I said anything, but we both nodded.

But I wasn't sure if Mamá was right. Being together with Papá was her dream. But for me, for Rodrigo? There was so much more that mattered.

8

THE NEXT MORNING I knew I had to get out of the house. I didn't want to think about what had happened between Abuela and my mother. Didn't want to worry about what it might mean for us. So, as soon as I finished breakfast, I headed across the street with the excuse that I had promised to help Teo with some math homework.

Teo's house was my refuge. I was almost *more* relaxed and comfortable there than in my own. I'd laugh at Nani's silly comments and smile at the banter between Teo's parents. And no one was a better friend than Teo . . . although Isabel was a close second. If she was still speaking to me.

"Buenos días, Miguelito. ¿Trajiste los limones?" Nani asked as I stepped on the porch.

"No, Nani. I'm Héctor, remember?" I gave her a small smile. "And I don't have any lemons today."

"Well, how am I supposed to make lemonade if no one

brings me lemons?" She shook her head and went back to whatever she was crocheting, still muttering about something.

I walked into the house through the wide-open door and stood in the empty living room.

"Buenos días," I called out. "Where is everyone?"

"¡Aquí!" Teo answered. "In the kitchen."

I walked in to see Teo hovering over the kitchen table flipping jigsaw puzzle pieces over.

"What are you doing?" I asked as he continued sorting the pieces by color.

"What does it look like?" he answered.

"Looks like a big waste of time," I said, chuckling.

He gave me a hard stare, then pointed to the chair next to him. "You going to help me? It's got five hundred pieces."

It wasn't exactly how I wanted to spend my Sunday, but it could be worse.

"Yeah, sure," I said, sitting down next to him.

"My dad found it a couple of days ago in the back of the closet along with some other stuff," Teo said as I began to look for matching color schemes. "Says it was his when he was young. It's a Nordic landscape. Check it out." He pointed to the box at the corner of the table. The cover had a picture of snowcapped mountains and a lake surrounded by little houses.

"Mm-hmm," I said, not overly impressed. Plus, after what had happened the night before, I didn't want to hear about foreign lands.

"This is why I want to travel the world one day," Teo declared. "Wouldn't it be cool to see snow? Imagine standing on top of a mountain and looking out at a sky so blue that it feels limitless. A place where you can do or be anything."

"Sure, I guess. But we have blue skies here." I put a corner section together. "And it's not like we can't be anything we want to be here."

Teo shook his head. "You just don't get it." He twirled a puzzle piece in his hand. "We're all equal, except some are more equal than others."

"What does that mean?" I asked. "Is this about my getting the chocolate?"

"No . . . well, yes . . . sort of. It's from a book my dad gave me." He lowered his voice and leaned across the table. "I'm not supposed to talk about it because it's banned, but I can let you borrow it as long as you don't show it to anyone. It's really pretty good."

"Um, I don't know." I hesitated even though I usually liked reading. "Why is it banned? Does it say bad things about the revolution?" Speaking out against the government was strictly forbidden.

"Nah." Teo focused on the puzzle again. "It was written way before the revolution, but it does remind me of Cuba. It's called *Animal Farm* and it's about these animals that take over a farm."

"Wait, so you think we live like farmers?" I scoffed, searching for a piece that would have the tip of a sunbeam. I didn't think Teo was making much sense. "We're not that far from Havana. This is not farm life."

"No," Teo laughed. "It's a metaphor. These pigs are in charge, and they pretend that all animals are equal, but the pigs actually live way better than everyone else. They basically end up controlling all the other animals. You'd have to read it to understand. There's a lot that happens in the book." Teo glanced up at me. "My dad and I had a good talk about it. He can explain it better than me."

Teo knew how much I loved discussing things with his dad. "I guess if your dad likes it, then sure . . . I'll read it, too." I paused for a moment. "Did Isabel read it?"

"Yep," Teo nodded. "Both of us did."

Now I was definitely not going to get left out. "Okay, then." I looked around. "Where is Isabel, anyway? How come she isn't doing the puzzle with you?"

"She doesn't have the patience. And she had to run some errands with my mom." He had a mischievous grin. "Girl stuff."

I didn't know what he meant by that, but I didn't care enough to ask.

After that, neither of us said much. But we were good enough friends that silence wasn't a problem. After a couple of hours of intense concentration, we were only halfway done with the puzzle and I was getting hungry.

"Want to have lunch?" I asked, hoping that Teo's mom had put some leftovers in their fridge.

"Sure. Whatcha got?" Teo asked without looking up from the pieces he was fitting together.

I knew there was a little bit of leftover fish at my house, but I really didn't want to go back there to eat.

"Just kidding." Teo gave me a little shove as he stood up. "I think we have some arroz con pollo from last night." He opened the refrigerator just as Isabel walked in carrying a bag of groceries.

"Are you still doing that puzzle?" she remarked, setting the bag next to the sink.

"It takes a while, but it's going faster since Héctor is helping." Teo closed the refrigerator door. "What did you guys get?"

"Food." Isabel glanced over at me, then quickly turned to Teo. "Is he staying for lunch?"

There was no one who could hold a grudge like Isabel.

"Of course he is," Teo answered. "Don't be so pesada. You're the one who insulted him first yesterday."

Isabel rolled her eyes, crossed her arms, and then stared at me.

If she thought I was going to apologize to her, she had another thing coming. There was no way I was going to back down first.

Neither of us said a word. Neither of us even blinked.

"You're both insufferable!" Teo declared.

"Who is?" Teo's mother asked as she walked into the kitchen.

"Who do you think?" Teo pointed at Isabel and me.

Teo's mother shook her head and held out a small white bag. "Isa, go put these away in your underwear drawer."

"Maaaaami!" Isabel snatched the bag and tore out of the kitchen as if she were on fire.

Teo smirked, for some unknown reason. He leaned over and whispered, "They're bras."

Teo's mother snapped a kitchen towel against his rear. "Teófilo Alejandro! There are things that we don't discuss!"

"But this morning you said it was all a normal part of growing up," he said with a sly smile. "And Héctor is like family, right? We can talk in front of him."

"Mira, no empieces con eso, Teo." She came over to the table and squeezed my cheeks. "You know we love you as if you were our son . . . but Isabel deserves privacy, right?"

I nodded.

"All right." Teo's mom looked out the window and then at Teo. "Now, where's your father?"

"No sé." Teo shrugged. "Haven't seen him in a while."

She opened the back door and took a step outside. "Evelio! Evelio!" she called out, before confirming that he wasn't in their small backyard. "¿Adónde se metió ese hombre?" She walked back to the bag of groceries. "I need to talk to him. He's not going to believe what I heard in town while waiting in those insufferable lines for our food rations."

"¿Qué?" I asked. "Does it—"

"Fidel opened the port of Mariel!" Teo's father announced

as he stormed into the kitchen. "I was over at Silvio's place helping him with a car when we heard the news." He shook his head in amazement. "It's incredible. I never thought I'd see the day."

"I know!" Teo's mother exclaimed. "I rushed home when I heard."

"What does that mean exactly?" Teo asked. "Aren't the ports open all the time?"

"Not for people who want to leave Cuba," Teo's mother explained. "The announcement said they're going to let anyone leave if someone comes to pick them up by boat at the port of Mariel."

I could feel the color draining from my face.

"So . . ." I swallowed the lump in my throat. "People can just . . . go?" I asked, aware that Mamá might already be making plans.

"Well, apparently, you still need to apply for a visa and have it approved." Teo's father took out several plates and set them on the table for lunch. "But the word on the street is that if you have a boat waiting for you, then they'll approve your paperwork."

"Free to travel the world . . . wow!" Teo's eyes were wide.

"But it could all be a trap to see who holds anti-revolutionary feelings," Teo's mother cautioned as she gave Teo's father a serious look. "Best we all stay quiet and give no opinion on the matter. You never know who's listening. Agreed?"

"Tienes toda la razón." Teo's father nodded. "Best not to speak of it with anyone."

I sat in the wooden kitchen chair motionless. Earlier that morning the idea of leaving Cuba was only a vague possibility. Unlikely at best, with the odds stacked against us. Now it seemed like it was just a matter of time.

And suddenly it all became crystal clear to me—I didn't want to go. I didn't want to leave my home, my friends, everything I cared about. I definitely didn't want to go in search of a father I barely remembered. But Mamá would be making plans . . . unless I did something right away.

"Um . . . I don't think I can stay for lunch," I said, pushing back the chair as I stood up. "I . . . um . . . forgot that Mamá wanted me to help her with something."

"What?" Teo eyed me suspiciously.

"A thing . . . in my kitchen." I waved to everyone. "I'll see you all later."

Without another word I rushed out of their house, across the street, and into my own.

"Mamá?" I called out, searching for her in her bedroom and then the kitchen. "Mamá!"

"¡Aquí!" I heard her respond through the kitchen window. I could see her taking down the laundry from the clothesline outside.

The radio in the kitchen was blasting some old song from before I was born, so I turned it down as I opened the back door. "Mamá, can you come here? I want to talk to you about something."

"Just a minute." She unclipped a bedsheet and then several pillowcases, dropping each into a laundry basket next to her.

I was anxious to talk to her, but I knew this wasn't something we could discuss outside where one of the neighbors might hear us. I tapped my foot, waiting for her to finish.

I had to convince Mamá that it was best for us to stay in Cuba . . . despite the fact that people were leaving through Mariel. I was going to present my arguments logically and beg her to reconsider.

I studied Mamá from a distance. She seemed to be in a good mood. Her hair was wrapped in a scarf and she was swaying her hips from side to side even though I'd turned down the music. As she took down the last towels and placed them into the laundry basket, I noticed that she was singing.

Only one thing could possibly make her this happy. . . . She'd already heard the news.

"Mi amor," she said, walking into the kitchen holding the basket with both hands. "You'll never guess what's happening."

"Mariel," I answered. "I heard. That's why I wanted to talk to you."

She put down the laundry on our small kitchen table and pointed to the back door. "Cierra la puerta. I don't want prying ears to hear."

I quietly closed the door, but as soon as I turned around, Mamá was already bouncing with excitement.

"Can you believe it?" Mamá came over and hugged me. "This is what we've been waiting for. A moment like this."

I pulled away. "But you know that we still need visas to be approved and—"

She waved off my comments. "That'll get done once we have a boat. . . . You'll see." She reached for one of the towels in the basket and began to fold it. "We'll be together soon."

I gritted my teeth. I had to stop this now if there was any chance of staying in Cuba. "But I was thinking that there might be another way for all of us to be together."

Mamá held the towel against her chest. "What do you mean?"

"If people are allowed to leave, then maybe things are changing for those who stay, too. Papá could come back and—"

"Come back?" She stared at me like I was crazy. "He's not coming back. Plus, this is our chance to be free."

"But things aren't so bad here," I argued. "I go to a good school, you have a job, we have this house—"

"Only because the government thinks that we play by their rules. Que somos buenos comunistas." She shook her head. "No, if we didn't comply and constantly pretend that we support everything Fidel says, we'd lose it all. I want us to go to where we can say what we want and be whoever we want without fear. Be given a chance to have more if we work hard. Our future is with your father in the U.S."

There was no other way around it. I had to tell her.

"I don't want to go," I said. "My future is here where all my friends are and I can make the national team."

Mamá's eyebrows scrunched together and she slowly put the towel on the table. "You think this life is fine because you're young and you've never known another way . . . but I have. I remember being your age before the revolution. Things weren't perfect then either, but it wasn't like it is now. As you get older, you'll understand." She rolled back her shoulders. "I'm sorry, Héctor, but we are going to go the first chance we get."

"But what if I want to stay?" I said, my voice rising along with my anger and desperation. "Why doesn't what I want matter?"

Mamá continued folding the towels, not even looking at me anymore. "I'm your mother and I know what's best for us. For all of us."

"You don't know anything!" I shouted, feeling completely defeated. "You're going to ruin my life."

I ran out of the kitchen before she could say anything more.

I slammed the door to my room shut and jumped on my bed.

I could feel tears stinging my eyes, but I refused to cry.

There had to be a solution to my problem, just like every algebra problem had an answer. And I had to find the best way to reach it quickly, because Cuba had everything I wanted and the U.S. had nothing. I just had to get my mother to see things like I did. Like Teo's dad had said, it was all a matter of perspective.

9

IT WAS ONLY Wednesday, but it felt like it had been one of the longest weeks ever. Being angry with Mamá was beginning to take a toll on me, but I wasn't going to give up. According to Mamá and her sources, Papá hadn't been able to find a boat captain willing to come pick us up, and rumors were flying around that some people's visas were not being approved even if there was a boat waiting for them. I still had time to change her mind.

As for my situation with Isabel . . . that was a different story. It wasn't too complicated. One of us had to give in and apologize.

And it wasn't going to be me.

"I don't even understand how this got to be such a big deal between you two. It's ridiculous." Teo sounded exasperated as we walked home from school. "Can't you just tell her you're sorry? Things aren't as much fun when we're not all together."

"Nope." I stared at Isabel's back as she walked by herself a half block in front of us. "She always gets her way and I'm done with that. She started it, so it should end on my terms. When she apologizes, then we can be friends again."

"You're being as stubborn as she is." Teo turned and walked backward to face me. "Isa no va a dar su brazo a torcer. She'll hold out as long as she has to. You've been around her almost as long as I have. . . . You know that I'm right." He paused. "And you did call her a stupid girl."

"So? She said I sucked." I narrowed my eyes as I watched her ponytail go around the corner. "I'm done with having people boss me around. I'm standing up for myself and what I want."

"Um . . . are we still talking about Isabel?" Teo asked as we turned onto our street.

I shrugged, not wanting to get into what was happening at home. "And we don't need her to have fun anyway. We're still going fishing Saturday morning, right?"

"Yeah, but let's leave really early. Last time, we got to the pier after sunrise and the fish weren't biting as much."

"That's because we waited for Isabel to get ready. This time we'll go without her," I said, watching Isabel approach her house. "She doesn't even like fishing that much anyway."

"Hold up." Teo stopped in the middle of the street between our two houses. "I'm not going to sit in my house again with you and Isabel glaring at each other. Let's go hang out at your house today."

"Sure." I glanced at Isabel staring at us from her porch. I wanted to make her feel jealous of the fun we weren't having. I threw my head back and laughed loud enough for her to hear me. "Oh, Teo, that's hilarious!" I exclaimed, and patted him on the back.

"Huh?" He looked at me as if I had lost my mind. Then he peered over his shoulder and saw Isabel. "Oh." He shook his head. "You two are more alike than you know. Guess that's why I'm one of the few people who can put up with both of you."

"Hey!" I gave him a light punch in the arm. "I have a bunch of friends."

"Mm-hmm. So does Isabel." He chuckled. "Yet both of you are always with me. Can't imagine what you two would do without me."

I rolled my eyes. "Let's talk about something else," I suggested as we approached my front porch. "Baseball, school, the weather . . . anything."

"Well, my dad quit his job at the high school yesterday." Teo said it as if it were no big deal.

I stopped in my tracks. *"What?"* It took me a second to absorb the news. "Why? He loves teaching."

"Yeah, but he can make more money fixing cars with his friend Silvio. Es todo por la izquierda, so he'll make more than what the government allows him to get from working at the high school." Teo shrugged. "It's like the taxi drivers that used to be doctors. Everyone's equally poor unless you get paid under the table for doing some sort of side hustle . . . or you're part of the government elite."

I sighed. I knew that there were two economies, the one that was controlled by the government and the illegal one that the government pretended didn't exist. I couldn't blame Teo's dad for wanting to provide more for his family.

"And . . ." Teo lowered his voice as I opened the front door. "I overheard my parents talking last night about Mariel. Sounds like *hundreds* of boats are showing up to get people. Can you imagine what that looks like? They said thousands may end up leaving. I keep wondering if someone we know will go."

I hesitated. I thought maybe I should tell him about Mamá's crazy plan. He was my best friend and there was no one I trusted more. He might even help me come up with a way to stay.

"You know . . ." I closed the door behind me. "I've been wanting to tell you something, but you have to promise—"

"Hey, your TV isn't working." Teo turned the knob, but there was no picture or sound.

"That's weird." I turned and flicked on the light switch, but nothing happened either.

"The power must be out," Teo said, plopping down on our sofa. "Oh well. What did you want to tell me?"

I was about to open my mouth and reveal our secret when Rodrigo walked in from the kitchen.

"What are you doing here?" I asked, knowing that Rodrigo never came home directly from school.

"I live here in case you forgot," he answered sarcastically, taking a seat in the chair next to the sofa.

"I wonder if we lost power, too." Teo looked out across the street to his house.

"Nah," Rodrigo kicked off his shoes. "This apagón is only affecting us. I think it might be our abuela's way of sending a message."

"A message?" Teo repeated.

"Reminding our mother that she can make life easy or hard. They had an ugly fight the other day."

"Oh." Teo nodded as if he understood, but he really didn't. How could he? He didn't know what Mamá was planning. Abuela was right to be angry.

"Abuela wouldn't do this," I countered. "Even if she was mad."

"So naïve." Rodrigo sighed, and shook his head. "I mean, come on, man . . . wake up. Listen to what people say and what they don't say. Open your eyes to what's really happening in this country. People are willing to risk everything to get out of here because they want to be free. 'Cause who cares if your jailer gives you scraps to keep you alive—you're still in jail. And we all deserve more. We deserve . . ." He paused his small rant and looked at Teo. "Never mind. Forget I said anything."

Teo stayed quiet.

"What's with you?" I asked, because this wasn't like Rodrigo. One, he never talked politics, and two, he never, ever hung out with us. "I'm surprised you're even home and not with your girlfriend."

"Marisol's gone," he answered.

"Oof!" Teo widened his eyes. "She broke up with you already?"

Rodrigo punched him in the arm. "No, bobo. She and her family left Cuba. They headed to Mariel last night. She left me a note."

"Oh," Teo replied, gently rubbing his bicep. "That's too bad."

Rodrigo slumped back in the chair. There was an air of defeat about him as he stared at his shoeless feet for several seconds.

"Sorry." It was the only thing I could think of saying, but now at least I understood his attitude. "I know you really liked her."

"Loved her," Rodrigo corrected me.

"Want to come to my house?" Teo offered. "We could watch TV over there."

"Nah, there's never anything good on either channel." Rodrigo propped his head against the side of the chair and closed his eyes.

"Unless there's a baseball game," Teo corrected him.

"Yeah, I guess," he muttered. "I'm just not in the mood. You guys go and have fun."

It was a choice between my brother's gloominess or Isabel's bitterness. Teo made the choice for me.

"Está bien." Teo stood and shook some imaginary dust off his pants. "Let's go, Héctor."

I glanced at Rodrigo, who was blankly staring out the window. I'd never really seen him like this.

"You want me to stay and keep you company?" I asked.

"Nah." He sighed. "I just want to be alone."

Teo motioned for me to follow him onto our porch. As we walked outside, Teo whispered, "Broken heart syndrome. Best to leave him be for a while."

I scoffed at his diagnosis. "And what do *you* know of broken hearts?"

"You don't have to experience it to recognize it."

I shrugged. "I guess."

"I think Isa's heart got a little broken the other day," Teo said as we crossed the street.

"You mean because I called her stupid girl? She's tougher than that."

"No." He pinched his lips together. "Maybe Rodrigo's right. . . . You *are* naïve." He stopped me before we approached the steps to his house. "It was when she saw Rodrigo with his girlfriend. She realized that he only sees her as a little kid." He looked at me. "Facing the truth hurts sometimes."

I scowled. "Since when are you this . . . um . . . *insightful*?"

Teo shrugged. "Being aware isn't a bad thing." He leapt up to his porch and stumbled as his foot caught the edge of the loose brick. "Ugh! That stupid thing is going to kill me one day!"

"It's not like you didn't know it was there, Mr. Perceptive," I mocked. "Now, let's go see what's on TV."

Nani shushed us the moment we entered the house. She was watching a Mexican telenovela.

"It'll be over soon," Teo whispered as I sat on his couch. "Want me to go get you that book I told you about?"

"Sure," I said, figuring that I'd read it later.

Teo left the room and came back with a folded hand towel.

"I hid it inside," he said, placing the towel on the table. "Like the spies do in the movies."

I nodded. The idea of reading something that was banned felt dangerous and exciting. Then again, it was just another secret of the many I had to keep.

We patiently waited for Nani to finish watching her show, but unfortunately, there was another she wanted to watch after, so Teo and I were relegated to playing checkers. After our fourth game, I tried to convince him to play a game of chess, but he refused. We were already halfway through our fifth game when Rodrigo knocked on the door.

"Change your mind about joining us?" Teo asked, letting him inside. "I've got a baseball—we can play catch outside if you want."

"Some other day." He walked over to Nani to say hello, but she batted him away, as she was intently watching an old movie on TV. "Just came over to get Héctor. Mamá wants him home."

"Right now?" I asked, looking at the checkerboard on the floor. "We're in the middle of a game."

"Yes . . . now." Rodrigo hovered over me.

"Go. We'll call this one a draw." Teo smirked because it was obvious I was winning. "And don't forget the towel."

"Right." I grabbed the hidden book.

"Later, Teo. Adiós, Nani!" Rodrigo called out as he left their house.

"Wow, he's in a rush," Teo remarked. "You better hurry."

I gave Teo a quick nod and dashed out.

"¿Qué pasa?" I asked Rodrigo after jumping down the porch steps to catch up.

"Mamá's going through our things, deciding what we should take with us to the U.S.," he warned as we crossed the street. "I think having the electricity shut off has flipped her out a little."

"She's not planning on leaving today, is she?" I was worried that Mamá might make a rash decision.

"Of course not," Rodrigo replied in a low voice as he opened the door to our house. "We don't have the visas yet, and Mamá knows that no one leaves until the government says it's time to go."

Once inside, I laid the towel-wrapped book on top of the TV and noticed that Mamá was sitting on the floor next to the dining room table with photo albums all around her.

"Look at this." She held up a picture of me as a baby

being carried in her arms while Rodrigo, wearing a sailor suit, hugged our father's leg. "I love this picture of the four of us. There are so few of them . . . but we'll change that soon enough."

"What are you doing?" I asked, unsure if I really wanted to hear the answer. She and I hadn't spoken much all week.

"When the time comes, we won't have a chance to gather our things. We'll need to be ready," she said, flipping through more pictures. "I want to take things that can't be replaced. You should go through your things, too."

"But it's not like we are definitely leaving, right?" I clarified. "At least, not right away."

Rodrigo got closer. "Wait, are we leaving soon?" he asked. "Because maybe I could try to find Marisol over there if we go."

Mamá stopped what she was doing and smiled at the two of us. "I do have something to tell you both."

We sat down on the floor next to her, light from the setting sun streaming in through the front window.

"I received a message from your father. He's looking for a boat captain to come get us. He doesn't have one yet, but it shouldn't be too long." She reached for each of our hands and clasped them. "Then we can leave all of this behind."

"But Rodrigo said it wasn't that simple," I said. "We need permission to go."

Mamá cupped my chin. "Mi amor, yo lo sé. We still have to be very careful, but we're getting closer and Abuela knows it. She's sending me a warning by having the electricity shut off, but she won't let anything really serious happen to us. . . . That's why I still have my job. She thinks I'll reconsider."

I looked straight into her eyes. "Is there a chance you will?"

Mamá let me go and turned back to her albums. "We already spoke about this, Héctor."

"Then can I at least tell Teo? He won't—"

"No!" She looked back at me. "We can't risk it. Not when we are this close." She took a breath. "I know Teo and his family are good people, but we can't tell anyone. It's already bad enough that your grandmother knows." She gave me a slight smile. "But from what I've been hearing, when the time comes, you'll have a few minutes to run over and say goodbye. You just need to make sure that I know where you are whenever you leave the house. No disappearing for the day to go hang out with friends . . . for either of you. I have to know where to find you."

Rodrigo pursed his lips. "Yeah, that's what happened with Marisol. Soldiers knocked on her door and gave them ten minutes to leave the house. She said goodbye to a neighbor and left me a note. That was it."

"Hopefully, you'll see her again," Mamá said, reaching out to touch Rodrigo's knee. "And I'm not surprised that her family left. Her father was at the Peruvian embassy, right? That's probably why they got approved to leave so quickly. The government wanted them out before they could stir up more trouble."

Rodrigo widened his eyes. "Wait. You knew about Marisol's family?"

Mamá laughed. "Abuela is not the only one who has her sources. But . . ." She stood, her eyes lighting up. "I just realized something." She began to pace around in the growing darkness of the house. "Maybe I've been too *quiet* with my plans. Maybe I need to stir up some trouble."

None of that sounded like a good idea. We'd always been told to follow the rules and not do anything to make us stand out.

"Mamá, what are you planning?" Rodrigo asked as he took out some candles for later in the night. "If you're arrested for anti-revolutionary activity, that won't help us."

"No, but there are other 'undesirables' that the government wants to get rid of. Prisoners, prostitutes, mental patients, dissidents, gay people . . . they're all being forced to leave whether they want to or not." She narrowed her eyes and gave us a grin that I had never seen on her face before—one I could only describe as devilish. "Can you imagine the embarrassment your grandmother would suffer if I were labeled as one of them? She thinks this little stunt with the electricity is going to get me in line, but she's only made me more determined to go."

"Mamá, please," I begged, not wanting to think what would happen to us if things went wrong. "Don't." I had to protect whatever slim chance I had of going to the Math Olympiad and of staying in Cuba—the only home I'd known. The place where my friends all lived.

She tapped my hand. "Don't worry, Héctor. I won't do anything for now. But at least I now have a plan B, if push comes to shove."

I wasn't reassured because, in Cuba, everything always seemed to end with a shove.

10

I SAT IN class the next morning staring at the empty desk in front of me. It was the second day that Pilar, a quiet girl who always wore her hair in tight braids, had been absent and rumors were swirling. Some said she had left for Mariel in the middle of the night, while others said that she'd simply moved.

"I bet more people will disappear like Pilar," Teo whispered as he took his seat in the row next to me. "Just *poof* and they're gone. No goodbyes or anything."

"Maybe," I said as the bell rang. "Or she might be sick and come back tomorrow or Monday."

"Yasmin," our science teacher, Señora Gómez, called out. "I want you to switch over to Pilar's old seat."

"Te lo dije," Teo said, a smug look on his face. "Pilar's gone for good, but look who's replacing her."

Yasmin was one of the most popular girls in school and rarely spoke to me or Teo. She had light green eyes that stood out against her tanned skin, and she always seemed bored by whatever was happening around her. I had known her since first grade, but it was only recently that I'd really noticed how pretty she was.

"Um, isn't Pilar coming back?" Yasmin asked. "Because if it's all right with you, Señora Gómez, I'd rather stay here."

"No, she's not coming back," Señora Gomez said sternly. "She's chosen to abandon her homeland. Now please move. You talk too much back there anyway."

Yasmin huffed and began to gather her things.

I made eye contact with Isabel, who sat near Yasmin, but she quickly turned her head.

Teo noticed.

"Can you please make up with Isa?" he asked me. "I can't take another week like this one. Please." He was almost begging.

"Have you asked her to make up with me?" I replied. "Because it seems like you're taking her side, and when you two fight, either I stay neutral or I secretly back you up."

"I'm not taking sides, and as for asking Isabel . . ." Teo pursed his lips and raised a single eyebrow. "What do you think happened?"

I knew that he had likely asked her and she'd probably ignored him.

"¡Silencio!" Señora Gómez slapped a ruler against her desk. "Why is there so much chatter in this class?" She stared straight at me, but didn't mention my name. There were certain benefits to being one of the top students, but I couldn't push my luck. "Now, I want to see everyone's homework out on their desk."

Yasmin bumped my shoulder as she passed by me.

"Sorry," she mumbled as she dropped her books on Pilar's old desk.

I felt a little current of electricity flow through my shoulder straight to my heart. Suddenly I was very hot. I adjusted the red kerchief that hung around my neck.

Yasmin glanced around at her new surroundings and when her eyes met mine, she smiled.

Suddenly Pilar's departure didn't seem like a bad thing at all.

As Señora Gómez started lecturing, my gaze drifted to the back of Yasmin's head. I noticed that her long brown hair had streaks of gold that shimmered when the morning sun hit it at the right angle. My mind wandered until I caught myself staring for far too long. I quickly looked down at my homework, and while Señora Gómez talked about electrons, I made sure to stare only at her and not Yasmin.

Before I knew it, the bell rang and everyone was getting up. Yasmin grabbed her things quickly and went over to her girlfriends, who were waiting for her in the back of the room.

"Glad that's over," Teo commented, picking up his books.

"Huh?"

"Class," he said. "It seems to get harder and somehow more boring every day, don't you think?"

I nodded. "Yeah, I guess."

Teo scoffed. "Well, school's always been easy for you, Mr. Straight As. I swear, sometimes I think we were switched at birth or something. You should've been the teacher's son and I . . ."

He didn't finish his sentence. How could he? Who would want to be the son of a traitor?

"No way that we were switched," I said, stacking my books on top of my notebook. "Only you can put up with Isabel full-time."

He raised a finger in the air. "Very true, compañero. Very true." He chuckled. "I think the army should count my entire life as some type of combat training."

"Combat training," I replied as we walked to the door. "You know Rodrigo is getting close to military age. Mamá's worried."

Teo waved off my concern. "Meh, your abuela will take care of him. Bigger question is what will happen when I reach that age. I've got no strings to pull." He glanced over at me. "Unless your grandmother can do something."

I thought about how Abuela said no when Rodrigo asked her for help with his girlfriend's brother. Would she help Teo?

"We'll come up with something," I said, stepping out to the hallway bustling with kids going to their next class.

"Yeah, sure." Teo had suddenly become unusually solemn. As he stopped by the water fountain, he said, "You know, sometimes families need to keep secrets and they don't even tell their closest friends. Like what happened with Rodrigo's girlfriend or Pilar." He paused and took a sip of water.

108

I clenched my books a little tighter. Did Teo suspect that we had plans to go? I couldn't afford to look at him for fear I might blurt it all out.

He lifted his head up and smiled. "But that's okay," he continued. "It's just the way things are in Cuba, right?" Teo stepped aside for me to get some water. "No one gets mad."

"Guess so," I replied, bending over the fountain.

Just as the cold water hit my lips, a hand grabbed the back of my shirt and pulled me away.

"Move, runt."

I turned around to see Tincho staring me down as a couple of his friends blocked Teo.

I couldn't understand how I'd managed to avoid him for years and now our paths seemed to cross all the time.

"Sure, Tincho." I stepped aside. "It's all yours. Sin ningún problema."

"Uh-huh." He kept staring at me. "And I heard about your brother's little girlfriend, Marisol. Turns out she's just like your father. Seems like there are a lot of gusanos circling around your family," he jeered. "Guess what that makes *you*."

"Wait, wasn't Marisol the girl who dumped you?" one of the boys asked Tincho.

Tincho spun around and glared at him. "I dumped her!"

"Excuse me, boys." Señora Andrade stepped in front of Tincho as if she were about to take a sip of water. She paused and looked back at us. "Is everything all right? Shouldn't you all be getting to class?"

Tincho and his friends pulled away. "Sí, señora."

"Héctor, I actually need to speak to you for a second," she said before I could take off as well. "It's about our math session. I'm afraid I have to cancel."

"Oh, that's fine," I said. "Do you want to meet tomorrow or just leave it for next Thursday?"

She glanced around as the hallway began to empty out. "No, I don't think I should continue tutoring you for the Olympiad anymore."

"What? Why?" Señora Andrade was the one who had encouraged me to try out in the first place, and no one understood what I needed to do to make the team more than her.

She took a deep breath as the bell rang for the next class. "It's for the best, Héctor. Things can become complicated in Cuba. Relationships can be judged simply by—" She stopped talking as Señor Linares approached.

Even though I was going to be late for class, I didn't care. I needed to know why she was abandoning me.

"I don't understand," I said. "Why won't you help me?"

"Señora Andrade, I think you have a class waiting and so does this student of yours," Señor Linares said, filling up a mug with cold water.

"Yes, of course." Señora Andrade had a tight smile as she looked at me. "I was just explaining to Héctor that his mother no longer wants me to tutor him and so I'm abiding by her wishes."

It felt like someone had thrown the cold water from the mug all over me.

I took a couple of steps backward, in a state of disbelief.

"Parents . . . who knows what any of them are thinking," Señor Linares scoffed as he and Señora Andrade walked away.

I couldn't believe what was happening. I felt anger churning in the pit of my stomach. Mamá was cutting off my future in Cuba. How could she?

How would she like it if I . . .

I took a deep breath.

Maybe it was time for me to do something drastic.

AFTER SCHOOL, I didn't wait around for Teo or Isabel. It was Thursday, so they'd think I was with Señora Andrade preparing for the Olympiad, but I was on a different kind of mission. A mission to save my dreams.

I raced down the streets of town, knowing what I had to do.

The moment I got home, I checked to make sure I was alone. I expected the house to be empty, but I had to be certain.

Then I began the search.

I started with Mamá's room. The electricity had come back that morning, so I turned on the lamp by her bed. She always kept everything neat and tidy, so I had to be extra careful not to mess anything up. I went through the drawer in her nightstand, looking for a piece of paper that would have Papá's contact information.

My plan was to call him and explain how much we were sacrificing to be with him. He probably didn't know how close

I was to getting on the national team or how well Rodrigo was doing on the school baseball team. I could even say that Mamá didn't really want to go and was only doing this because he wanted her to leave. That last part might be a lie, but I was desperate.

I flipped through Mamá's address book but couldn't find his phone number, and there wasn't anything else in the drawer that might provide a clue. I searched in her closet, chest of drawers, and couldn't find anything. Scanning the room, I thought about where I might hide something if I were Mamá.

My eyes fell on her bed.

I walked over, lifted up the mattress, and found several envelopes addressed to Mamá, but with an address different from ours.

A twinge of guilt filled my chest at the invasion of Mamá's privacy, but I brushed it aside. This had to be done.

I opened the envelope with the most recent postmark and it was from my father, as expected.

I skimmed over the parts where he talked about how much he loved her and how he missed all of us. Even reading fast, I could feel the energy and truth in his words, and it made my heart soften a little. I missed him, too, but I didn't want to give up everything I knew to go live with him. Maybe there was a way he could eventually come back here.

Then I read his description about being in prison. He didn't go into detail, but he mentioned being beaten and how happy he was now that he could celebrate being free. I sighed. The odds of him returning were close to zero and I knew it. We'd never be together in Cuba.

I shook my head to scatter away the creeping doubts about what I was doing. Papá's experiences weren't mine. I had to focus on what *I* wanted . . . just like he had.

I flipped the page over and at the bottom Papá had written his address in Miami with a phone number.

I checked the alarm clock on top of Mamá's nightstand. It was almost five-thirty and there was a chance Papá might be home from his factory job. It'd be risky because Mamá or Rodrigo could be home at any moment, too. But I couldn't take the chance of waiting two more days until the weekend.

It was now or never.

I took the letter and ran to the phone in the living room. Mamá never called him from the house because she thought government agents would be listening to the calls and it could come back to hurt us. But at this point, what did we have to lose? She was already asking for the visas and I wasn't going to say anything against the government. In fact, if someone was listening, they'd hear how much I wanted to stay.

I dialed the number, keeping an eye on the door.

The phone went through a series of clicks and tones, then began to ring.

I held my breath, waiting.

On the fourth ring, someone picked up.

"Ha-lo?" a deep voice responded.

"Papá?" The word sounded strange coming from my lips. I had only spoken to him once in the last six years, and it had been that brief call a few months ago from a stranger's house. I wasn't sure how he'd react to my calling him now. "Es Héctor."

"No," the man replied.

My heart fell. Had I dialed the wrong number or had Papá moved? I hadn't even stopped to consider the different possibilities. What kind of mathematician was I when I ignored the probabilistic logic?

"Pero espérate un minuto," the man instructed. I could hear him put the phone down and then heavy footsteps running somewhere. "¡Raúl! ¡RAÚL!" he shouted. "Creo que es tu hijo. . . . ¡Apúrate!"

A couple of seconds later I heard the phone being picked up again. "¿Hola? ¿Quién habla?"

I took a deep breath, this time recognizing the voice. "Papá, it's me . . . Héctor."

"Héctor! It's so good to hear your voice. I've missed you so much! Is everything okay?" His voice changed from surprised to worried. "Where is your mother? Where are you?" He was speaking so fast that I couldn't answer his questions. "Is your brother all right? Did something happen?"

"No, no. Todo está bien." I braced myself for what I was about to do. "I'm calling because Mamá told us about the plans and—"

"I know. It won't be long now, mijo. Thinking of us being together, being free, is the only thing that got me through those long years in prison." I heard his voice, filled with emotion, begin to break. "It was hard, but worth it. And now the time is here. I can't wait to see you all."

"Um . . . about that. I don't know if Mamá told you about the math team and—"

"¡Claro que me lo dijo!" he gushed. "She's so proud of you. And I've been bragging to all the guys at the factory about how gifted you are. I told your mom that you get that brilliant brain of yours from her, but she won't believe me." He chuckled. "We'll have to convince her together." He paused. "But why are you calling? Does your mother know you're doing this?"

I stayed quiet. This wasn't how I expected the conversation to go. I was supposed to convince him to tell Mamá that we shouldn't leave, but now all I wanted was to see him.

"Héctor, are you still there?" Papá asked.

"Yes," I answered. "I . . . um . . . I just wanted to make sure you wanted us all there."

"¡Ay, Héctor!" Papá exclaimed. "There's nothing I want more in this world. I love you with all my heart. Con toda mi alma." He paused. "You know, I've been taking chess lessons so we can play together when you get here. Your mother told me that it's your favorite game and I know you're too old for the piggyback rides I used to give you."

Starting from deep in my chest and rising to my head, I felt an enormous urge to cry. There had been a huge hole in my heart that I hadn't even realized was there. I wanted to be a family of four. I wanted for us all to be together, too. But I also wanted to stay in Cuba. I could feel myself being torn right down the middle. "Yo te quiero también, Papá," I said.

Out of the corner of my eye I saw Mamá picking something up from the porch.

"I have to go," I said in a rush. "Please don't tell Mamá I called."

I hung up the phone before Papá could respond and stuffed his letter in my pocket just as the front door opened.

"You left one of your books outside, Héctor," Mamá said, putting it down on the coffee table. "You need to be more careful because . . ." She paused to study me. "Are you all right?"

"Yeah, sure." I could feel a small bead of sweat forming at the edge of my forehead. I needed to act normal. "And that's not my book. Maybe Rodrigo left it?"

Mamá leaned over and read the title. "*Differential Equations and Advanced Linear Algebra for the Modern Era*. Does that sound like something your brother would read?"

"Huh?" I walked over to look at the book, not recognizing the title.

"I'm going to go start dinner." Mamá headed toward the kitchen, stopped, and turned around. "Did something happen at school today?"

I opened the math book and saw a note from Señora Andrade.

"Héctor . . . ," Mamá called out.

117

"I'm fine. Just a long day," I answered. "Thanks for bringing in the book."

I sat down and read the note as Mamá left the room.

Héctor,

I'm sorry I couldn't say a proper goodbye at school, but I had to keep my leaving Cuba a secret. I hope that blaming your mother for canceling our arrangements helps distance you from my actions. I'm sure your grandmother can smooth things over with the math team. I will be rooting for you from afar.

Enjoy the book, and may your dreams always follow you wherever you go.

I couldn't believe it. Señora Andrade had left . . . probably through Mariel.

Everything was changing and there was nothing I could do to stop it.

How many more signs did I need?

No matter how much I fought it, my future was no longer in Cuba.

12

THE ALARM CLOCK next to my bed sounded, startling me out of a dream about hot-air balloons lifting me up into the clouds. My hand slapped the button just as Rodrigo stirred in his bed.

I put on my glasses and got up, careful not to make noise so as to avoid Rodrigo's wrath. He didn't understand how great it was to be by the water and see the sun come up over the horizon. How exhilarating it was to feel the fishing line being tugged by a yellowtail at the hidden fishing spot Teo and I had discovered a few months back. Or how the sound of the tiniest waves hitting the shore battled for attention against the wind rustling the leaves of the mangroves. I hated the idea of leaving this behind.

And the only person who really appreciated it as much as I did was Teo, and he was expecting me to be outside in ten minutes.

I tiptoed across the room, the moonlight streaming through

the window, and grabbed my lucky fishing shirt . . . being extra careful not to make the hole under the left arm any bigger. It was starting to get a little small on me, but I didn't care. It was a faded red and it had the word CUBAVISIÓN in blue and green across the chest, with the TV station's slogan, EL CANAL DE TODOS, underneath. It was a promotional item that Abuela had managed to get for me a couple of years ago, and every time I'd worn it fishing, I'd caught something good. So I was not going to mess around with fate.

I picked up the fishing pole I'd left by the sofa the night before, walked to the front door, and slowly turned the knob.

Outside, I took a deep breath, inhaling the damp pre-dawn air.

I felt lucky to even get to go fishing. Mamá had not been thrilled to learn that I had made plans with Teo, but Rodrigo assured her he could find me if for some reason our visas were granted while I was out. It was strange to have my brother take my side, but maybe the whole thing with Marisol had softened him up a little.

"Psst. Vámonos," Teo whispered, the wind carrying his voice from the middle of the street. "The fish are waiting."

I jumped the porch steps and hurried over.

There was nothing like going fishing with your best friend.

"Where's your lucky shirt?" I asked, noticing that he was wearing a plain white undershirt and not the bright yellow T-shirt he usually wore when we went fishing.

"Couldn't find it. I think my mom may have thrown it out or something." He tugged on his brown-checkered shorts. "Think I'm going to make these my lucky fishing shorts."

"Hmm." I wasn't convinced. Luck wasn't something you could simply replace. "You sure you don't want to go back and look for it?"

"Nah." He started walking down the middle of our street. "I want to get there before sunrise."

I glanced up at the full moon hanging low in the sky.

"¿Viste la luna?" I said, pointing up to it.

It had a foggy halo around it. It was a sign that there was too much moisture in the air, and that could only mean one thing . . . a storm was coming.

"Yeah, but hopefully, the rain will hold till after we catch enough for dinner." He turned the corner past all the darkened houses. We were likely the only ones up at this hour.

"So, are you going to talk to Isabel today?" he asked. "Make up with her?"

"Yeah, yeah," I said.

"That's what you said before and you didn't do it."

"Well, she didn't walk home with us yesterday, did she?" I countered.

"Um, we live across the street. You could've done it at any point in the afternoon."

I shrugged. "I'll do it when we get back."

"Promise?"

I rolled my eyes. "Promise."

Teo stopped me from taking another step. "Seriously. You have to do it."

"Tranquilo. I said I would, and I will."

He nodded as if satisfied.

"And what's the deal with Yasmin?" he asked, a slight snicker in his voice.

"I have no idea what you mean," I said. "Is something going on with her?"

He laughed so hard that he scared a nearby bird, making it flutter away into some nearby mangroves. "You are the worst liar."

"Lying about what? I haven't even said anything."

"Pretending that you don't like her . . . c'mon. I sit next to you and I've seen you staring at her back for two days now." He looked at me with puppy-dog eyes and pumped-up lips. "Ah, young love."

"Shut up." I gave him a push.

"Just admit it," he insisted. "She *is* pretty."

"I haven't really noticed," I said, not breaking my stride. "Guess you must be the one who likes her."

"Nice try, but she's not my type."

"What is your type?" I said, hoping to change the conversation.

"Haven't quite figured that out yet. Un flechazo hasn't struck my heart yet. Cupid is still holding back that arrow."

I acted like I was gagging on his words. Teo was the only

person I knew who talked like that. If Isabel were with us, she'd be making fun of him right now, too.

I kicked a small rock down the street.

Teo was right. Everything felt off when a piece of our trio was missing.

Even the most annoying piece.

As we approached the gravel side road that led to an abandoned pier, my thoughts drifted to the phone call with my father. Hearing his voice had stirred something up inside of me. I'd nearly forgotten him. I felt guilty for having focused only on wanting to be on the math team. Family was more important . . . but Teo was like family and I'd be leaving him behind.

I didn't know how to feel anymore.

We reached the end of the main road and were now pushing aside the overgrown bushes that hid our secret fishing spot from view. There were some thorny bougainvillea and dense mangroves to navigate, but as soon as we made it through, I spotted the rickety old pier. Most of it had been washed away in one of the hurricanes from long ago, but some pylons and part of the platform remained standing. It was in bad shape for anyone to walk along, but the fish seemed to love it.

"Let's set up," Teo said, dropping his pole and bucket.

We had developed a system over the past couple of years. I would catch the hermit crabs that lurked around the mangroves and Teo would place them on the hook.

After a few minutes we had our first two pieces of bait and

our lines were in the water. Now it was just a matter of being patient.

Minutes ticked by with Teo and me silently casting and recasting our lines, trying to entice the fish. But there wasn't a single bite. Not even a nibble.

Soon the sky began to lighten up with streaks of pink and orange.

I looked at our empty bucket. We'd been at this for a couple of hours and things weren't looking good.

I blamed Teo's shirt.

"Let's try a different spot," I suggested, the hermit crab still dangling from the tip of my fishhook. "They're not biting over here today."

"Want to go to the bridge next to the boatyard?" Teo reeled in his line. "It's a little far, but I'm willing to walk over and try."

"Can't be worse than here." I bent down and grabbed a couple more hermit crabs and tossed them into the bucket. "It might be crowded, though, by this time. It's a popular spot."

"Yeah, I know." He slung his fishing pole over his shoulder and picked up the bucket. "I probably should've worn my lucky shirt," he said as we ducked under the overgrowth and walked back onto the side road. "Ahora estoy sala'o."

I tugged on the bottom of my shirt. "Meh, I have mine on and I haven't caught anything either."

"Maybe I jinxed the two of us," Teo replied as we walked quickly to the main road to make up for lost time. "Now we'll probably—"

"¡Mira a quién nos encontramos!" a voice from behind us exclaimed. "Anyone need some worms as bait?"

I turned to see Tincho and his friends on bikes.

As if we needed further proof that we were having an un-lucky day, they circled around and stopped directly in front of us.

Teo loomed silently behind me like a giant shadow.

"Listen, Tincho." My feet crunched on the gravel as I stepped off the road and onto its shoulder. "We don't want any trouble."

Tincho laughed. "Yeah, but I have a feeling trouble wants you."

"¿Y tú?" One of the larger kids eyed Teo. "¿Qué tú miras?"

Teo dropped his gaze, not wanting any type of confron-tation.

Tincho shook his head. "¿Ese? He's just grande por gusto, but the other one . . . he's got quite the story." He leaned over and whispered something to one of his friends, who simply raised his eyebrows in surprise.

I imagined that he was saying who my father and grand-mother were, but I didn't care. Not anymore.

The three boys hopped back on their bikes. "See you later!" Tincho shouted, his face twisted with a somewhat evil smirk.

Teo stepped out from behind me. "Let's go."

"Why do you always back down? You let him call you 'grande por gusto' and did nothing."

Teo shrugged. "But I am a 'big for nothing' and I don't care. Fighting doesn't solve anything."

"But some things are worth fighting for," I argued. "Your honor. Your pride."

Teo rolled his eyes and walked away. "An idiot like Tincho can't hurt either of those things. Now, let's go catch lunch."

As one hour became two, then three, and finally four, it became clear that our luck was not changing, even at the bridge. Our day of fishing had been a complete bust and it was already close to lunchtime.

We headed home with a new plan. Find Teo's lucky fishing shirt and try again the next morning.

"Did you look in your dirty-clothes hamper?" I asked as we walked down a main street about a block away from our houses.

"Of course I did," Teo insisted. "And in Isabel's and outside on the clothesline. It wasn't in my drawers or in the closet either."

"Hmm. Well, we'll ask your mom. I bet she'll know. Moms always seem to—"

I stopped talking as we rounded the corner and saw a crowd gathered in the middle of our street. Their voices carried on the breeze and I could hear the anger in their chants, although I couldn't make out what was being said.

"This can't be happening," Teo muttered.

We both approached slowly, careful to keep our distance.

As we got closer, we could see a few of our neighbors standing in front of my house along with many other unfamiliar faces. They were shouting insults and taunting my mother to come outside.

"It's against you," Teo whispered, his voice filled with shock.

I nodded, thinking back to the phone call I'd made to my father. Had someone been listening? Was this my fault?

"Welcome home, gusano!" Tincho called out as the crowd turned to look at me.

"Run!" Teo gave me a shove. "Now!"

IT WAS AS if my shoes had melted into the asphalt beneath me and my legs refused to move. I was paralyzed by what I was seeing. People I'd known my whole life were standing side by side with strangers who hated us without even knowing us. The mob would turn on me any second, so if I was going to get away, it had to be now. But how could I leave my family? I couldn't choose my own safety over the people I loved.

Tincho's smile among the angry stares made my decision all the easier.

I ran through the crowd as several people spit at me and called me *gusano*. As I reached the porch steps, the front door flew open and Mamá pulled me inside.

"Are you okay?" Mamá inspected me from head to toe. "No one hurt you?"

"I'm fine," I said as the shouting outside got louder. The chant of "¡Gusanos, ratones, salgan de los rincones!" was now on repeat.

"I've had enough!" Rodrigo declared, slamming the dining room table with his hands as he stood up. "I'm going out there and tell them what they—"

Mamá spun around to face him. "You sit back down," she ordered. "I will not have you out there with those people. I don't trust a single one of them." She pointed me to the table. "And you, too. Go be with your brother. We'll wait them out."

I took two steps when a splat against the door stopped me in my tracks. Then a flurry of pops and more splats hit the house.

"It's just eggs," Mamá said, her voice quivering a bit. "We can clean it up later." She pulled back the closed curtain to take a peek outside. "Let them do their worst."

Rodrigo had snuck over to the door without Mamá noticing.

He yanked it open and took a step outside.

Mamá jerked back her head, but it was too late. "NO!" she yelled as Rodrigo stepped onto our porch.

I raced over to join him, but Mamá grabbed me by the arm and had me stand next to her in the doorway.

Rodrigo now stood in front of the crowd. "Any of you cowards want a piece of me? Come up here." He pounded his chest with his own fists.

"¡Gusano! Just like your father!" someone yelled.

"And his girlfriend!" Tincho added.

Rodrigo ducked as an egg came flying toward his head, smashing against the window.

I looked across the street and saw Teo, Isabel, and their parents watching the scene unfold. Teo's dad was holding Isabel by the arm. I could tell that they all wanted to help, but they were powerless. Any action could turn the mob on them.

"¡Que se vayan!" an older man wearing a white tank top shouted while pumping his fist in the air. "¡Escoria!"

"With people like you here," Rodrigo answered back, "who wouldn't want to leave!"

Another egg was thrown, hitting Rodrigo in the leg.

"¡Basura!" a woman yelled.

I scoured the faces in the crowd. There were several people hanging out around the edges who seemed uncomfortable being there. They were probably going through the motions just like I had done a week earlier.

It gave me an idea.

I pulled away from Mamá's grip and stood next to Rodrigo.

"Listen . . . I know many of you are angry," I shouted, the mob growing momentarily quiet. "But isn't it better if we argue about baseball?" I glanced around, hoping to find some receptive faces. "Tell me . . . who here likes Los Industriales?"

"Me!" I heard Isabel's voice from across the street, and then I saw her father drag her inside. Teo's eyes locked with mine and he gave me a quick nod.

Several people in the crowd looked at each other for a moment, then quickly the chants about us being traitors and scum started again.

My idea hadn't worked. Maybe I had to pick another team.

"No, listen—" I tried speaking over the crowd. But Mamá stepped out in front of me.

"Por favor!" she begged, raising her arms in the air. "Many of you have known us for years." She pointed to me and Rodrigo. "You've seen these boys be born and grow up in this house. You *know* us. Please stop this!"

A skinny man drenched in sweat yelled out a vile insult toward Mamá. Words that we were never allowed to say.

It was the last straw for Rodrigo. He jumped into the crowd and charged at the man who had insulted our mother.

"RODRIGO!" Mamá screamed, holding me back by the arm.

It became total mayhem.

Many in the crowd had stepped away, not wanting to be part of a fight, but others seemed to enjoy watching the spectacle as if it were a real boxing match.

Rodrigo got in a couple of good punches against the man, but now several people were ganging up on Rodrigo.

I broke free of Mamá's grasp and ran to help my brother.

I pushed through the crowd, but before I could get to him, Tincho pushed me to the ground and kicked me hard in the stomach.

I gasped.

"Told you that you wouldn't always be protected," he sneered.

Every ounce of air had been forced out of my lungs and I couldn't seem to get any back. Black dots floated in front of my eyes. I curled up in self-protection, but I could still see my mother in the middle of the throng of people.

"¡¡¡BASTA, ANIMALES!!!" Mamá screamed. "They're only children!" She stood over Rodrigo, whose face was bleeding.

The crowd began to disperse.

Suddenly I felt an arm sweep under my rib cage to help me stand.

Teo.

"You touch him again and I will beat the hell out of you," Teo threatened as he held the loose brick from his porch in his hand. "Now get out of here!"

Tincho stepped back, glaring at both of us.

Mamá was already pulling Rodrigo back into the house, even though he seemed to want to stay and fight some more.

I tried to breathe, but my lungs didn't want to work. I took in short, shallow breaths as Teo propped me up.

The crowd seemed to have had their fill of humiliating us. For most of them, there was no need to waste more of a Saturday afternoon with gusanos like us and so they were drifting away. Ready to go on with their normal lives as if nothing had happened.

But for me, everything had changed.

I didn't think even Abuela could help us after this. I would never be a math Olympian.

I struggled to simply adjust my glasses and take a few steps, but at least I could finally feel the warm, humid air filtering into my chest.

"Gracias," I croaked out, still leaning on Teo for support. "Can you help me get inside?"

"Of course. Brothers forever, right?" Teo said, dropping the brick before we headed back to the porch littered with broken eggs. "You were right—some things are worth fighting for."

I smiled as we climbed up my steps, Teo's arm still holding me up.

As I grabbed the doorframe for support, Teo let go of me.

"You gonna be okay?" he asked.

"Yeah," I said meekly, not really sure if I would be. "Guess our family's secret is out. . . . Mamá is planning to leave."

"Mm-hmm." Teo took a step back and glanced down at the eggshells around his feet. One of his shoelaces was undone and was dragging along a piece of yolk.

"I'm sorry that I couldn't talk to you about it," I said as Teo bent down to tie his sneaker.

Teo glanced up at me. "I get it. Sometimes even best friends can't share everything."

"Yeah." I looked out at the few stragglers still milling around. They didn't matter to me anymore. "I better go check on Rodrigo," I said, turning away from him.

Then someone shouted, "Broken glass is better than broken eggs!"

I spun back around.

Teo heard it too and darted up to see who had said it.

That was his one mistake. He should've ignored it. He should've kept tying his shoe.

Instead, the trajectories of two objects in motion intersected at the worst possible point.

The brick slammed into the side of Teo's head.

"NOOOOOOO!" I screamed, seeing it all happen in slow motion.

I darted forward as Teo's body lurched sideways and then crumpled down the remaining steps.

"TEO!" I heard his mother screech from across the street and saw her sprinting toward us as everyone else ran away.

I jumped down to where Teo was lying, blood from his head already pooling on the cement walkway and onto his white T-shirt.

"Teo! Teo! Talk to me!" I said, crouching next to him. I took off my lucky fishing shirt and pressed it against his head.

Teo didn't move.

I looked at his chest. He wasn't breathing.

"¡Ay no!" Mamá exclaimed, rushing out of our house. "¡Dios mío! ¡No!"

"Teo . . . please," I begged, panic beginning to overtake me. "Someone get a doctor!" I yelled as Teo's mother pushed me aside and I fell backward onto the grass.

I stared up at the sky, then back at Teo and his mother.

I refused to believe what I was seeing.

It was unthinkable. Unimaginable.

Then Teo's mother let out the most piercing wail I had ever heard and my world screeched to a stop.

14

IF ONLY I hadn't called my father.

If only I hadn't told Teo on our way back from fishing to fight back sometimes.

If only I hadn't gone out into the crowd when there was a fight already brewing.

If only I hadn't asked Teo to help me inside the house.

If only . . .

But it was no use to keep thinking about all the things I could've done differently. Nothing changed the fact that my best friend in the entire world was gone.

And it was my fault.

Or at least my family's fault.

It had been only a day since Teo died, but time had become irrelevant. It felt like only a few minutes had passed, and in the same instant it felt like I'd been stuck in this nightmare for years. I kept reliving every moment.

I didn't know how we were going to face his parents. How could they and Isabel even look at us, knowing that he died because we had planned to leave Cuba?

"Maybe we shouldn't go over there," I suggested as Mamá put together a platter full of food. "They may not want to see us."

"It would be completely understandable if that's the case. And then we'll respect their wishes and leave," Mamá replied, picking some lint off her black blouse. "But they are like family, so we need to see if there is anything we can do for them." She took a deep breath, and I could see tears forming once again in the corners of her eyes.

Normally, seeing my mother cry might make me uncomfortable, but not this time. Now I wanted everyone to feel the same exhausting sadness that I felt.

Rodrigo stood silently by the door. A quiet guard between us and the rest of the world. A world that hated us.

Mamá dabbed her eyes with a white handkerchief. "I can only imagine the anguish . . . to lose a son like that." She stared at Rodrigo and then me, clearly imagining. Then she took another deep breath to regain her composure. "Whatever happens, however they react, we accept it. Understood?"

Rodrigo nodded and opened the door.

For the first time in my life, my stomach churned at the thought of going across the street. I didn't want to see Isabel or her parents, but I knew I had to.

I swallowed the lump in my throat and followed Mamá as she carried the platter of food.

It was time to face the people whose family I had destroyed.

Rodrigo closed the door after me, and I noticed that Mamá had cleaned up all the eggs from the porch. In fact, you couldn't tell that anything had ever happened in our yard.

We marched across the street like a mother duck with her ducklings behind her.

Silently we went up the steps, the missing brick a glaring reminder.

I glanced at Nani's empty rocking chair.

I wondered if she grasped what had happened or if she'd retreated into her own world where Teo was still laughing and giving her pecks on the cheek.

Mamá knocked gently on the door.

We waited.

A few seconds passed and Mamá knocked again, a little stronger.

It was exactly as I had feared. They didn't want us there because they blamed us for what happened. It was a mistake to come over.

I was about to tell Mamá that we should go when the door swung open and Teo's father stood there, staring at us. He had dark circles under his eyes and his shoulders were slumped.

Before we could say anything, Teo's mother came running

over to hug Mamá. Mamá thrust the platter into my hands so that they could embrace.

"Entren, entren," Teo's father said, motioning for us all to come inside quickly.

I didn't want to look at him, so I kept my head down, following Mamá into the living room. Without saying a word, I sat down on the couch and stared at my hands holding the platter.

"Lo siento tanto," Mamá said. "We loved Teo so much. I can't . . ." Her voice cracked, and she couldn't keep talking.

Teo's mother uncontrollably sobbed into Mamá's shoulder as Mamá stroked her hair. I imagined that she hadn't stopped crying since it had all happened.

"He was an exceptional boy," Teo's father added.

A few seconds of silence passed.

"We brought over some food," Rodrigo said, pointing to the platter. "Give it to them, Héctor," he said, tapping my leg.

I lifted it up, but I just couldn't look at Teo's father.

"Héctor, you know where everything is," he said. "Just take it to the kitchen and bring everyone some water, please."

"Yes sir," I whispered. I stood up and realized that it was probably the first time I had ever called him *sir*.

I carried the tray into the kitchen, where Isabel was sitting with Nani at the table.

"Teo!" Nani proclaimed upon seeing me, her face lighting up.

Hearing Nani call out his name was like a dagger straight through my heart.

"No, Nani," Isabel said, gently stroking Nani's arm. "That's Héctor."

"Ah, sí." She smiled at me. "You do look a lot like Teo when he was shorter and thinner. You two could be brothers." She glanced around. "¿Y dónde está Teo?"

Isabel sighed. "We told you, Nani. He's in heaven now." She paused to let the words sink in. "He died yesterday."

Nani's lips quivered as she nodded. "Ah, sí." She stared down at the cup of café con leche in front of her.

"Your dad asked me to put away some food that my mom brought over," I explained, holding the platter. "I think it's some croquetas and empanadas."

"Just put them here." Isabel pointed to the table.

"Hay croquetas?" Nani asked, her attention now focused on the food.

"Yes." I took off the linen napkin to reveal an assortment of croquetas, empanadas, and little papas rellenas. "Have whatever you like."

Nani suddenly seemed content again as she reached for a croqueta. "¡Qué rico! Mi mamá hacía las mejores croquetas de bacalao. ¿De qué son estas?"

"I think those are made with ham," I said.

"Mmm." Nani took a bite and smiled.

Isabel locked eyes with me.

There was so much to say and yet I didn't know where to start.

"You doing okay?" she asked.

I nodded. "You? Your parents?"

She shrugged. "The doctor had to give my mom some pills to help her calm down, but I guess we're doing okay, considering. Doesn't seem real, though."

I sat down next to her. "I'm really sorry," I said. "About everything."

"It's not your fault," she replied, but her voice was flat. It was as if she didn't believe her own words. Or maybe I couldn't believe them.

I thought about my final promise to Teo. I had to make things right with Isabel.

"I'm also sorry about last week," I said. "You were being honest with me and I just got mad. I should've apologized days ago."

"Teo convinced you, huh?" She chuckled. "He was telling me a couple of days ago that if by any chance you said you were sorry, then I was supposed to follow up with an apology, too." She gave me a halfhearted smile. "So, I'm sorry, too."

"Teo . . ." I shook my head. "Don't know what I'm gonna do without him."

"*You* don't know?" She widened her eyes. "I've never even existed without him being with me."

She was right. Even before being born the two of them had been together. It was a stupid thing to say in front of her.

"I'm sorry. I didn't mean—"

"It's okay." She took a deep breath. "You loved him as much as I did. This is hard for all of us. I just miss him already, you know?"

"He's still here," Nani said.

"Okay, Nani," Isabel answered, not wanting to go through telling her again.

"No." Nani looked at me, then Isabel, then back at me. "Teo is here." Her wrinkled old hand pointed to her heart. "And here." She touched her forehead. "He lives through us. Our memories of him and how we choose to honor him while living our lives." She smiled as her eyes glistened. "One day we will see him again and then we can once more share in all the stories."

It was such a wise and non-Nani thing to say that Isabel and I sat dumbfounded, not knowing how to respond.

Then I did what felt right in my heart.

I got up and gave Nani a kiss on the cheek.

She stroked the back of my head and then said, "Remember, always be careful of the dragons."

Isabel broke out laughing and I did, too.

It was a laugh born out of sadness. A momentary relief.

"Asere." Rodrigo joined us in the kitchen. "What's going on in here? I thought you were getting us all some water."

"Oh, yeah." I stood up and got several glasses from the cupboard.

"Siento mucho lo de Teo," Rodrigo said to Isabel and Nani. "He was a really good kid. He deserved better."

"Mm-hmm," Isabel replied.

"Gracias, mi amor." Nani gave him a sweet smile. Then she leaned over to Isabel. "Who is he?" she asked.

"That's Rodrigo," Isabel explained. "Héctor's brother."

"Ah . . . yes." She nodded. "Héctor, the one with the dragons."

"Dragons?" Rodrigo questioned, glancing over at me.

"It's just something Nani says." I handed him two of the glasses.

"Give me one more and leave my water in here," he said, pointing to the glasses I was holding. "I'll come back and hang out with you guys."

I expected Isabel to like the idea of Rodrigo wanting to spend time with us, but she didn't seem to care. In fact, she seemed a little bit irritated.

The moment he walked out with the drinks she turned to me. "Does he have to come back here?" she asked, clearly annoyed.

"Um . . . I guess not," I said. "Why?"

"It's just if he hadn't started that fight, then Teo might not have gone over and . . . and . . ."

She didn't finish.

"Teo came over because of me," I said, relieving Rodrigo of the blame. "It was my fault. You should be mad at me. You should hate me."

"You were trying to protect your brother," she corrected me. "Just like Teo went over to protect you. But Rodrigo . . ."

"He was defending my mom."

"From insults." She spat out the words. "Stupid words that didn't mean anything ended up costing my brother his life."

I didn't know what to say. She was right and at the same time she was wrong.

"I know," I muttered. "But it was an accident."

"It wasn't," she countered. "Someone threw that brick on purpose, even if they didn't mean to hit Teo with it." She shook her head in disgust. "And you know the police won't do much. They're all in on it."

"I guess." I thought about the police. What if they'd been listening in to my phone call to my father? And then ordered the action against us? Maybe *I* set everything in motion?

I felt like throwing up.

Isabel started to pace around the kitchen. "Soon it'll be like nothing happened. Whoever did it might not even feel guilty about it. Teo will be buried and forgotten."

"No," I countered. "He'll never be forgotten because—"

"¿Quieres una empanada?" Nani asked as Rodrigo came back in.

"No, gracias, Nani." Rodrigo motioned for me to get up. "We have to go."

I looked over at Isabel standing in the corner with her arms crossed over her chest. Rodrigo was oblivious to the change in how she saw him.

"Now?" I questioned.

"Maybe Héctor can stay and you can leave," Isabel suggested.

Rodrigo shook his head. "Mamá said both of us," he replied, and walked back out.

"Do you want me to stay a little while longer?" I asked, unsure if she really wanted me to. "I can talk to my mom."

"Yeah." She dropped her arms by her side. "That'd be good."

We headed into the living room together and noticed that everyone was already standing by the door. My mother came over to Isabel and gave her a big hug while whispering something in her ear.

I could see Isabel nod as she pulled away.

"Mamá," I said, looking at my mother, who had her arm in the crook of Rodrigo's elbow. "I think I'm going to stay here a little while longer, okay?"

Isabel's father put a hand on my shoulder. The air in the room felt heavy, like stepping outside right before a big downpour.

"Héctor." He paused for a moment. "I think it's best that you all go home. We appreciate that you came over . . . but we can't take chances."

"Chances?" Isabel looked at her parents.

"We've been marked as traitors to the revolution," Mamá answered.

"I'm sorry, but we can't afford to be seen as sympathizers." Isabel's mom's bottom lip quivered. "We have to protect Isabel—she's all we have now."

"But you mean for today, right?" My eyes darted from Mamá to Isabel's parents.

None of them wanted to look at me.

"We'll let you know when you can come over again," Isabel's father replied.

"But that's not fair!" Isabel protested. "Héctor's done nothing wrong."

"We know," Isabel's mother said softly. "It's just the way things have to be. It could change in time."

"What about the funeral?" I asked.

"We won't be there. Teo would understand," Mamá said. "We need to protect Isabel and her family."

"Protect them from . . . us?" As I said the words, I knew that this was exactly what we were doing. We were their biggest threat.

"Sadly . . . yes." Isabel's father put both hands on my shoulders and stared straight into my eyes. "You must promise me that you will do right by Teo and protect Isabel. That means, as far as anyone is concerned, our families have had a falling out and parted ways. We'll have no more contact with each other."

I couldn't believe it.

I hadn't only lost Teo, I'd lost Isabel and her family, too.

"NO!" Isabel shouted. "Héctor's my best friend. I don't care what other people think."

"Héctor?" Isabel's father gave my shoulders a squeeze. "You understand, don't you? We have to do this. It isn't personal."

I wanted to argue, but there was no fight left in me. And even though I thought I was done crying, a tear slipped from the corner of my eye. I nodded and glanced at Isabel.

She seemed shocked that I would agree to this.

Mamá pulled me away. "We understand. We each have to do what is best for our families."

Isabel had fire in her eyes, but she folded her arms against her chest. "Fine. If everyone agrees . . ." She gave me a flick-of-the-wrist type of wave. "Then that's it. Bye."

I wanted to say something else, but what could I say that would make a difference?

We all stared at each other for a couple of seconds. Adults and kids. No one knowing what else to do.

We'd always said we were like family to each other. A Venn diagram of two families where the circles overlapped Teo, Isabel, and me. The three of us were part of each set of families.

But friends weren't the same as family.

Our Venn diagram had been pulled apart and I was no longer a member of their family circle.

I turned to leave, knowing that my last reason for wanting to stay in Cuba was gone from my life.

15

WAITING.

It was all that we could do, now that we were stuck at home. Mamá had been fired from her job early on Monday morning and neither Rodrigo nor I was going to school anymore. The worst part was that none of us knew how long we'd be waiting for whatever was supposed to happen next.

Because anything was possible.

It might be something good like being allowed to leave, or it could be something bad like another repudiation act.

Or worse . . . nothing at all would happen and we'd be trapped in limbo forever.

"I'm going outside," I announced to Mamá, who was washing the dishes from dinner. "I need some fresh air."

"Just be careful." She cast a worried look in my direction. "Neighbors are watching."

It had been three days since the mob had shown up at our

house, and Mamá had become fearful that they might return. I, on the other hand, had lost all fear when I'd lost Teo.

"I'm sitting in our backyard. . . . It'll be fine." I opened the back door and stepped into the darkness.

A feeling of emptiness enveloped me as I sat down by the clothesline and tilted my head to the heavens. I stared at the sprinkling of stars and felt the gentle breeze rustling the nearby palm fronds.

I missed Teo.

I missed Isabel and her family.

I missed how life used to be.

Earlier that afternoon I'd seen people wearing dark, somber clothing go in and out of Teo and Isabel's house. It was obvious that they were paying their respects to the family after Teo's burial. A final goodbye that didn't . . . couldn't . . . include me.

"I'm sorry, Teo," I whispered, my eyes fixed on the North Star. "You were such a good person and you deserved so much better. A long life with your family . . . next to me." I wiped away a tear. "You were my best friend and you were always there for me. I hope you know that I really wanted to be there today to tell everyone how amazing you were, but your parents want me to stay away to protect Isabel."

I sighed. "But you probably already knew that because you're watching over us from heaven." I paused, thinking back to the little bits of Catholic teaching I'd picked up from Teo's parents. Those discussions, like so much in Cuba, had been in secret because being religious was something else the government didn't allow . . . even though most people seemed to still believe in God. "I think that's how it works, right, Teo?"

I stayed quiet as if expecting an answer . . . but none came.

Instinctively, I clasped my hands together and silently asked God to take care of Teo wherever he was. I had never really prayed before, but it felt like the right thing to do.

Then, somewhere in the distance, I heard a door slam and a dog began to bark.

The realities of life in Cuba flooded my brain and I quickly pulled my hands apart, looking around to make sure no one had been watching me.

I had to be careful.

For my sake and my family's.

As the days passed, we all realized that we had to find a way to function in this new normal of being unwanted by our own country. By Thursday, we knew we had to adapt in order to survive.

"Niños," Mama said, her purse in one hand and an umbrella in the other. "I'm going to run some errands. I'll be back later."

I didn't answer. Instead, I just stared out our window at the dark and gloomy sky. It was as if Mother Nature were mourning Teo along with me.

"I'm going to go out, too," Rodrigo announced, finishing his café con leche from breakfast. "I can't be cooped up in here anymore."

"Ten cuidado," Mamá cautioned. "We don't want any more trouble."

"I know," he said, returning to the kitchen. "I won't do anything stupid."

Minutes later it was quiet again.

I had tried to read through the math book Señora Andrade had given me, but I couldn't concentrate. Even challenging algebraic equations no longer appealed to me. It was as if my love for math had died with Teo.

I turned on the TV just to have some noise. Unlike Rodrigo and Mamá, I didn't want to leave the house. I wanted to stay locked away, because here I could pretend that Teo was alive and out in the world somewhere. My self-grounding wasn't a great punishment for what I'd caused, but at least it was something.

Minutes turned into hours while I stared out the window. As a slight drizzle fell against the glass, small beads of water chased each other along the windowpane. I imagined them to be Teo, Isabel, and me.

Nothing would ever be the same again.

I wondered how Isabel was dealing with Teo being gone.

Every day I missed him more and more, but I also missed her. She was just across the street, but I was going to keep my word and not see her. Plus, she seemed pretty mad when I left her house.

I glanced at the clock on the side table. If Isabel had gone to school, she'd be coming home soon. I could at least check on her from a distance.

I perched myself on the corner of the sofa to get a better view out the window.

The front door opened, letting a cool breeze rush in.

"What are you doing?" Rodrigo asked, coming inside and shaking the rainwater from his hair. "Watching telenovelas?" He pointed to the TV.

"No," I said, slouching against the arm of the sofa but keeping an eye on the street. "Not really doing anything."

"Uh-huh." He peered out the window and nodded. "You're waiting for Isabel."

I shrugged. "Just want to see if she's okay."

"You can't talk to her. You know that, right?"

"I know."

"I mean, even some of my friends told me that they have to be careful around me."

"Wait, you went to see some of your friends?" I was starting to get angry. "That's not fair."

"They don't live around here. The watch committees in their neighborhoods don't even know who I am." He plopped down in the large chair next to the sofa. "Not that it matters. They also thought it was a bad idea to be seen with me."

I nodded; the anger I'd felt for a moment evaporated. No one wanted to take a chance with traitors.

"I also heard some stuff while I was out," he said in a softer tone. "Not that you should believe any of it, but it's better that you know."

"What?" I asked, looking back at the street and not really interested in whatever Rodrigo had heard from his friends.

Rodrigo leaned forward, his elbows on his knees. "I think it's just people gossiping and making things up, but it sort of makes sense."

"Just spit it out," I said, knowing that Rodrigo sometimes talked in circles without getting to the point.

"It's about Isabel," he said.

I sat up and looked at him.

"Well, it's really about her family." He paused. "There are rumors that they're blaming us for Teo's death. I know that was their plan to pretend that they're mad and all, but I was told that they really do hate us and . . . well . . . there might be some truth to that."

I swallowed the lump in my throat.

Maybe it wasn't an act and they *were* blaming us. Rumors often had a grain of truth at their core.

"Anyway . . ." Rodrigo stood up, having finished his mission of ruining my day. "Thought it was important for you to know in case you 'accidentally' planned to run into them outside."

Just as he said this, I spotted Isabel walking quickly down the street. Her head was hung low and I couldn't tell if she was crying, trying to avoid the rain, or both.

I knelt on the couch so that if she happened to look at our house, she'd be able to see me, but she didn't even cast a quick glance in my direction. Instead, she kept her eyes down and walked straight up the walkway to her porch. I watched as she paused for a moment to notice the missing brick, then quickly went inside.

And that was it.

My only glimpse into her life. Not even Nani was on the porch anymore.

I curled back down on the sofa and hugged my legs. There was nothing for me to do and nothing I wanted to do. I closed my eyes hoping to disappear into the darkness of sleep.

I wasn't sure how long I'd been out, but I was jarred awake by Mamá coming into the house excited about something.

"¡Niños!" she called out, closing the door behind her. "I have big news!"

Rodrigo sauntered out from our room. "What's up?" he asked as I lifted my head from the couch and rubbed my eyes.

Mamá looked around as if there might be someone else in the house. "We're alone, right?"

I let out an exasperated sigh. "Who else would be here?"

Mamá ignored my comment and smiled. "We got a boat." Her voice cracked with excitement. "I spoke with Manolín, he's one of your father's primos, and he got word that a boat was being sent. The captain has his family's names and ours on his list."

"¿En serio?" Rodrigo's eyes widened. "Do you know the name of the boat or when it'll get here?"

"It's called *The Lovely Lady,* and Manolín thinks it could be here any day." Mamá squeezed her hands together in an attempt to maintain control. "We need to pack a small bag with whatever we're taking. There won't be much room on the boat." She walked over and put an arm around Rodrigo, giving him a tight squeeze. "And I'm going to see about the paperwork tomorrow. Do whatever needs to be done to get it approved."

None of this felt right to me. It seemed so rushed. I wasn't ready.

"How come I've never heard of this guy Manolín?" I asked, unsure why no one else was suspicious. We didn't have much extended family in Cuba and none that lived close by, so it was strange to hear a new name. "How do we know he's not lying? That we're not being set up?"

Mamá's shoulders relaxed a bit and her eyes softened. "Nadie nos está engañando, mijo." She walked to the couch and sat next to me. "Manolín isn't a stranger. He's more of a distant cousin to your father, but he has family in the U.S., too. He feels the same as we do about Cuba."

I could see a certain level of pity in her eyes and it bothered me . . . a lot. She couldn't know how I felt about Cuba because I didn't know how I felt. I'd been pretending for so long that I wasn't sure if I loved or hated it anymore.

"I know leaving right now is hard," she continued, pausing to search for the right words. "Especially after everything that's happened, but—"

"You mean after Teo died," I interrupted, backing away from her. "Say what happened. He died because of us and now we're leaving like it didn't matter."

"That's not true," Mamá said calmly. "I would do anything to have Teo be with us again. But staying here isn't going to bring him back."

"It doesn't feel right . . . ," I muttered.

"Mamá, but about the visas . . ." Rodrigo sat in the chair by the sofa. It seemed like we were now having an official family meeting. "I know you talked about a plan B, but I don't think you should do anything. I'm the man of the house, and if someone has to pretend to be one of the 'undesirables' that they're deporting, then it should be me. I can—"

"¡Ni lo pienses!" She shook her head vehemently. "I won't have you be labeled. It—"

"¿Pero tú sí?" he argued. "It's okay for you to be labeled?"

"I'm old and married. What's a label to me?" She stood up. Our brief family meeting was over. "Plus, we're not there yet. I have a couple of other things I'm working on. People who might be willing to help."

"But—"

"Enough." Mamá cut him off, slicing the air with her hand. "I'm your mother and I make the decisions."

It seemed that between Rodrigo declaring himself the man

155

of the house and Mamá playing the I'm-your-mother card, I was being left without any say at all.

Mamá marched across the room. "Listen, things may get harder before they get better . . . but they will get better once we're in the U.S." She looked over at me. "I promise."

I lay back on the couch, turning away from her empty promise.

She didn't know if it was ever going to get better. . . .

But I believed her about things getting worse.

OVER THE NEXT few days, Mamá began giving away our things. It was strange to see stuff we'd always had disappear, but it made sense. Everyone knew that once the government officials showed up to send you to Mariel, the house would be sealed, and all of its contents confiscated. At that point, the government would simply take everything. So Mamá had put most of our belongings in one of two categories . . . things that she wanted friends to have and things that would be left behind. Over the weekend, people had shown up at our back door, in the middle of the night, to collect whatever Mamá promised them. It was somewhat comforting to know that at least people we knew would be using our stuff.

Assuming that we were actually allowed to leave.

A part of me still wasn't convinced that it would happen. A gnawing feeling in my gut told me that we didn't deserve to go. That it wasn't fair for my family to be reunited when Teo's family would always be broken.

"Héctor, I told you to sort your clothes," Mamá said, coming into my room. "You haven't done anything." She picked up an old T-shirt and tossed it into the hamper.

"I will," I replied, not looking up from the banned novel Teo had given me. I was reading *Animal Farm* knowing that I'd never have the chance to discuss it with him or with his dad. But I was figuring it out on my own. I now understood what Teo had meant about the book mirroring Cuba's own revolution and how the animals were fooled into accepting the illusion that everyone was equal. I just wished I could talk about it with him.

Mamá plucked the book out of my hands and placed it facedown on the bed next to me. "No," she said. "Now."

I rolled my eyes and sighed. I didn't want to clean my room. "Can't I wait for Rodrigo? It's his mess, too."

"I need your things," she said, picking up a pair of Rodrigo's socks and adding them to the mound of dirty clothes. "Separate what's in good condition and what's not. Even if it's dirty. Put whatever needs to be washed by the door." She opened the armoire and surveyed the clothes inside.

"I'll do it after dinner," I said, bargaining for more time. "Please."

"Héctor, no te pongas malcriado." She had her hands on her hips. "Cuqui is coming by later tonight, and she has a friend whose son is about your size. He could use your school uniforms and whatever else is in good shape. But I need time to wash and pack it all up before she gets here. Just keep your favorites. We'll get new clothes once we are in Miami."

I glanced at some of my shirts. I didn't really care about any of them and I knew we'd be limited with what we could take with us. I'd rather have books than clothes anyway.

"Fine, but what about Rodrigo's things?" I asked. "Doesn't he have to do it, too?"

She waved me off. "He already promised his things to someone. Now move."

I slunk off my bed and went to the open armoire.

I grabbed a suit I'd worn to one of Abuela's events and flung it onto the bed, hanger and all. "Won't be needing that anymore," I muttered.

I kept going through my things, taking out most of them and putting them on my bed. Then I tackled the dirty clothes piled up in the hamper.

I tossed the first few shirts on the floor. They were Rodrigo's and they reeked. Mom would have to wash them later, because no one would want them with that smell.

I pulled out a couple of old T-shirts that I didn't think were nice enough to give away and formed another pile on the floor. I dug down and grabbed some towels and underwear, adding them to the mound. Then I got to my school uniforms.

I inspected each of the shirts and shorts before stacking them together. As I got to the final white shirt, I held it up to the light and, although it was a little dingy, it was still good enough to give to Cuqui. The last thing in the hamper was a pair of crumpled-up school shorts.

I shook them to try to get rid of some of the wrinkles when I heard something tumble to the floor and roll toward my bed. I looked over and saw the rock I'd stuffed in my pocket at the teacher's acto de repudio.

I stared at it . . . a reminder that I had been one of those people in the crowd throwing rocks. Back then I was willing to do anything to be accepted, to be seen as loyal. At the time the Math Olympiad seemed to be the most important thing in my life. . . . Now it felt like a stupid, insignificant dream.

I bent down to grab the rock when I saw something bright yellow rolled up under the back of my bed.

My heart stopped as I realized what it might be.

I slithered under the bed frame and pulled it out with the tips of my fingers.

And there it was.

Teo's lucky fishing shirt.

He'd left it behind when he slept over a couple of weeks ago. I laid it out on the floor, smoothing out the wrinkles. It had a smear of dirt along the bottom, and I could smell the musty mix of sweat and seawater. A reminder of one of our many days spent together.

For a moment I could see Teo wearing the shirt and lying on my floor, his hands behind his head, as he laughed and talked baseball. My ears strained to hear the voice that only existed inside my head.

Tears pricked my eyes and one silently rolled down my cheek. I clenched my fists, wanting to hit something . . . anything.

I wiped my eyes and the image of Teo seemed to vanish, once again leaving the shirt empty on the floor.

It wasn't fair. None of this was.

He deserved to be here.

I deserved to be with him.

I hated leaving and hated staying.

I sighed and picked up the shirt, gently placing it next to the math books on my desk, turning my attention back to the clothes—the life—I was giving away.

That night I heard Cuqui talking to my mother in the kitchen, but I didn't leave my room. I didn't want to see what other things Mamá was giving her. All the things that actually made our house a home were slowly disappearing. What was left felt like a fake version of who actually lived in the house. Then again, maybe the house fit who we were now. People just going through the motions. More pretending.

At least, I was.

It was well past midnight when a light tapping noise woke me up.

I sat up in bed, unsure if I'd really heard it.

I looked over at Rodrigo, who was still asleep. I tried to

listen for the sound again, but the night had grown quiet with only the light chirping of cicadas outside.

I lay back on my pillow and closed my eyes, believing that the noise had just been my imagination.

"Héctor," a voice whispered in the darkness.

My eyes flew open.

This was not a dream.

"Héctor." I heard my name again.

I grabbed my glasses from the nightstand and darted to the open window. Isabel was standing there in the moonlight.

"I couldn't sleep," she said. "Want to come outside and talk?"

I nodded and pointed for her to go around to the backyard.

Tiptoeing out of my room, I snuck through the kitchen and out the back door. Isabel was already sitting on the small bench next to a flowering gardenia bush.

"Everything okay?" I asked her, noticing that she was still in her pajamas.

"No," she responded, tugging on the sash of her robe. "But I'm guessing you feel the same way."

I sighed and plopped down on the cool grass in front of her. "I miss him so much," I murmured, finally saying the words out loud.

"Me too," she responded. "But I felt better when you came over. I miss having someone annoy me." She gave me a half-hearted shrug.

"I'm sure there are plenty of people at school that annoy you," I said, trying to get her to smile.

She scoffed. "They do, but not how you think. Everyone is super nice. Too nice." She pointed to the white gardenia. "Like I'm some sort of delicate flower that will wilt any day now." She rolled her shoulders back. "I'm not like that."

"Oh, I know." I chuckled. "No one messes with . . . or pities Isabel Fuentes."

Isabel grinned, proud of the comment and my evaluation of her. "And *this* is why I had to come over. We're friends forever, right?"

"Definitely." I smiled, feeling a little of the weight I'd been carrying lift off my shoulders. But I had to know something, and I knew Isabel would always tell me the truth. "Listen, I need you to be completely honest with me about something."

"Okay, what is it?"

"It has to do with your family." I studied her face for a reaction, but so far there was none. "Do you blame me for what happened with Teo?"

"No." She kicked the blades of grass under her shoes. "I guess I was mad at Rodrigo for a little while, but not anymore."

"But what about your parents? They blame me, don't they? I saw it in your father's eyes the other day."

"Honestly?" Isabel took a deep breath. "I think they do. Sometimes."

Her words cracked whatever tough shell I'd been keeping around my heart. Knowing that her parents now saw me that way was almost too much to bear. Tears welled up in my eyes and plopped to the ground.

"Thanks for being honest with me," I croaked out.

"But it's not just you," she explained. "They blame everyone else, too."

She gazed up at the heavens, as if searching for answers, while I wiped my eyes.

We stayed quiet for a few seconds until Isabel broke the ice again.

"My parents blame a lot of people. They blame Teo for going over after they told us not to. They fault my dad for not being there to stop Teo. Yo cargo con la culpa también."

"¿Tú?" I asked. "Why should you take any of the blame?"

"Because it was my shouting that caused my dad to drag me inside the house and leave Teo on the porch. And my mom feels responsible for not having acted quickly enough to grab Teo before he ran over. But, of course, the main person who should carry the blame is the one person we'll never find . . . the one who threw the brick."

"Yeah, but the whole thing started because my mother wants us to leave Cuba."

Isabel pursed her lips and seemed to mull things over in her head. "How is that going?"

"Who knows." I plucked a blade of grass and split it down the middle. "Mamá went to see about getting our exit visas again, but I don't think it went very well. She said they told her she'd have to wait her turn, but a boat is on its way here, so we need to get them quick."

"Don't you worry about the boat?" she asked. "I mean, have you seen some of them on TV?"

"Yeah, some aren't very big."

"It's not the size, it's how many people are on board." She shook her head. "Even the big ones are completely overflowing with people. They all look like they're about to sink."

"Guess that's why the government doesn't care." I leaned back on my elbows. "Let all the traitors sink to the bottom of the ocean."

"My dad said that the reason the boats are so full is because they're forcing boat captains to take a bunch of people who either want to leave or the government wants to kick them out. And it's not just regular people either. He said that there are criminals and people from the asylums being mixed in with everyone else." She chewed on one of her fingernails. "You're going to have to be careful when you get on the boat. It's not like a fishing trip or something."

"Oh!" I sat up. "Speaking of fishing. I found Teo's lucky T-shirt in my room earlier today. Mamá washed it. Do you want me to get it for you?"

Isabel shook her head. "Nah, you keep it." She smiled. "Maybe it'll bring you luck with getting your exit visas."

"Thanks." I bit my lip. "You think if Teo would've been wearing it, then maybe—"

"Por favor." She rolled her eyes. "Don't even think about that. The shirt wouldn't have changed anything."

"You know what could have changed things." I paused, before finally saying all the things I'd been keeping inside. "If I'd been honest with you and Teo from the beginning. Told you both about what my family was doing."

"It wouldn't have made a difference," she said. "Plus, families have to keep secrets sometimes."

"That's exactly what Teo once told me," I said, remembering our conversation while walking to class. "I think he might have even suspected."

"I don't think he did," Isabel mused.

"Then that's even more reason why I should've told him. He was like family. You both are."

Isabel looked away. "Sometimes you can't trust family either."

"What do you mean?"

Isabel stayed quiet.

I tapped her leg. "Dime," I said, wanting to know what she meant. "Come on, tell me. There's something you're not saying."

"It's just that . . ." She stopped for a beat. "Like Nani. I wouldn't tell her a secret and expect her to keep it quiet. But she's family."

"Well, yeah. Eso se cae de la mata." I knew Isabel too well to think she was only referring to Nani. There was more to what she was saying. "And . . . ," I prodded.

"And then there's your grandmother."

"Uh-huh."

Isabel widened her eyes at me as if I was being dense. "Hello? She lives and breathes the Communist Party."

"Yeah, but she'd never do anything to hurt us." I thought about everything that had happened in the last couple of weeks. "I mean, she probably had the electricity shut off for a little while, but that was just to prove a point." I realized how bad it all sounded. "It's only because she'd had a fight with my mother when she found out Mamá wanted to leave."

Isabel's eyebrows scrunched together. "So . . . she knew about your plans?"

I nodded.

Isabel stood up. "And then there was an acto de repudio against you."

"But Abuela didn't have anything to do with that." I stumbled getting up but was now face to face with Isabel. "She'd never put us in harm's way. She wasn't even in town. She's been gone all week."

Isabel cocked her head to the side. She wasn't convinced.

"De verdad. She wouldn't," I explained, not wanting another family member to carry the blame when it was actually my fault.

I took a deep breath and looked down at my hands. "The acto de repudio was because of me," I said, not able to look her in the eyes. "I was stupid and called my father from the house phone two days before . . . before . . ."

"Stop!" she commanded. "It's not your fault."

"It is, though. Someone was probably listening and—"

"Doesn't matter," Isabel insisted. "My parents asked around, and the acto was originally planned for early in the week, but the CDR didn't think enough of our neighbors would show up. That's why they changed it to Saturday—so that they could bring in strangers." She gently touched my arm. "It wasn't you, Héctor."

A wave of relief swept over me. I began to shake and couldn't control the tears that ran down my face. Isabel hugged me as I tried to regain control.

"You've been thinking that all this time?" she asked, stepping back as I adjusted my glasses.

I nodded. "But it's still my family's fault for wanting to leave."

"No." She refused to accept my guilt. "It's whoever threw the brick and whoever ordered the acto in the first place. That's it." She bit her lip. "And it could happen to anyone who wants to leave."

"But we're the only ones trying," I mumbled.

"Not necessarily." Her eyes locked with mine as if she was trying to telepathically tell me something.

Suddenly I realized what Isabel was hinting at. "You? Are you talking about your family? Are you trying to leave, too?"

"Shhhh!" Isabel covered my mouth with her hand. "I didn't say that," she said without any conviction. "Those words did *not* come out of my mouth."

"You are!" I declared. "But why wouldn't you or Teo tell me?"

Isabel folded her arms and cocked her head to the side again.

"Yeah. Guess I didn't say anything about it either."

Isabel widened her eyes as if telling me to think about it a little more.

"Oh . . . and my grandmother." I nodded, fully understanding what she and Teo had meant about keeping family secrets. "Well, don't worry. I won't say a word to anyone."

Isabel smiled and gave me a wink. "And technically, I haven't said a word either."

THE NEXT MORNING I couldn't stop thinking about my late-night visit from Isabel. Talking to her again had made things better. And knowing that there was a chance that we'd *both* go to the U.S. filled me with hope. Maybe once we were over there her parents would allow us to be friends again.

Not that anyone could ever really stop us.

She had said it. We were friends for life.

"You seem different today," Rodrigo observed as I changed the sheets on my bed. "Even at breakfast you smiled. What's going on?"

"Nothing," I answered, not bothering to look at him as he swept the room.

Mamá had left us a list of things to do before she got back from going to see Manolín about the boat. I didn't understand why we had to clean when we were going to have it all taken away, but Mamá insisted.

"¿Niños?" a voice called out from the living room.

Rodrigo and I looked at each other. The voice sounded like Mamá's, but we knew it wasn't her.

It was Abuela. She was back.

"Where is everyone?" she called out.

I rushed over and grabbed Teo's book, *Animal Farm,* from my desk and hid it under my mattress.

"You go," Rodrigo said, focusing on his sweeping as if it were the most important thing in his life.

I hesitated.

"Dale," Rodrigo ordered. "Don't keep her waiting. I'll go in a couple of minutes. Just want to clean things up in case she comes into our room."

I relented, knowing that Abuela would start searching for us if one of us didn't go out there.

"Aquí," I said, walking over to the living room.

"Ay, Héctor." She stretched out both arms as she approached me. "I was so sad to hear about Teo. What a horrible thing to have happened." She wrapped me up in her arms and kissed the side of my head. "If I hadn't been out of town, I would've gone to the wake and burial with you."

"I didn't go." I squirmed my way out of her embrace. "Their family didn't want us there."

"Oh." She grimaced and shook her head. "I'm sorry to hear that. I know how close you were to their family. Maybe with time . . ."

I shrugged.

She sighed. "So much loss over such a selfish decision." Abuela glanced around. "And where is your mother?"

"She went out this morning, but she'll be back later if you want to talk to her."

"Actually . . ." She pulled me by the hand over to the dining room table. "It's better if we talk without her here."

I had a bad feeling about this conversation.

"Buenos días, Abuela." Rodrigo came over and gave our grandmother a quick kiss on the cheek.

"Siéntate, Rodrigo." She tapped the chair next to her, having taken a seat at the head of the table. "I want to talk to both of you about something important."

Rodrigo shot a quick glance across the table at me as he sat down.

"You both know that I love you very much and only want what's best for you, right?" Abuela said, her eyes gazing at us with tenderness. "And for your mother as well."

"Mm-hmm," I said, nodding.

Rodrigo stayed silent.

"I know she loves you boys, but she's going about things all wrong," Abuela continued. "Look at the situation she's put you all in. She's—"

"Abuela," I interrupted. "I don't think we should be talking about—"

"We absolutely need to talk about these things," Abuela

corrected me. "Your mother is a good woman who loves deeply, but that love causes her to have blinders sometimes. She isn't looking out for your best interests anymore." She let out a deep breath. "She's always been obsessed with Raúl—to the detriment of everything else."

"Mamá is a good mother," Rodrigo said, defending her.

"Oh, I know that." Abuela nodded in agreement. "She's had to be both mother and father because Raúl never showed any real type of responsibility for you."

"That's not true." Rodrigo pushed his chair back. "He was in jail. You can't do much for your family when you're behind bars."

"Tranquilo, Rodrigo," Abuela chided. "I'm not saying these things as insults but as facts. You two are old enough to know the whole truth. Your parents are simply human beings with faults like everyone. Your mother views the world through your father's eyes and he . . . Well, his choices have not put his family first."

"He loves us," I insisted.

"Oh, I suppose he does in his own way." Abuela looked at the two of us before continuing. "But despite what your mother believes, your father chose to go against his government and then tried to take off on a raft, abandoning all of you. That's not putting his family first." She paused. "His time in prison wasn't for some noble cause, it was because he was deserting his country and his family."

I'd never heard it described this way. Mamá always said it was because he was fighting for a better life. And when I spoke to Papá on the phone, he sounded excited about all of us being together.

Abuela had to be wrong about him.

"But what about him being sent to the U.S.?" Rodrigo asked. "Wasn't it because he refused to conform? Because he had his own beliefs?"

"Conform?" she scoffed. "Refused to conform to being a good citizen, a good father? I guess that's one way to put it," Abuela continued. "You have to understand, even in prison he still had choices. He refused to make any type of atonements in order to reduce his sentence and come back to his family."

She sighed. "And now that brings us to today. It breaks my heart to say this, but if your mother wants to follow him down a path of destruction . . . I can't stop her." Abuela gave us a slight smile. "But I can save my two precious grandsons."

"What do you mean, save us?" I asked.

"You're both old enough to renounce her foolishness," she explained. "You'll come live with me. I'll arrange everything." She gave my hand a squeeze. "Things will go back to how they were before. You can still try out for the math team, Héctor, and Rodrigo, you can return to the baseball team. It'll be even better than before."

"No." I shook my head. "I'm not going to move out of our house and leave Mamá here by herself."

"No, that's not what she means." Rodrigo looked from me to Abuela. "You mean she'd go to the U.S. by herself and we'd stay in Cuba, right?"

"Sí." Abuela nodded. "You let your mother do as she wants and you would live your own lives . . . in your homeland." Abuela reached for both our hands and held them as if we were about to say some sort of prayer around the dinner table. "Think about it," she said. "You could remain with everyone you know and I'll make sure you get all the benefits that our government provides. You could leave with me now or, if you don't want to deal with your mother being angry, you can wait a little longer and just tell the authorities when they show up with the exit visas. You'll be taken care of and—"

The front door slammed open.

Mamá stormed in and looked at the three of us sitting at the table. Her eyes blazed with fury.

"What are you doing here?" she demanded of Abuela. "You're not welcome in this house."

Abuela stood up. "I was talking to my grandchildren. Giving them options."

"We don't need any options from you." Mamá glared at her, but Abuela showed no emotion. "I've already made plans for us."

"With Manolín? On his boat?" Abuela smirked. "Ha!"

"Wha—? How did you . . ." Mamá was caught off guard.

"I knew it," I muttered. "It *was* a setup."

"Setup?" Abuela shook her head. "No, but . . ." She wagged a single finger in Mamá's direction. "You should know better than to think you could plan something that I wouldn't know about. Cuando tú vas, ya yo vengo. And that boat isn't taking you anywhere."

"What did you do?" Mamá's eyes narrowed. "They're good people. Did you hurt their chances of leaving?"

Rodrigo and I were now watching the back-and-forth like spectators at a tennis match.

"Yo?" Abuela feigned ignorance. "I only helped Manolín's family. Got their visas expedited so they could catch their boat . . . *The Lovely Lady,* I believe it's called. It arrived this morning." She checked her watch. "In fact, Manolín and his family are probably already headed to Mariel by now. The military officers were just waiting for you to leave their house to give them their visas."

Mamá's face dropped. But only for a moment.

"That's fine," Mamá replied. "If we don't get our visas before that boat leaves, we'll just leave on another one. And starting tomorrow, I'll do whatever it takes to be declared undesirable. Make sure everyone knows I'm your daughter. I'm sure your compañeros in el partido will love gossiping about the whole thing. In fact, I'll show up at your work. I'll go every day. Two can play at this game."

"You think this is a game?" Abuela was seething. She looked over at us. "You see? Nothing is above her love for that man."

She paused, making direct eye contact with me. "Nothing and no one."

"What are you talking about?" Mamá stepped closer to us.

"You don't see it," Abuela said, shaking her head. "You never have."

"Please." Mamá waved her arms open. "Enlighten me."

Abuela gritted her teeth. "You're willing to leave everything, take your children from all that they know, and endure untold hardships in that wretched country . . . for what? A man that hasn't been in your lives for years. It's pitiful! Pathetic!"

Mamá pointed to the door. "Get out!"

Abuela stood up, tugged on her linen shirt to smooth out any creases that had formed. She was in no hurry to obey Mamá's order.

"Think things through very carefully, Ivette. This decision can't be undone later," Abuela cautioned. "This is something you'll come to regret."

"The only thing I regret is that you found out," Mamá retorted. "Now go!"

Abuela took a few steps toward the front door, which had been left open. "Ay, mija. There's simply no reasoning with you." She shook her head and then paused in the doorway. "Perhaps it's time you discovered that getting what you want isn't always the wonderful thing you imagined. I can see to that."

"What do you mean?" I asked, noticing Abuela's demeanor had changed. "What are you going to do?"

She looked at me and gave me a half smile, then turned her attention back to Mamá. "You won't have to declare yourself anything, Ivette. I'll make sure you get your permits tomorrow. You'll be on your way to catch the boat before sunset." She narrowed her eyes. "But trust me, you'll soon be like all the others, wishing you'd never left."

Mamá glared at her with a fury that I'd never seen before. "Really? You think Lucía and her family wish they hadn't left? They've probably had a great life in the U.S."

"You're still bringing up those gusanos?" Abuela scoffed. "¡Le ronca! It's been twenty years!"

"She was my best friend and you ruined it all," Mamá replied.

"I saved you from her corrupt ideology." Abuela scowled. "Or I thought I had. But it doesn't matter . . . not anymore. Boys"—she looked at Rodrigo and me, her face softening once again—"remember what I told you. *You* have a choice."

Mamá glanced over at us and in that instant Abuela walked out of the house, not giving Mamá a chance to have the last word.

"What does she mean that you have a choice?" Mamá asked.

"She wants us to stay with her," I explained. "And not go to the U.S. with you."

Mamá drew closer to us. I could see by the look on her face that this was something she hadn't considered. "And what did you tell her?" she asked.

Rodrigo stood up and put an arm around Mamá's shoulders. "That we're not leaving you."

Mamá let out a deep breath.

"Yeah," I agreed. "We stick together. The three of us."

Mamá relaxed and smiled. "Good. And tomorrow we will hopefully get out of this place."

The three of us held each other in a tight group hug.

It felt like this was a moment that would become ingrained in my memory. Our final night at home. Possibly our final night in Cuba.

I glanced out through the big window in the living room to the small house across the street. There was only one person I had to see before leaving.

18

IT TOOK A few hours after we had all gone to bed for the house to become perfectly quiet. I had been waiting to hear Rodrigo's slight snores to make sure he was sound asleep before venturing out. While I lay in bed, I'd had the idea of giving Isabel a gift to remember me by . . . my prized 1953 Miñoso baseball card, the one Teo had always wanted.

Like a snake slithering through the tall grass, I slid out from beneath my bedsheet and crouched over the small duffel bag next to my desk. It was packed with the few things we'd each be taking to the U.S., including the math book Señora Andrade gave me, my best baseball cards, and a picture of Teo, Isabel, and me.

There was enough moonlight filtering through the wooden slats on the window shutters where, if I held up each card at a certain angle, I could tell which one I was holding. I had finally found the Miñoso card and slipped it into my back pocket when Rodrigo woke up.

"Planning to sneak out?" he asked from across the room.

"Huh?" I spun around and could see him propped up on one elbow. "Oh, no," I said. "I'm just checking to make sure I have everything for when we leave."

"Uh-huh, right." He dropped his head back on the pillow. "Say bye to Isabel for me."

"Um . . . okay." I zipped up the bag and grabbed my sneakers.

Even though Rodrigo was awake, I still tiptoed around until I was out of the house. In the distance I could hear some tree frogs and the light hum of cicadas, but the houses in the neighborhood were dark and still.

I crossed the street and made my way to the side of Isabel's house where her room was. I lightly knocked on the open window. "Psst. Isabel . . . ," I whispered. "Wake up."

I waited.

Nothing.

"Isa," I said more forcefully. "Wake. Up."

"Héctor?" I heard her ask from the darkness of her room.

"Of course," I said. "Who else? Meet me out back."

I ran around the house and sat down on the steps off their kitchen.

About a minute later, Isabel opened the door and walked outside.

"¿Pasó algo?" she asked. "Because I don't think we can sneak out every night. I have school in the morning."

"We're leaving," I said. "Maybe while you're in school tomorrow. Our boat is here."

"Wow." She sat down next to me. "It's really going to happen, huh?"

Neither of us said anything for a little bit.

There wasn't much we could say.

"Any word about your family leaving?" I asked.

"No." She sighed. "My dad asked for permission to leave right after Mariel opened up, which is why he got fired from the high school, but—"

"He got fired?" I repeated. "I thought he quit?"

She shook her head. "He told us that he'd quit, but it wasn't true. We're kind of in limbo right now because our family in the U.S. hasn't found a boat that'll take us. Papá thinks there's a chance the authorities will just send us out on a random boat."

"No, you don't have to wait. . . . You can come with my family." I perked up thinking how we could all go together. "You've seen how they're putting tons of people on all the boats—what's four more on ours?"

Isabel shook her head. "That's not how it works."

"Why not?" I persisted. "If you get the exit visas, we could make it work. Rodrigo says that some of the boats have to wait a week out in the bay before they're loaded with all the passengers."

"Even if we did get our visas, unless you're on a captain's list, you don't get to choose the boat. My parents already warned me that the trip could be pretty bad. We could be placed on anything that floats."

"Yeah, I actually don't know what kind of boat we'll have either. All I know is that it's called *The Lovely Lady*. It might be one of those really tiny ones that hold four or five people." Now I was worried about what kind of boat would have that name and whether it could make the ninety-mile trip to the U.S. The waters between Cuba and Florida were notoriously bad, and there were plenty of stories of people drowning trying to make it across.

"Four or five people might be what normally fits, but at Mariel they'll probably put two or three times that," Isabel mused.

I thought about the images I'd seen on the news. She was probably right.

Both of us sighed at the same time.

She turned and faced me. "I guess this is it, then. We say goodbye now and then you write to me with your address in Miami or wherever you end up living."

"We should have a code or something," I suggested. "In case the censors screen our letters."

"Well, don't write anything political even in code," she said.

"I know, but still. How about when I write that my cousin Ismael is doing well in school then that means everyone is fine?"

"Why not just say we're all fine?" Isabel yawned. "The censors won't care about that."

"Then what do you think the censors would care about?"

"They might be curious to know if someone is leaving or if it's about someone in the Communist Party." She paused, looking like she was mulling something over. "How about when I write to you saying that I'm going to visit Pilar, then that's a code meaning we're finally leaving."

"Ooh, that's good." I nodded, already liking the idea. "And if you ever have to write something that's not true, add something about my beating you in a race."

"Why would I write to you about something that's not true?" she asked. "And you never beat me in races," Isabel reminded me.

"I know, that's how I'll know the whole letter is fake," I explained. "My mom told us that my abuela made her write a super-mean letter to her best friend, who left for the U.S. when she was around fifteen. I just want to make sure that doesn't happen to us."

"It won't." She smiled. "We're friends forever."

"Oh, speaking of being friends." I reached into my back pocket and pulled out the baseball card. "I want to give you this."

Isabel took the card and looked at it, clearly not impressed.

"It's my Orestes Miñoso card from the Chicago White Sox," I said. "It's the card Teo always wanted."

She stretched out her hand and gave it back to me. "You should keep it, then. I don't really like baseball and that was more of your thing with Teo."

"Oh, okay." I took back the card, wishing I'd given my gift a little more thought and brought her something she actually liked.

She snatched the card out of my grasp. "On second thought, I'll keep it and give it back to you when we see each other in the U.S.," she said with a small smile. "Deal?"

I was about to agree when the kitchen light turned on.

"You have to go," Isabel whispered, giving me a quick hug and then pushing me away. "Have a safe trip and we'll see each other soon, okay?"

"Okay," I said, and pulled into the shadows as Isabel opened the back door of her house.

Through the window, I could see her talking to her father.

For a moment, I thought he might open the door and invite me inside. But he just glanced out the window and then turned off the light.

Clearly, it was time for me to go.

19

I TOOK ONE last look in the mirror before walking out of the bathroom. My hair was still wet from the shower, but it was perfectly combed. I had carefully chosen what to wear for the boat trip, knowing that I had to both be comfortable and make a good first impression when we arrived. The short-sleeve green button-down with Teo's lucky fishing shirt underneath seemed to check off both requirements. I was good to go.

"Took long enough," Rodrigo complained as I joined him and Mamá in the living room.

"Are you in a rush?" I answered, stepping around our small duffel bag. "It's not like we're going anywhere right now."

"Cálmense," Mamá said as she concentrated on filing her nails. "We don't know how long we'll have to wait."

I sighed, sitting down on the couch, which now faced the empty spot where the TV used to be. There was really nothing left for us to do except wait. The house was clean and tidy, just like the three of us. I noticed that Rodrigo had chosen his favorite plaid shirt with the pointy collar, and we were both wearing identical khaki shorts. Mamá had done her hair and was wearing a flowery pink blouse with white pants. On any other day, it would have seemed like the three of us were going to someone's birthday party in the park.

But not today.

Today we'd be walking out of the house and never coming back.

We sat listening to the radio all morning. The minutes and then the hours ticked by without anything happening.

None of us wanted to say it out loud, but we were all beginning to think the same thing. What if Abuela had lied? What if our exit visas weren't approved and we were waiting around for something that wasn't going to happen?

"I'm going to make us some lunch," Mamá announced, walking to the kitchen. "Any requests? I still have most of our food. I kept it just in case things don't go as we expect."

"Whatever you make is fine," I said, having moved to the dining room table to play a game of solitaire.

"Yeah, anything," Rodrigo agreed, looking over my shoulder and tapping the last row of cards as I flipped over the four of hearts.

"I know how to play, and it's called solitario for a reason," I said, plunking the card down exactly where he had pointed.

Then the rumbling sound of an engine and the loud squeal

of car brakes made us both freeze. Rodrigo rushed to the window and I was right behind him.

"They're here!" Rodrigo exclaimed. "This is it!"

I watched as two soldiers got out of the military jeep. One of them was speaking to one of our neighbors, an older woman who we knew was the head of the CDR in our neighborhood and had been present the day Teo died. She pointed to our house and said something before turning away from them.

"We need to go fast," I said, turning away from the window. "Julia Ramírez was talking to them. She's probably plotting another acto de repudio before we leave."

"I doubt it," Mamá said, pulling out our identity cards and all our other papers. "She spoke to me last week and apologized for being involved. Said she didn't want to be a part of it, but that she had no choice that day. She was just following orders."

"Yeah, well, maybe she doesn't have a choice today either," I replied as one of the soldiers pounded on the door.

Mamá glanced at Rodrigo, who was already holding our bag. "Ready?" she asked, putting on a white jacket that matched her pants.

"Listo," Rodrigo and I said in unison as she opened the door.

The first soldier stepped into the house without Mamá even having a chance to invite him in. "Señora Ivette Marina Fulgeira," he said in a gruff voice. "Based upon your request, it's been determined that you are to leave Cuba immediately.

This house and all its contents are being seized by the govern-ment." He glanced around, inventorying in his head what we had. "You have ten minutes to gather a few things and head to the Centro Abreu Fontán for further processing."

"It's not needed," Mamá said. "We can leave right now."

The soldier held his hand up to stop us from moving while he looked back at his jeep. I could see that the other soldier was standing by the driver's-side door and seemed to be waiting for something . . . or someone.

"Is something wrong?" Rodrigo asked, causing the soldier to look back at us.

"No, gusano." His face hardened. "Are you two going to be traitors and leave with her as well?"

"They are." Mamá took a step forward, picked up her large purse, and swung it over her shoulder. "If I can have our papers"—she handed the soldier our house key—"we'll be on our way."

The soldier thrust the papers at Mamá's chest and Rod-rigo responded by tensing, as if to attack, but Mamá quickly squeezed his arm. It was a reminder that we all had to be on our best behavior and not get provoked . . . no matter what anyone said or did. We couldn't give them a reason to deny us permis-sion to leave.

"Gracias," Mamá said, and motioned for us to follow her out.

I already knew that the Centro Abreu Fontán was the

processing center just outside of Havana where everyone had their papers and identity cards inspected. Mamá had packed food for us in case there were long lines and was bringing every piece of documentation that she could think of. Her marriage license, a letter from her work saying she'd been fired, birth certificates, and even photographs. We'd just have to walk a couple of blocks to one of the main streets to get a taxi to take us there.

"Good riddance." The soldier driving the jeep spit at the floor as we walked by. "Too bad you're leaving before your neighbors give you a going-away present."

Mamá kept her head held high and looked straight ahead.

I, on the other hand, looked everywhere, trying to engrave it all in my memory. The sound of the jeep's motor idling while birds sang in the nearby trees and bushes, the scent of gardenias carried in the light breeze, and our neighbors' faces peering out from behind curtains.

But most of all, I gazed at the little house across the street.

I could see Teo and Isabel's mother standing at her living room window watching us.

She didn't move.

She was a statue observing us as we abandoned our past.

My heart pounded as we rounded the corner.

I wanted to turn around and run back home, but I couldn't. It was no longer our home. Just another house on the block.

We were already gone.

The taxi we were in pulled over just as we approached an inter-section. We'd been driving for about thirty minutes in an old man's beat-up Chevrolet from the 1950s. It was a leftover from before the revolution, now being used as a makeshift cab.

"Why are you stopping?" Mamá asked the old man. "This isn't the center."

"The Abreu Fontán is at the end of the next street," he an-swered. "You and your sons can walk the rest of the way."

Rodrigo and I exchanged a worried look. We could see a small crowd of people gathered about a block away. Even from a distance you could tell that it was people protesting those who were leaving. It would be the acto de repudio all over again.

"No, take us all the way to the door," Mamá insisted, point-ing ahead. "The price we agreed upon was to get us there. All the way there."

"You're close enough," he replied, taking a puff from the cigar hanging between his fingers. "Anything more will cost extra."

Mamá opened her purse and handed him more money. "That'll cover the washing of your car if they get it dirty. Now, please . . . I'm a single woman with two children. Por favor . . . ayúdanos."

Mamá hated using the poor-me, single-mother excuse, but she clearly could see we wouldn't make it on foot.

"Está bien," he said, folding the bills and putting them into the front pocket of his guayabera. "Put your windows up, though," he ordered.

Mamá nodded, but then turned to look at Rodrigo and me.

"I just want you two to know that things may get tough for a little bit, but we'll get through it together." She smiled and I could see the love oozing out of her eyes. "I'm so proud of you boys. You're young men and I can't wait for your father to get to know you."

"Get those windows up!" the old man ordered as the car got closer to the crowd. "They've got tomatoes ready to be launched."

I rolled up the window and tried not to think about what we were heading into.

20

THE CENTRO ABREU Fontán looked nothing like what I'd imagined. Instead of some nondescript office building, it resembled a small castle that had fallen on hard times, with peeling paint and broken windows. As we got closer, a group of about fifteen people began to pelt the car with rotten food and garbage while yelling insults at us. Then suddenly they all stopped and rushed over to a bus that had pulled up behind our taxi.

"Go now!" our driver urged. "While they're busy with the people on the bus."

Mamá didn't waste any time. She opened the door and we tumbled out of the car, hurrying up the steps to the front entrance. A guard stood at the top of the stairs holding a rifle, but before Mamá could show him the documents in her hand, he waved us through. Apparently, he was more concerned with the people who were still inside the bus.

Stepping through the large door, I could see how elegant the building must have once been. Tiled floors and stucco columns and grand archways that led to a large courtyard outside . . . I could imagine the fancy events that had taken place here.

But that was a different time. Now there were hundreds of people just like us sitting on the floor waiting for the next step in the journey. A journey out of Cuba.

"I'm guessing we have to notify someone that we're here," Rodrigo said, casting a long look out toward the crowded courtyard and beach area beyond. "And find a place to hang out."

"But who do we tell?" I said, searching the room for some sort of administrative area.

"Let's ask someone." Mamá pointed to a nearby family that was sitting together next to one of the columns. They had a young toddler who was falling asleep sucking on a pacifier while his head rested on his mother's lap. "They look nice enough."

"I'll stay here," Rodrigo mumbled. "I'm looking to see if there's anyone we know out there."

"I'll stay with Rodrigo," I volunteered.

"Fine, I'll be right back. Don't move," she warned as she walked toward the family.

I wiped the back of my sweaty neck. I couldn't understand why there were so many people inside where it was so warm and stuffy. The only air circulating in the room came from the open doors along the back that ushered in the sea breeze.

"Let's make sure we find a spot outside," I suggested, looking at the courtyard and beach, which were also full of people waiting around. "Doesn't make sense to be in here."

"It does if it rains or if we want to avoid baking in the sun all day," Rodrigo said, his eyes going from group to group outside.

"We can come in if the weather changes. Plus, how long could this all take?" I said. "A couple of hours?"

Rodrigo turned to stare at me, one eyebrow raised.

"Oh." I realized that it was a silly thing to say because we had no idea how long we might be here. It could be an hour or it could be all day. All we knew was that our boat had supposedly arrived and was hopefully waiting for us.

"I'm sure everyone here thought it would be just a couple hours. And yet here they are." Rodrigo turned his attention back to the crowd. "Ooh!" he exclaimed. "I see a friend of mine from school." He gave me a slight nudge. "Go tell Mamá. We can ask them what we should do next."

"You go tell her," I retorted.

"Don't be stupid." He pushed me a little harder. "Go!"

I huffed as I marched over to where Mamá was crouched down talking to the family. I didn't know why I let him boss me around so much.

"Permiso," I said, interrupting their conversation. "But Rodrigo spotted some friends outside."

"Oh good," Mamá said, standing up. "These nice people were just telling me to get a good spot because it might be a while before we get called up. They've been here since yesterday morning."

"¡Ayer!" I exclaimed, causing the toddler to lift his head up from his mother's lap.

"Shush, shush, shush." The toddler's mom patted the bottom of his diaper, coaxing him back to sleep.

"Perdón," I mouthed, not wanting to make another sound, but still surprised that they'd been here so long.

The father gave me a sympathetic half smile. "Hopefully, you won't be here that long. For some people they're only here a couple of hours—for others it's days. No one knows why and if you ask . . . well . . . no one wants to add to the risk of not getting their final approvals. I've already seen several people get rejected."

"But if we have all our papers, there shouldn't be a problem, right?" I didn't want to think about getting turned away at this point. We had no house to return to or . . .

The mother must have seen the concern on my face. "Tranquilo, mijo," she said in a hushed voice. "I'm sure you'll be fine. It's usually professionals, like doctors or engineers . . . or kids that are of military age that get turned back."

I glanced over at Rodrigo. He was close to military age. I couldn't imagine what we'd do if he got denied permission.

"Mamá! Héctor!" Rodrigo caught me looking at him and motioned for us to follow him outside.

"Well, thank you for all the information and good luck," Mamá said, stepping away from them. "I hope they call your names soon."

"You too!" they both replied as we went to join Rodrigo.

"They seem nice," I mentioned as we walked out into the large, noisy courtyard where Rodrigo was standing.

"Por fin." Rodrigo let out an exasperated sigh. "You took forever. And look. . . ." He pointed to a group of people huddled under the shade of a sea grape tree trying their best to escape the hot afternoon sun. "I spotted a friend of mine walking over there."

"Well, we can—"

A voice over the loudspeaker began calling out names. "Markel Laguna, Felicia Guzmán, Javier Mare, Eloy Oliveros, Erich de la Fuente, Bernardo Pacheco, Sandra Rodríguez, and all corresponding family members . . . report for inspection."

I glanced over at the family we'd been talking to, but they were still sitting. Their names hadn't been called.

"You two go find us a good place where we can wait since we may be here a while," Mamá suggested, stepping away from us and following a few of the families that had been called. "I'm going to make sure the powers that be know we're here."

"All right." Rodrigo headed out, making a beeline for his friend.

At least one of us had found a familiar face among all the strangers.

I followed Rodrigo and trotted down the courtyard steps toward the beach. That was when I saw her.

I wasn't a hundred percent sure it was her, but the back of her head looked all too familiar.

She turned to hand something to an elderly woman sitting next to her and then I knew.

It was Yasmin.

She was in the same group of people seeking shade from the sun as Rodrigo's friend.

My first instinct was to try to calculate the actual odds of this happening, but instead my heart skipped a beat and I froze. My brain was no longer even able to make my feet move, let alone solve a math equation.

Rodrigo glanced back and saw me standing still at the bottom of the steps. "Kleto, come on!"

Kleto? Had he just yelled out Kleto in front of everyone? Where Yasmin might hear him?

Immediately my cheeks grew warm with a combination of embarrassment and pure fury. My temporary brain glitch was over.

I balled up my fists and ran to catch up to Rodrigo. It took all my self-control not to punch him.

"Don't call me that again," I said under my breath as we stepped off the concrete and onto the sand. "Ever."

"Paco!" Rodrigo shouted, completely ignoring my threat, and focused on the group under the sea grape tree.

A dark-skinned boy sprang up and raced across the sand. "¡Asere!"

Rodrigo dropped our duffel bag as the two boys slapped each other's hands and then hugged.

Paco looked at Rodrigo incredulously. "¿Pero qué haces aquí?"

Rodrigo laughed. "What do you mean what am I doing here? Same thing you are. Trying to get to Miami."

"Uh-huh." Paco took a small step back. "Yeah, but your grandmother . . . Delegada Fulgeira . . ." He looked over at me with suspicion. It was too many years of not being able to fully trust anyone that made Cubans doubt everything. "She's here, too?"

"Are you kidding?" I chuckled at the mere thought of it.

"It's just my mom and my brother," Rodrigo explained. "Abuela is most definitely not supportive of us leaving, but she really couldn't stop us."

Paco nodded in understanding. "Well, your grandmother is definitely hard-core in her beliefs. I still remember when she visited our class last year." Paco smiled at me. "You know that we spent the rest of that day doing this to your brother." He clicked his heels and saluted Rodrigo.

"Don't remind me." Rodrigo rolled his eyes and picked up our duffel. "So, is your whole family here?" He pointed to the group under the tree.

"A lot of them are. We've got my parents, my little sister, my grandmother, some aunts and uncles, and a few cousins. I have an uncle that's been living in New Jersey for about fifteen years. He's coming on a boat to pick us all up."

"Is Yasmin your cousin?" I asked.

"Yeah." He glanced back at her. "Oh, wait . . . are you two in the same class?"

"Mm-hmm," I said nonchalantly.

"¡Oye, Yasmin!" Paco called out. "Look who's here!" He pointed at me.

She gave me a polite wave and continued talking to the old woman next to her.

"She's not too thrilled to be here right now," Paco whispered. "She didn't even know her parents were thinking of leaving."

"When did you get here?" I asked.

"Late last night." He pointed to the tree. "We got lucky with the shade because my dad's friend was sitting over there with his family, and when his name got called, he had us come over and take his spot. Believe it or not, some people have been here for a week!"

"A *week*?" Rodrigo's eyes grew wider.

I looked around at the hundreds of people outside. There were several sea grape trees, but it was obvious that shade was a luxury. Some families had created makeshift tents with sheets, while others had simply resigned themselves to being in the sun.

"Yep, and I hope you brought some money, because you'll need it to buy the little food they sell here. And . . . whoooweee!" He let out a long whistle. "Mi hermano, it is soooo bad and expensive. You have no idea. From what I've seen, it might be better not to eat."

I hadn't thought about bringing money, not that I had any. Nor had I thought we'd need to worry about food for more than a few hours.

"I've got some cash and so does my mother," Rodrigo said. "We can help get food for your family if you need it." Rodrigo gave him a little poke. "Especially since you're inviting us to sit under the shade with you . . . right?"

"Yeah, of course. It's just the three of you. . . ." He looked over his shoulder at his family. "But I better check with my dad. Hold on."

Paco raced back to the sea grape tree and I saw him talking with a man wearing a straw hat. I wasn't sure what he was telling him, but a woman holding a baby was now staring at us.

And so was Yasmin.

The man in the straw hat nodded and Paco waved for us to come over.

Maybe this place wasn't as horrible as it had first appeared.

AT ANY OTHER time the shade of the large sea grape tree would have been a perfect spot to catch a nap while listening to the surf and the seagulls. I could imagine myself running around the beach, laughing with Teo and Isabel as we splashed each other along the ocean's edge.

But that would never happen again. Not here, not any-where.

"Come, I'll introduce you to mi familión," Paco said as we followed him to where his family had laid two large sheets in the shade of the tree. The women in the group were all sitting cross-legged on the sheets while a couple of the men were perched on nearby tree roots.

"Bienvenidos." One of the men greeted us with a warm smile. "Paco tells me you're friends from school. I'm his father, Gonzalo Giménez."

"Buenas, señor." Rodrigo shook hands with Paco's father. "I'm Rodrigo and this is my brother, Héctor."

"Thank you for making room for us," I added.

"Por supuesto," he replied. "Just find a little space under the leaves and claim it for yourselves."

"Paco, no seas mal educado." A thin woman wearing a polka-dotted scarf over her hair waved Paco over. "Introduce your friends to us."

"I was just about to do that, Mami." He pointed to his mother. "That's my mother . . . obviously." He continued around the group, pointing to each person. "Swinging from the branches is my little sister, Patricia."

A little girl who was about six waved at us as she took a break from climbing the tree and plopped down on the sand again.

Rodrigo and I waved back.

Paco continued. "Sitting on the branches are my tíos, Chucho and Roberto, and"—he pointed to the ocean—"my tía Ines is out there somewhere looking for shells with my younger cousins, Yaniel, Andrés, and Silvio. You'll meet them later."

I glanced over at the two men and noticed that they both looked a lot like Paco's father, with the same dark skin, lanky build, and straw hats. The three of them were probably brothers.

"Esta es mi abuela, Lupe." Paco had walked around the large bedsheet and put his hands on the shoulders of the old woman who in turn gave his fingers a quick pat and kiss.

I gave his grandmother a slight nod.

"That's my tía Mercedes." Paco motioned over to a woman with very fair skin and blond hair who was rocking a baby in her arms. "And those are her daughters, baby Daynaris and . . ." He paused to glance at me for a second. "Well, you already know Yasmin."

Yasmin gave me a halfhearted smile.

It wasn't much, but it was enough to make my chest feel like it was going to explode. Suddenly the chatter coming from the other nearby families, the sound of the waves in the distance, the screech of seagulls flying overhead, all seemed to disappear. For a moment it was as if I were sucked into a soundproof tunnel where I lost all sense of time and place. The only things that existed were Yasmin and me.

"Héctor . . ." Yasmin's voice seemed to bring me back to reality. "When you were inside, did you hear if they were going to be selling milk or formula for the babies again? We heard they sold some yesterday."

"Um . . . ahem . . ." I cleared my throat, which for some strange reason had decided to go dry. "No." I glanced at her mother and baby sister. "But I did talk to a family inside that had a little kid and they've been here since yesterday morning. They might know."

Rodrigo pointed to our mother, who had just walked outside and was scouring the area looking for us. "There's our mother over there." He waved to capture her attention. "She might have some information."

Mamá gave us a nod to show that she'd seen us and began walking in our direction.

"Hey, why don't Rodrigo and I go on a milk-finding expedition once his mother gets here?" Paco thumped Rodrigo's chest. "What do you think? 'Cause I'm getting a little tired of just sitting here."

"It's been less than a day and you've been sleeping most of the time," Yasmin pointed out. "I think you can deal with it."

Paco edged closer to us. "Like I said before," he whispered. "Super cranky."

"Why don't you boys open up that extra bedsheet from the family that left this morning." Paco's mom pointed to a white sheet with small pink flowers leaning against a blue suitcase. "We were going to use it as extra shade, but I don't think we need it."

"Yes, ma'am." Rodrigo motioned for me to go with him to get it. "Gracias."

Paco's grandmother pushed Yasmin to get up while we unfolded the sheet. "Help the boys out," she instructed. "Put their sheet next to ours so they overlap and sand doesn't get caught in between. We may all be getting to know each other for a while."

Yasmin sighed, but got up dutifully.

As we stretched out the sheet and placed our duffel bag on one of the corners to keep the wind from lifting it up, Mamá arrived.

"Buenos días," she said hesitantly.

"Mamá, this is my friend Paco and his family," Rodrigo explained. "They said we could set up here with them."

"Oh, that's very kind." Mamá smiled. "Thank you."

"Yo soy Dolores, la mamá de Paco." Paco's mother stood, took Mamá by the hand, and walked her over to the empty sheet. "And this area is for you and the boys. Not much, but not too bad, considering."

Mamá dropped her large purse on top of it. "It's wonderful. Thank you again."

"Mamá, did you hear anything about milk?" I asked. "They wanted some for the baby."

"Our decision to come was a little last-minute," Tía Mercedes explained. "And I didn't bring enough baby formula."

"No, I'm sorry." Mamá bent down, unzipped her bag, and pulled out something wrapped in a towel. "But I have some food that I prepared last night." She unwrapped the checkered cloth to reveal a stack of slightly squished ham sandwiches. "The baby may not be able to eat it, but perhaps the rest of you would want some?"

The men quickly demurred, but Paco's little sister came running over. "Yo quiero," she announced as she hid behind her mother's leg.

"Of course." Mamá handed a small square to Paco's mother, who in turn gave it to her daughter.

Paco looked to the water's edge. "Rodrigo, let's go get my cousins. They're going to want one of those." He bent down and took a sandwich, motioning for Rodrigo to follow suit. As soon as Mamá handed it to Rodrigo, the two of them took off.

"The kids should eat it," Yasmin's mother suggested. "We can always have whatever they sell here."

"Quizás para ti," Paco's grandmother replied, reaching over and taking one of them. "But I'm not going to insult this kind woman's generous and delicious offer by not having at least a little."

"It's only bread with a little ham, but please . . . enjoy." Mamá passed her a small sandwich square. "It's the least I can offer."

Yasmin reached over and took two, giving me one. "Better eat when you can," she said. "Because who knows what comes next." She stared intently at her mother. "Some of us didn't get to plan things out."

"Yasmin." Her mother said her name through clenched teeth. "Enough." She widened her eyes. "We have company."

It was clear we'd arrived in the middle of an argument that had been going on for a while.

"And having them here changes things somehow?" Yasmin stood up. "You treat me like I'm a little kid, maybe I should start acting like one."

As if sensing the increased tension, the baby began to cry. Not just the normal baby-like bawling, but a blasting-out-her-lungs type of wail.

Yasmin grabbed my hand and pulled me away from the

group. "Héctor, let's go talk to those friends of yours with the little kid and see if we can get some milk for Daynaris," she said, not bothering to ask me or her parents about leaving.

I didn't say a word since all my thoughts were focused on the fact that Yasmin was holding my hand. I could sense that my feet were moving and I was willing to go wherever she was taking me. After a few steps, I looked back at Mamá, who signaled that I should go.

"Can you believe them?" Yasmin complained as she dropped my hand and we walked toward the main building. "I don't know about you, but I wasn't even told that there were plans to leave." She shook her head. "I didn't even get a chance to say goodbye to anyone. Did you?"

"Um . . . well . . . I've kinda known for a while," I replied. "Word got out, too."

She glanced over at me. "Oh . . . right. I heard about all that," she said, realizing that Teo had died at the acto de repudio against us. "Sorry. I know you two were close."

"Yeah," I muttered, feeling a sharp twang of pain in my chest as all the memories of that horrible day flooded back. "He was my best friend. Him and Isabel." I took a deep breath. "But at least I did get to say goodbye to her."

"That's good," Yasmin mused as we went up the steps. "She's a sweet girl."

A slight smirk crept across my face.

"What?" Yasmin asked, noticing my grin. "You don't think so?"

"Yeah, I guess," I said. "It's just that's not the first thing I'd think of to describe Isabel. She's more of an in-your-face, echada pa'lante kind of person. Sweet?" I chuckled. "Not exactly."

Yasmin shrugged. "If you say so." She looked around as we walked into the building. "Bueno, where is this family that you're friends with?"

"I never said we were friends," I clarified. "I just talked to them for a minute when we got here." I pointed to the far wall, where they were still sitting. "But that's them over there."

"So, wait." Yasmin pivoted to face me, her hands on her hips. "If you're not friends, what are we doing here?"

"You were the one who wanted to find out about the milk situation," I reminded her. "I just said that they might know something."

Her eyebrows scrunched up and she looked frustrated. "But that would be true of anyone who's been here a while." She threw her head back. "Ugh! I thought that you had some connection to them. That they would want to help us."

"They still might," I insisted, walking over to the family. "They seemed nice."

"Lots of people 'seem' nice," she replied as we got close. "Nice doesn't mean much these days."

I gave the family a little wave as we approached.

"Find a place to settle down outside?" the father asked, looking up at me from his spot on the floor.

"Yeah, we ran into some friends." I motioned to Yasmin

standing behind me. "She has a baby sister, and we were wondering about getting some milk or formula."

"We don't have any to spare," the mother said quickly. "I'm sorry."

"Oh, no. I wasn't asking that," I explained. "We just wondered if they were going to sell some again today and for how much."

"No idea," the father said. "And prices . . . they fluctuate. It's whatever they want to charge, but I'd plan on about five or six times more than the black market."

"That's a lot," I said. Things on the black market could be ten or twenty times the usual price. But it was often the only way to get things. The government rations were never enough, and in Cuba everything got rationed . . . everything.

"Meh." The father shrugged. "It's not like Cuban money is going to do us any good over there."

Over there.

In the U.S.

I thought about all the conflicting stories I'd heard about life there. Abuela and my teachers always made it sound horrible. But Mamá described it as a paradise where we could do, say, or be anything we wanted. I figured it was probably somewhere in between.

I stared at my feet, lost in thought while Yasmin asked a couple of questions about where to get the milk.

I wiggled my toes inside my black sneakers. They were in

pretty good shape and I'd been lucky that Abuela had been able to get them for me after I'd outgrown the yearly pair that was allocated to me in our ration book. No matter what Mamá said, Abuela *had* always tried to look out for us. She'd been our backup with all her government connections. Now she wouldn't be around to help make things better. We'd be on our own.

Sink or swim.

"Hello?" Yasmin gave me a nudge. "Aren't you listening? Let's go."

"Oh, yeah. Sure." I had missed the last bit of their conversation, but I wasn't really that interested in the milk logistics anyway.

I thanked the couple and chased after Yasmin, who was already headed down the hall instead of going back to the beach.

"What are you doing?" I asked as she stood by one of the columns, watching a side door where two soldiers entered from outside. "Why are we here?"

"Your friends over there mentioned that the soldiers bring the food through that door," she said, looking like a tiger ready to pounce.

"Uh-huh." I followed her gaze. "So?"

"So . . . ," she replied. "We're going to intercept them and get some food before they sell it to anyone else."

"I don't think—"

Before I could finish my sentence, she'd already made a dash for the door and was walking out. For a second I thought about letting her go by herself, but I wasn't about to spend the rest of my time here having her think I was a coward.

I darted after her, hoping no one would say anything.

As I stepped outside, I realized Yasmin hadn't waited for me at all. She was already sneaking around a parked flatbed truck with nobody inside.

My stomach tightened as I looked around, but there was no one in the parking lot. We were alone . . . for the moment.

"Yasmin!" I whispered loudly. "Yasmin!"

She sauntered out from the other side of the truck with a big smile on her face. She was holding something behind her back.

"¿Estás loca?" I asked as she got closer. "You know we could get in big trouble."

"Here!" She tossed me an orange. "Now stop complaining."

I stared down at my hands holding the fruit. Stealing from the government soldiers was a really bad idea. Yasmin might not care about getting in trouble, but I did.

"Relax," she said, shifting a couple of oranges that she'd stuffed down her shirt. "There's a big box of them in the passenger seat. They won't miss a few. It's sálvese quien pueda."

She was so close to me now that I could see the little freckles that dotted the bridge of her nose. She did have a point about no one missing a few pieces of fruit, and it was about survival. But her eyes were scouring the area in search of more things. We couldn't press our luck.

"Fine," I said, putting the orange in my pocket. "But we really shouldn't risk—"

Yasmin's lips were suddenly on mine as she pushed me back against the nearby wall. I had never kissed a girl in my life, but somehow this wasn't what I had envisioned. I'd thought it would be softer and more planned out. My heart was beating so hard that I almost didn't even hear the door bang open.

"What are you two doing?" a soldier's booming voice called out.

22

WE WERE BUSTED. Not only were we not supposed to be in this area, but if they checked our clothes, we'd be labeled thieves. I could feel my insides begin to shake. After everything we'd gone through, I might have ruined it all for a stupid orange.

Yasmin slowly pulled away from me and sheepishly looked down at the ground. I, in turn, couldn't stop staring at the bearded soldier wearing his green army fatigues standing in the doorway. There was a heavyset woman wearing regular clothes right next to him.

Once again, I didn't know what to do. My mind was calculating the odds of us getting kicked out of Centro Abreu Fontán versus the odds of being thrown in jail for stealing.

"We're sorry," Yasmin spoke in a soft voice. "I just wanted a little privacy for my first kiss."

The woman began to chuckle as she elbowed the soldier in the ribs. "Love at the Fontán . . . Pretty funny, don't you think?"

"Hmph!" The bearded soldier didn't seem to be buying the

young-love story. "I'm going to have to report the two of you," he declared. "And your families."

"No, please," I begged, knowing that if we got kicked out, we'd have nothing to go back to. "We weren't doing anything bad. Our parents don't even know we're out here."

"You're all scum." The soldier scoffed and spit on the ground.

"¡Ay, qué gruñón!" the woman chastised him. "Love should be encouraged . . . even in times like this." She took a set of keys from her pocket and began walking to the truck, shaking her head all the way.

"I'm so sorry," Yasmin said meekly, batting her eyes at the soldier. "Por favor."

"Mira . . ." The woman paused, turned around, and looked back at the soldier. "If you overlook their little indiscretion, I'll let you have one of the oranges in my truck."

I was shocked at the woman's offer.

"No te sorprendas," she said, giving me a wink. "Even old women like me remember that young love sometimes needs a little help."

The soldier rubbed his beard and glanced over at us again. "Dos," he demanded. "Since there's two of them."

The woman rolled her eyes and let out a deep belly laugh. "I'm such a sucker. Come." She motioned for the soldier to get the fruit. "But these two can leave right now with no problem . . . yes?"

"Yes, fine." He nodded and walked toward her truck. "They're just stupid kids anyway. What do I care?"

"¡Gracias!" I shouted, grabbing Yasmin's hand and sprinting back inside the building.

We continued running and weaving around groups of people until we hit the courtyard, where we stopped to catch our breath and Yasmin promptly yanked her hand out of mine.

"That. Was. Awesome," she said, tucking in her shirt a little more to keep the oranges in place. "She didn't suspect us at all." Yasmin giggled. "She fell so hard for the whole sappy love nonsense that it cost her two more oranges. What an idiot!"

"Yeah." I was starting to feel a little guilty about stealing from someone who had gone out of her way to help us. "But she really didn't have to do that. It was extremely nice of her, don't you think?"

"Meh." Yasmin tossed her hair back with a flick of her wrist. "It worked because of my great acting. I had her convinced."

"Mm-hmm," I said, my heart beginning to settle down. "Acting, right."

"What?" Yasmin gave me a side-eye look. "You thought some of that was real?"

"No," I replied quickly. "I knew it was all fake. It's just that before they got there . . ."

Yasmin raised her eyebrows. "The kiss?" She paused to gauge my reaction. "You don't think that I like you or something?" Her lips twisted and she scrunched up her nose. "Ugh, no. I'm super popular and you're a math nerd." She shook her head as my heart dropped. "I saw the door opening and knew we needed to have a cover story. It was quick thinking . . . that's all."

"I figured," I said, trying to hide my feelings. "Just didn't want you to get all weird about any of it now."

"Why would I?" She shrugged. "We barely know each other. It's not like we're even friends."

She was right. We weren't friends . . . just former classmates and now co-conspirators. A pair of thieves.

It all made me feel a little sick to my stomach.

We continued walking toward the beach, Yasmin with a little skip in her step. Suddenly she stopped and turned to me. Her eyes narrowed and she pointed a finger at me.

"Listen, you can't tell anyone about that kiss," she demanded, her mood having quickly changed. "I don't want it to somehow get back to my friends. I have a reputation to maintain."

"No problem," I replied.

"Not a word to anyone," she insisted. "Not even to your brother."

"I got it." I paused, feeling the weight of the orange in my pocket. . . . It reminded me of the rock I'd had during the acto de repudio. "But if someone asks, we say that an old woman was giving them away," I said. "I don't want anyone to know what we really did either."

Yasmin rolled her eyes at me. "Seriously?"

"In fact, here . . ." I pulled out my orange. "You can have mine. Is it a deal?"

"Fine!" She snatched it out of my hand. "More for my family."

The rest of the way back we didn't say much more to each other.

When we got to our group, Yasmin presented the oranges to her family with much celebration. She stuck to the story of finding a woman who was handing them out and no one seemed to question it.

For the rest of the day and night, Yasmin ignored me . . . and I didn't care.

Mamá had given Paco's dad some money and he had managed to get us all a few crusty old sandwiches to share and some milk for the baby. As we ate under the setting sun, our families began telling stories. Some were funny and made everyone laugh, helping us forget where we were for a little while. But pretending that this was some strange beach outing was useless. The undercurrent of fear and worry couldn't be ignored.

Once night fell, everyone grew more and more quiet. There was nothing to do except stare at the stars and listen for the names being called periodically. Always hoping to hear your own family's name and feeling disappointed when the night grew silent once again. We began taking turns going to sleep, making sure someone was wide awake in case our names got called. But as many families left, even more arrived. The Abreu Fontán was *packed* with people.

By dawn I couldn't even pretend to sleep. All I wanted was to get to the boat and the next step in our journey.

I stared up at the leaves fluttering in the early morning breeze.

My green button-down shirt was rolled up under my head like a pillow as I shifted my body to try to get a little more comfortable. It was no use. The sheets were all covered with a dusting of sand that had blown over us during the night, making everything extra scratchy.

"¿Dormiste?" Mamá whispered, her eyes open and watching me. She had curled up next to me during the night, her white jacket covering her like a small blanket.

"A little," I said. "On and off. Kinda hard to sleep and listen for our names."

"Yo lo sé." Mamá sat up and smoothed down her hair. "I'm going to go to the bathroom before the lines get too long. Paco's mother says the ones on the other side of the baseball field are cleaner. Want to join me for a walk over there?"

"Sure." I grabbed the green shirt, which was now completely wrinkled, and put it on, leaving it unbuttoned, with Teo's lucky shirt peeking out. "Should we bring some money in case they sell food again?"

"If you want to call that food." Mamá gave me a wink as she covered a sleeping Rodrigo with her jacket.

"Better than nothing," I said, my stomach already grumbling.

"True." She picked up her large purse. "Let's hope they have something."

As we made our way in between groups of sleeping people

strewn all around the beach and then the grassy area around the baseball field, I noticed how it looked and felt like a battlefield. We were in a fight with an enemy that completely controlled our fate. We could be stuck here for however long they'd want.

"Ivette?" someone called out as we began to cut through third base to get to the building where the bathroom was located.

We turned around to see a clean-shaven officer in army fatigues stepping out of the dugout and walking quickly in our direction.

Mamá was puzzled for a moment, then a wave of recognition crossed her face. "Osvaldo?" she said, smiling as he got closer. "Is that really you?"

"¡Sí!" The officer thrust his arms wide open about to hug Mamá, then quickly pulled back when he remembered where we were.

He looked around awkwardly for a moment to see if anyone was paying attention to the exchange. Confirming that no one had noticed or at least no one cared, he seemed to relax. "Who else do you know who has red hair and this many freckles?" he said, chuckling.

"Wow, Osvaldo Cepero." Mamá shook her head in disbelief. "How long has it been? Nineteen . . . twenty years?"

"I left Puerto Mijares over twenty years ago," he replied. "Can you believe it? Time goes by so quickly. What about you? Are you . . . were you still living there?"

"Oh, no. My father and brother passed away when I was

seventeen and my mother moved us to the outskirts of Havana. I've been there ever since. Got married, had kids . . ."

"Ahem . . ." I cleared my throat to remind Mamá I was still there.

"Oh." Mamá put an arm around me. "This is my son Héctor." Mamá looked at me. "Osvaldo was one of my neighbors growing up. We were sort of like you and Isabel. Uña y carne when we were young. Inseparable. Knew each other's secrets and everything."

"Those were good times," he said wistfully. "As for me . . . I got married, then divorced. No kids, though."

"Married, huh?" Mamá mused.

"Yeah, well . . ." He shrugged. "Didn't last long."

Mamá gave him a strange look. "Well, I hope you find someone more . . . compatible. Tu otra mitad, because you deserve happiness," she said.

Osvaldo sighed, but didn't say anything else.

"Listen, I have a favor to ask." Mamá lowered her voice. "We're with some friends over by the beach and they have a baby. Do you think you might be able to get us some more milk? We'd pay for it, obviously."

Osvaldo nodded. "I'll see what I can do, but don't let my rank fool you." He tapped the stripes on his shoulder. "I'm not in charge over here. I only came by to see how much space there is and then I'm headed back to the port." He smiled. "But I'll ask around."

"Anything you can do," Mamá said. "I'd appreciate it."

Osvaldo leaned a little closer. "Ivette, *you* also need to eat while you're here . . . not just the kids. Don't save any of your money for later. Spend it all here because there's no buying food once you leave."

"You mean there's no food to buy at the port?" I asked.

"I mean at El Mosquito," he answered.

"El Mosquito?" I repeated, unsure of what he meant.

"That's the nickname it's been given. It's a holding area next to the port where people are kept until their boat gets called up. Boats can be anchored in the bay for days or weeks."

I blinked, confused by what he was saying. "But I thought that's what this place was . . . a holding area until we could leave."

"No, this is where they check your papers, verify that you can leave. Bureaucracy at its best." He pursed his lips and looked at Mamá. "El Mosquito is something completely different." He lowered his voice and got closer to us. "I'm not sure what's going on at that place, but it isn't good. Most people are stripped of anything of value before going in and then they aren't being given much food to eat while they wait there." Osvaldo shook his head. "It's a tough place. I see how the people look when they finally get to the boats. Hopefully, you won't be there too long, but you need to prepare yourself."

Mamá nodded, but I could see the worry in her eyes.

He reached over and gave Mamá's hand a gentle squeeze. "I'll see what I can do about that milk and getting you some food," he said. "Be strong. You can do this."

"I don't think I have much choice." Mamá chuckled nervously. "It's too late to go back now."

Osvaldo grimaced. "I need to go. It wouldn't be right for me to be seen talking to you for so long."

Mamá agreed. "It was good to see you again, Osvaldo. Take care of yourself."

"Tú también, Ivette." He glanced over at me. "Make sure to take care of your mom, Héctor. There aren't many like her."

"I will," I answered as he turned away from us.

Mamá and I didn't say much after he left. We quietly walked to the bathrooms, which reeked of urine and poop. I decided to wait outside for Mamá, choosing to do my business later . . . either in the ocean or behind a tree somewhere.

Thankfully, Mamá didn't take long.

"¡Qué peste!" she exclaimed, holding her nose as she walked toward me. "Y es un asco adentro."

"I know. It's really bad," I said. "Even upwind you can smell it."

We could see a few people crossing the field, having gotten up early as well to beat the bathroom rush. In the heat of the day, this place was going to get much worse.

As we walked back to the beach, Mamá fanned her nose to try to get rid of the lingering stench. It was as if the smell had become lodged inside our heads. Neither of us wanted to speak because then we'd be able to taste it, too.

Finally, a strong gust of wind blew away the remnants of bathroom air. I took a deep breath and let it out slowly, happy to once again be surrounded by just the slightly unpleasant smell of too many people crowded together.

"What do you think of what Osvaldo told us?" Mamá asked as we made our way around the different family groups. "About El Mosquito."

"Um . . ." This was one of the first times I could recall Mamá asking for my opinion. "It sounds pretty bad, but . . ." I shrugged. "How do we know we can trust what he says?"

"He's my friend," Mamá replied. "He wouldn't lie."

"He would if he gets a kickback from us spending money here." I glanced at Mamá and, for the first time, thought that she might be too trusting. "You know that friends lie all the time."

"He's not like that," Mamá insisted. "I just wonder if I . . ." Her voice trailed off.

"If you made the right choice?" I asked.

Mamá bit her lip and nodded.

"You did," I said matter-of-factly. "A few hard days isn't going to kill any of us. You said it yourself—Rodrigo's almost of military age and he could get shipped to Angola. Then in a few years it would be me. Plus, Papá is waiting for us and . . ." I thought about the book Teo had given me and how much had changed recently. It felt like a pair of blinders had been taken off my eyes and I was seeing things with a different perspective. "And soon we won't have to pretend anymore or be afraid that we'll be jailed because of something we say. We'll be free." It sounded like I was repeating everything Mamá had been telling me, but for the first time I believed it myself. "Mamá, this is our chance. We *have* to take it."

Mamá leaned over and gave me a kiss on the top of my head. "When did you get so grown-up and wise?"

I smiled. "I've always been like this—you're just starting to notice."

"Speaking of noticing . . ." Mamá arched a single eyebrow. "What do you think of Yasmin? She's very pretty."

"Yeah." I shrugged. "But I thought she was a lot prettier before I got to know her."

"Ah." Mamá chuckled. "That happens sometimes. It can—"

"Milagros García, Serafin García, Rogelio Betancourt . . ." A voice announced names over the loudspeakers.

Mamá and I fell silent and picked up our pace to get back to our group.

"Niurka Veranda, Mario Cantor, Carlos Cespedes . . ." The laundry list of names continued. "Jesús Giménez, Martín Giménez, Gonzalo Giménez . . ."

"That's Paco's dad and uncles," I said, starting to run-walk.

There were even more names announced as the loudspeaker crackled and hummed.

Then the last name on the list was announced . . . ours!

Suddenly it felt like a hundred butterflies were all batting their wings inside my chest.

I couldn't believe it. We were really going to leave this place.

Mamá and I broke into a full-fledged sprint, but she quickly fell behind.

"Hurry!" I urged, not wanting to leave her. "Come on!"

She came to a full stop, her hands on her hips as she took huge gulps of air. "Go." She waved me on. "I'll catch up."

"But . . ."

"¡Dale! Get your brother!" she shouted. "Before it's too late!"

I turned around and ran faster than I ever had before.

But as the sea grape tree came into view, I stopped and stared.

Everyone I knew was gone.

23

FOR A MOMENT I thought I'd made a mistake. That I was looking at the wrong spot, but no . . . there was no doubt that our sea grape tree was now sheltering a group of strangers. In fact, I could see some of them shaking the sand off our old bedsheets.

I spun around, scanning the area for Rodrigo or a member of Paco's family. How could they have all disappeared so fast?

"Héctor!" Rodrigo called out. "Over here!"

He was standing by the steps holding our bag.

I let out a huge sigh of relief. We couldn't afford to waste time searching for each other once the names got called. Everyone had to be ready immediately or else your chance to leave might be denied.

"¡Espérate!" I shouted, looking over my shoulder for Mamá.

A minute later I saw her emerge and flagged her over. She was out of breath, but full of energy. We hurried over to Rodrigo, who was tapping his foot impatiently.

"Come on," he said, thrusting the small duffel bag into my chest. "We're going to be the last ones."

"Hey, we came as fast as we could," I said. "It hasn't even been ten minutes."

"It was my fault," Mamá said, huffing and puffing as we hustled through the courtyard that led to the main building. "I had to go to the bathroom and thought the one by the baseball field would be empty."

"Well, I was worried when I didn't see either of you," Rodrigo complained. "And Paco's family took off to try to get in line fast." He shook his head. "Next time, you need to tell me before you go somewhere."

"You're right," Mamá agreed as we walked inside. "We stick together from now on."

Rodrigo's shoulders relaxed as we made it to the back of the long line of people who'd had their name called. There were at least a hundred people in front of us, so it would take a while before our papers would be inspected. I could see Paco standing with his family toward the front of the line, and some families were already being questioned by officials sitting behind a long table. A few guards holding rifles flanked either side of the table, probably to ensure there'd be no outbursts as the officials reviewed the paperwork each family presented.

I hoped there wouldn't be any problems with everything Mamá had brought with her.

As if reading my thoughts, Mamá rummaged through her purse and pulled out a folder. She was double-checking that we had everything we'd need. "You let me do the talking," she said, flipping through the papers and pictures. "Unless they ask you a direct question and then every reply is extra polite. No matter how rude they are . . . understood?"

"We both know how this works," Rodrigo answered. "We're not stupid."

"Well . . . ," I snickered. "Some of us aren't stupid."

Rodrigo glared at me but stayed quiet as another family with two small children got in line behind us.

The minutes ticked by and the line inched slowly forward. At this rate we'd be here for at least an hour.

We continued watching from afar how each family was being questioned when they got called to one of the officials at the table. It seemed pretty straightforward, and the first few families didn't have any issues. In fact, there was a certain level of excitement as each group left the table and headed toward a back door.

But now there was a soldier making his way down the line questioning people.

I could see people shaking their heads as he approached each group.

He was looking for someone.

We held our breath as he got closer.

"Ivette Marina Fulgeira?" the soldier asked Mamá.

"Yes," Mamá answered, her voice shaking.

He glanced at me and Rodrigo. "These are your sons?" he asked as our eyes met.

I quickly dropped my gaze and stared down at his black boots with the olive-green pants tucked inside.

"They are," Mamá replied. "Is there a problem?"

The people around us had all stepped back. No one wanted to be associated with us.

"There's no problem, but you need to come with me," he explained. "Your sons can keep your place in line."

"Wait," I said, looking up at him. "Where is she going?"

"I don't have to answer to you, gusano," the soldier sneered.

"No," Rodrigo argued. "We stay together, so we'll go with you."

"That's not a choice right now," the soldier stated. "I was asked to bring your mother, not you."

Mamá glanced around, taking stock of the situation. "You boys stay here." She gave Rodrigo the folder with all the papers. "I'll come right back."

"I don't think that's a good idea." Rodrigo eyed the soldier, then Mamá. "We should go with you."

Mamá smiled, but I could tell it was all an act. "It'll be fine. No one's done anything wrong. Just stay in line." She nodded to the soldier. "Let's go."

The soldier escorted Mamá away, but her words haunted me. She thought no one had done anything wrong . . . but I had. What if this was about what happened with the oranges? Could this be my fault? But if so, why wasn't Yasmin's family in trouble?

I had to find out what was going on.

"Stay here," I said to Rodrigo, dropping our bag on the floor. "I'm going to follow them."

"No!" Rodrigo reached out to grab me, but I was too fast for him. I slipped away, leaving him standing in the line. He had no choice; I knew he'd stay there because otherwise we'd lose our spot.

I had no plan except to blend into the crowd and see where they were taking my mother.

Keeping my distance, I could see Mamá as she walked alongside the soldier, and people stared at them as they cut through the crowd.

My stomach turned when I saw them head toward the same side door where Yasmin and I had snuck out the day before. As the door opened and Mamá stepped outside, I caught a glimpse of the soldier who'd caught Yasmin kissing me. Or at least fake-kissing me.

The door closed and I quickly became aware of how many more people were now in the packed hallway. They'd be able to give me some cover so that I could sneak closer to the door, but I had to be careful because if I got caught, it would definitely make things worse.

I tried not to attract any attention as I made my way over.

I reached for the doorknob, hoping there wouldn't be anyone standing on the other side.

Suddenly the door flew open and I stood in front of a familiar face.

"Mamá!" I exclaimed, surprised to see her.

She immediately pulled me aside. "What are you doing here?" she whispered.

"I was worried," I replied. "Is everything okay?"

"Yes." She glanced behind us as we hurried back to the line. "It was Osvaldo. He heard my name being called and wanted to get us some food before we left." She tapped her purse. "He warned me again that we need to eat before we get to El Mosquito."

"Well, first we have to get out of here," I said as we wove through the crowded room.

"And that's what matters," Mama said. "Getting out."

She stopped and grabbed me by the shoulders. "Héctor, you have to promise me that you won't be so reckless again. It's not like you. You're supposed to be my logical thinker." She shook her head. "Taking off to follow me . . . That could have been a disaster for all of us."

"I know." I shrugged. "But sometimes I don't want to be the logical one."

She cupped my chin in her hand. "Mi amor, be who you are. The world needs more thinkers. People who can view a math problem from different angles. See the entire chess game, not just the next move."

I sighed as Mamá gave me a kiss on the cheek. Thinking

about chess games and math problems seemed like something I'd done in another life. Maybe one day I'd get back to all that . . . but not today. Today I was focused on getting out of this place.

As we headed back, I noticed that the line had moved up, with Paco and his family now speaking to one of the officials. We were all getting one step closer to leaving.

Rodrigo's face lit up when he saw us strolling back to him. Then, as I got close, his eyes narrowed and he clasped my arm, squeezing it as hard as he could. "You're an idiot!" he said under his breath. "Never do that again."

I jerked my arm out of his grasp. "Don't touch me."

"Boys . . . stop," Mamá warned. "Don't make a scene. There's—"

The sound of fists banging on a table and raised voices made everyone stop to see what was happening at the front of the room.

Someone *was* making a scene—and it wasn't us.

I stepped out from the line and saw a guard pulling Paco's dad away from the table.

"He's not of age yet!" he yelled. "And we've already been approved!"

Paco's aunts and uncles also began arguing. There was shouting and I could see Paco's mom crying.

"I'm not leaving him!" his mother shouted.

More guards rushed over from other parts of the building to maintain order.

Even from the back of the line, we could tell what was happening. The officials weren't going to allow Paco to leave Cuba.

"Oh no." Mamá covered her mouth with her hand. "Los pobres."

Everyone in line was transfixed. We all felt sorry for them and at the same time fearful that it might happen to us, too.

"That isn't right," Rodrigo whispered. "Paco's only a few months older than me. And he's not of military age yet either. They shouldn't be doing this to them." He started shifting his weight back and forth like a boxer about to go into the ring. "I should do something. . . . He's my friend."

"Ni lo pienses," Mamá warned. "Those officials are looking for any excuse to deny us." She shook her head with pity as Paco and his father said goodbye to the rest of their family. "There's nothing we can do for them."

I watched silently as Paco's family was separated. His uncles and cousins, including Yasmin, were all crying but they were walking away. Paco stood in a corner, his head hung low. His father was trying to convince Paco's sister and mother to go with the rest of the family, but they were refusing.

Paco's mom locked her arm with Paco's and headed to the front entrance of the Abreu Fontán building.

They were going to stick together.

Just like us.

No matter what.

24

IT WAS FINALLY our turn. The room had cleared out and a large man with a thick mustache was reviewing all our papers. Mamá had warned us not to say a word unless absolutely necessary, so Rodrigo and I stood behind her trying to make ourselves invisible.

We were all worried that Rodrigo would get denied just like Paco. During our time in line we'd seen at least ten other people flagged and denied permission to leave. In fact, the man standing next to us at the long table was currently being refused because he was a dentist. I could hear him arguing that he only worked as a taxi driver, but none of it seemed to matter to the woman inspecting all his documents.

"¿Esos son tus hijos?" The mustached man peered around my mother. "Where's their father?"

"He's in Miami," she said. "I have papers where he gave me full authority over the boys." She pointed to the folder.

"Everything is there. We're supposed to be on a boat called *The Lovely Lady*."

"Mm-hmm," he muttered, flipping through our documents. "That boat already left."

"What?" I blurted out.

The government official lifted his head and studied me. "You're . . ." He looked down at the papers again. "Héctor?"

I nodded, already regretting having said anything.

"Well, little escoria . . . we're getting rid of you by putting you on a different boat." He checked a list on the table. "You'll be on . . ." His finger ran across the page. "*Delta Queen*. They'll make room for you there."

"That's fine," Mamá said, pushing me behind her again.

"Hmph." He stamped some papers and then shoved the folder across the table. "Dale. The bus is outside."

We had made it.

We were getting out.

The three of us.

"Gracias," Mamá mumbled, taking the folder and quickly leading us to a door being held open by a guard in full uniform.

Outside there was a bus riddled with splatters of eggs and tomatoes. It was filled with people who, like us, had passed inspection and were now one step closer to getting to the port. As we boarded, I noticed there was a quiet sense of excitement and hopefulness, one that no one wanted to express for fear it would be quickly snatched away.

We silently walked to one of the last empty seats near the back . . . the three of us squeezing together with Mamá in between me and Rodrigo. There was a slight breeze coming through the bus since all the windows had been removed, but there was still a strong smell of rotten food inside. I was sitting closest to the aisle and could see the squished pieces of eggs and tomatoes leaving a trail along the floor. Without a doubt there'd be a crowd of "patriotic revolutionaries" ready to bombard us with garbage and rocks the moment we cleared the front gate.

"We're waiting for a few more and then we'll go," the driver announced, standing at the front of the bus. "Anyone changing their mind better do so now. Next stop is El Mosquito."

No one moved.

The driver shrugged and took his seat. "Está bien," he said, and turned on the engine.

The bus rattled and shook, but we were still waiting for the last people in line.

"Here." Mamá took out some sandwiches and gave them to us. "Eat this now before we get to El Mosquito."

"Is this from Osvaldo?" I asked, taking a bite of the stale bread.

"Yes," she answered.

Rodrigo had his mouth full as he talked. "Who's Osvaldo?"

"A friend of Mamá's that we saw on the way to the bathroom," I said. "He warned us that El Mosquito was going to be bad."

"He was the reason they pulled me out of the line," Mamá said, keeping an eye on the soldier sitting in the first row behind the driver. "He said they'd take all our money once we got to El Mosquito."

"Do you believe him?" Rodrigo asked, finishing his sandwich with one more big bite.

"I don't think he'd lie," Mamá replied as the final people boarded. "I trust him."

"We should keep our heads low," I suggested as the bus began rambling forward. "I'm pretty sure this bus gets pelted with stuff every time it goes out."

"Good idea." Mamá hunched down and covered her head with her big purse.

Rodrigo and I did the same, covering ourselves with our hands as the bus went out onto the street and into a crowd of people armed with projectiles. The driver moved us slowly through the crowd, letting those doing the acto de repudio against us have their fun. An older man a few seats in front of us got into a shouting match with someone outside and was promptly hit with several eggs.

After about a minute the bus broke free of the protesters and we stopped at the nearby intersection. We all began poking our heads up to catch what could be our last views of the streets of Havana.

"Look!" Rodrigo pointed to the opposite street corner. "It's Paco and his family." Rodrigo leaned out of the bus and waved, making eye contact with his friend as we waited at the red light.

"Our money," I whispered, noticing that the guards were speaking with the driver. "We should give it to them if we're not going to be able to use it."

Mamá nodded as Rodrigo motioned for his friend to hurry over.

Paco shook his head. It was too risky. He couldn't be seen making contact with scum like us. They were already in a bad situation; contact with us would probably make it worse.

"He won't come over," Rodrigo said as Mamá took out her blue wallet with all our money in it.

"Just show him the wallet and toss it out the window as we leave," I suggested. "He can get it once we're gone."

"Someone else might get it," Rodrigo pointed out.

"So?" I countered. "At least, it's someone other than those guards."

"Do it," Mama urged as the bus shifted gears. "Quickly."

Rodrigo glanced at the soldiers, who were still distracted with the driver. He leaned his arm out the window holding the wallet so that Paco could see it and then he flung it onto the sidewalk, where it skidded toward a nearby building.

As the bus pulled away, the three of us turned around to look out the back. We could see Paco running across the street, but the bus turned the corner before we could make sure he picked it up.

"I think he got it," Rodrigo said.

"I'm sure he did," I answered, turning back around.

"It should help them at least a little bit," Mamá added. "I've been saving up for a while."

As if on cue, one of the soldiers from the front of the bus walked down the aisle, kicking aside some of the broken eggshells with his boot. Everyone stayed quiet as he stopped in the middle to make an announcement.

"Mis estimados pasajeros . . ." The tall, skinny soldier's voice had a mocking tone as he called us his esteemed passengers. "We will be arriving at El Mosquito very soon. Your exemplary driver and my fellow colleague and I would like to offer you the chance to donate, directly to us, any money or valuables before they are confiscated at the inspection point."

A murmur went through the bus as people began to whisper and look at each other.

"Your experience with the inspection officers will be much quicker and easier if you are not seen trying to take anything of value from the motherland," he continued as his partner in crime, a short man with a beard, began passing around an empty black bag. "Better to give it up now than be accused of trying to steal Cuba's treasures."

One by one people emptied their pockets and removed any jewelry they might have. The fear of being turned back over something like a watch or a little bit of money was too great.

As the short, bearded soldier reached us in the back,

Mamá dropped a small gold chain she was wearing into the black bag.

"That's it?" the soldier questioned. "You don't have money?"

Rodrigo reached into his back pocket and dropped a few bills.

"We gave everything else to friends who were still at the Fontán," I explained.

The soldier shrugged and continued to the row behind us.

. They were making out like bandits.

I hoped we weren't all being suckered, but it seemed like most people had heard the same rumors about El Mosquito and were giving their things up now.

As the bus slowed down, I could see a small building with a line of people outside.

"Paco's uncles may already be inside," Rodrigo mused. "We'll search for them when we get through. Stick with them."

"Safety in numbers," I said, staring at what would be the next stop in our journey.

The Fontán was an overcrowded old place, but this was much worse. We were entering what looked like a prison. The whole area was surrounded by a high chain-link fence with barbed wire on top, and there was only a small building with a long line of people waiting to get inside.

I scoured the line and, at the very front, I saw a few familiar faces from when we got called up at the Fontán, but everyone behind them looked like they had gone through much worse than us. I noticed that they were all skinny men with shaved heads and their clothes looked worn. They were flanked on either side by police officers with guns at the ready.

"Bienvenidos a El Mosquito," the soldier holding the bag full of our valuables snickered. "May your stay be exactly what you gusanos deserve."

25

THE BRIGHT SUN beat down on us as we stood in line outside the small building. It had been almost two hours, but we were finally getting close to going inside. Behind us the line never got shorter, as there was a constant stream of buses bringing more gusanos like us and also bringing men who had guards surrounding them. The rumor was that the men with shaved heads were either criminals from a prison a few hours away or patients from a mental institution in Havana. No one knew for sure. All we knew was that they were being sent to the U.S. with the rest of us. Whether they wanted to go or not.

"Neither of you brought anything of value, right?" Mamá asked us, touching her bare ring finger where her wedding band used to be. She'd given it to Cuqui for safekeeping, hoping to get it back one day. "You're not hiding anything in your underwear."

"I don't own anything of value," I said as one of the guards opened the door and motioned for us to go inside. "Except for my baseball cards . . . and those are inside the math book that's in our bag."

"All right," Mamá whispered, stepping into the hot, muggy room. "You just do as they say and remain silent."

Rodrigo clenched his jaw but nodded in agreement.

"Bags there," a female soldier shouted from behind a small wooden table. She pointed to a table where two men were looking through someone's small suitcase. "You know the name of your boat?"

"*Delta Queen,*" Mamá said as she motioned for Rodrigo to hand over our duffel bag and she fished out the folder of documents from her purse.

"Listen for the name of your boat. When it gets called, you'll be put on a bus and taken to Mariel." The woman glanced over at us as we dropped our bag on the table. "Do you have any valuables on you?"

"No," Mamá replied. "None of us do."

"Mm-hmm." The woman paused to study Mamá's face. "Let me have your purse," she ordered.

Mamá gave it to her and the woman dumped all the contents on the table. She checked the large purse's lining and then went through each item, setting aside a lipstick and small mirror. She then rifled through the papers and photographs my mom had brought, before shoving them all back into the purse.

"You two." She pointed to Rodrigo and me. "If you have anything on you, put it on this table."

Rodrigo dug into his pocket and pulled out a little bit of money that he'd been saving and slapped it onto the table.

"Hmph." The woman raised an eyebrow. "That's it?"

The three of us nodded.

"No wedding ring?" she asked Mamá.

Mamá shook her head.

"¡Inspección de varones!" the female officer yelled, and looked back at a line of guards talking in the back.

"An inspection of the boys?" Mamá asked, visibly worried. "What for?"

"Are you sure you're not hiding anything?" The woman leaned back in her chair, her arms crossed in front of her chest, evaluating our reactions. "Now would be the time to turn it over before we search for ourselves and discover that you're lying to us." She gave me a cold, hard stare. "And we dislike liars even more than traitors."

"We don't have anything," I proclaimed. "We already told you."

"Fine," she answered as a male guard showed up next to the desk. "We'll make sure of that." She pointed to Rodrigo and me. "Search them," she ordered.

"Let me go with them," Mamá said. "Please. I beg you."

Mamá's heartfelt plea seemed to soften the female officer's tough demeanor. She handed Mamá back her bag. "Listen, I'm going to let you keep your purse with your photos and papers, assuming you don't have anything else hidden on your body. Your sons will be fine—they'll be together." She pointed to where several women were standing next to a screened-off area. "Just go over there with those other women. Follow the rules and you'll all be out of here in a few minutes."

Mamá's eyes filled with tears, but she didn't say anything. She only gave us a simple nod for us to do as instructed.

I didn't want to go. Once again, my feet felt like someone had nailed my shoes to the tiled floor.

"Come, Héctor," Rodrigo called, having already taken a few steps away from the table. "Fuerza."

Strength.

Rodrigo was right. We needed to be strong even if our plan to stick together was falling apart.

We walked into an empty room and the officer promptly closed the door behind us.

"Take off your clothes and toss them into a pile next to me," he said, sitting down on a stool in the corner of the room. A small uncovered window next to him allowed sunlight into the room. In the distance I could see row after row of temporary tentlike shelters.

I took off my wrinkled green shirt and Teo's lucky fishing shirt and tossed them both toward the guard, who was now lighting a cigarette.

As I undid the button of my shorts, I stared out the window

at a soldier with a guard dog patrolling the perimeter of our building.

I decided to keep my eyes focused on the scene outside, refusing to look at the guard or Rodrigo, as my shorts dropped to the floor.

"Everything . . . socks and shoes, too," the guard stated as Rodrigo and I both tossed our shorts over to him.

Tears started to press against my eyes, but I fought against them. I would not give this stranger the satisfaction of seeing me cry. I kicked off my shoes, slid them over to the corner, and pushed back my glasses as I bent down to peel off my very smelly socks.

Standing up again, my fingers touched the rim of my underwear . . . the last piece of clothing on me.

I began to shake uncontrollably. I could feel every rib sticking out of my skinny body as I stood almost naked in the room. I took a deep breath, trying to regain control, but all I seemed to inhale was the smoke from the guard's cigarette.

"Keep the underwear," the guard said, kicking our clothes back to us after having patted them down. "Just get dressed and join me outside."

He marched out of the room, leaving Rodrigo and me to get dressed in silence.

When we walked back into the main room, I spotted the guard casually smoking his cigarette next to a few other men. "¡Niños!" he called out. "Over there." He pointed to a door that led to the outside. "You'll wait for your mother outside."

"What about our stuff?" Rodrigo asked, pointing to our duffel bag piled on top of other bags and suitcases. "There's nothing valuable in it."

"Then you shouldn't miss any of it," he snickered, nudging the guy next to him, who started to chuckle. "Now go."

Rodrigo wouldn't give up. "But I've got pictures and things that are important to me," he insisted.

"Not my problem." The guard tossed the cigarette on the floor and stubbed it out with his boot. "They stay, you leave."

I pulled Rodrigo by the arm. I was losing all my baseball cards and the math book Señora Andrade had given me, but none of it was worth getting into trouble with these guards. We had come too far to get sidetracked by this.

"Déjalo," I said, dragging him with me toward the exit. "It doesn't matter."

"It matters to me." Rodrigo was seething. "It's the only picture I have of Marisol."

"Seriously?" I rolled my eyes at what it was he wanted. "You can look for her when we get to Miami," I said. "And you can take more pictures there."

"You don't get it." He shook his head. "What if I can't find her? What if her family goes somewhere else? The U.S. is a big place. What if I never see her again?"

"The only *what if* you should worry about is what if those guards decide to not let you leave?" I retorted, stepping outside. "Then for sure you won't see her again."

He knew I was right.

I stopped to look out at the sea of people ahead of us. There were so many more than we'd seen at the Fontán, and here there were guards with guns patrolling the entire area.

"Keep moving!" a guard shouted at us. "You can't stay near the building. Families are that way." He pointed to the make-shift shelters.

Rodrigo and I took a few steps toward the ones closest to us. There were dozens of them and none seemed too sturdy. They were just large tents with no side panels, but they covered the rows and rows of cots beneath them. Maybe we'd find Paco's uncles or someone else we knew in one of them.

"Héctor! Rodrigo!"

We spun around to see Mamá. She was rushing toward us with her arms outstretched.

We hugged, happy that our separation had only lasted a few minutes.

"You okay?" I asked, noticing the tear rolling down Mamá's cheek.

"I'm fine," she said, wiping it away. "We are almost out of here. That's what matters."

"We should try to find a place to wait," Rodrigo suggested.

I nodded, having noticed that another group of men was being escorted by guards toward the far side of the camp. "Families are on that side," I said, pointing to the nearby tents.

"Then that's where we will go," Mamá said.

As we got to the tent area, I noticed how packed it was. There were families sitting together on a single cot and even more people huddled together on every spot of bare ground. A few looked clean and fresh, as if they had left their house a couple of hours earlier, but most looked like they'd been homeless for weeks. I glanced at Mamá and Rodrigo. We were starting to look as ragged as most of the people around us.

"I don't see any space for us," Mamá said after walking through four different tent areas. "And no familiar faces."

"Atención . . ." The loudspeaker at the top of one of the poles crackled and hummed before the voice was heard again. *"Sea Party, Rascal Love, Pat River, y Some Believe."*

I was sure that they were the names of boats, but the person announcing them was mangling the English words, so they all sounded like some strange version of Spanish.

"Look for anyone getting up," I suggested, scouring the nearby tent for movement. "People will be leaving to get on those boats."

"There!" Rodrigo pointed to a group on the other side that was standing.

"Go get their spot!" Mamá pushed us forward. "Before someone else does."

Rodrigo and I chose different paths to try to get there. I ran around the outside of the tent while he wove in between the rows of families huddled next to each small bed. I managed to get there first and quickly sat on the mattress, claiming it for our family.

I smiled at the woman next to us, but she turned her head and ignored me.

Even though there wasn't much room between each cot, I quickly noticed that there was a distinct separation between each family. People were talking in hushed tones with those in their own group.

The fear that there were watchful eyes trying to catch anyone who didn't support Fidel ran deep. Anyone could turn you in. A family member, a teacher, a friend.

Even here at El Mosquito, where we were all making a public declaration that we wanted to leave, there was fear. It felt like at any minute the whole thing would be revealed to have been an elaborate trap to catch anti-revolutionaries.

Or maybe . . . the real fear was that it wasn't.

26

THREE *DAYS* PASSED and we had barely ventured away from our coveted spot under the tent. The cot had become a prized commodity as more and more people arrived every hour. I had run a few calculations in my head and estimated that there were well over two thousand gusanos like us waiting for the next step in the journey. But even with so many people, I felt more alone than ever.

I didn't even want to talk to Mamá or Rodrigo.

I just stared at the gates on the far end of what had become our prison, where a steady trickle of people would exit once their boat's name got called. I watched their tired and haggard bodies transform with excitement as they finally stepped away from El Mosquito. They were heading toward freedom while the rest of us continued to wait. There was no reason or pattern that I could decipher as to why some only had to wait a few hours and others were waiting for days.

No one knew what was really happening on the outside, and questioning things was simply not tolerated. The guards had made certain of that by keeping us all in check with threats and intimidation.

In fact, I had already seen several instances where a guard had grabbed someone, even for a minor offense like complaining too loudly about the lack of food, and then that person wasn't seen again. Some said that the guards would take these people to the cordoned-off area of the camp reserved for criminals and those that the government labeled "undesirable." Others theorized that those taken away were simply thrown out of El Mosquito completely, left to fend for themselves like Paco and his family. No one wanted to say what we all were thinking . . . that perhaps those people were being "eliminated" in a more permanent manner.

So we all just sat on our cots, sweating in the stifling heat or trying to avoid the afternoon downpours, always hoping that our boat's name would be called next. The only thing left to do was think about the lives and homes we had abandoned.

For me, my thoughts of home always went back to Teo and Isabel.

I missed them. I missed going to school. I missed my house and my room. I missed the idea of going to the International Math Olympiad.

I even missed Abuela.

We hadn't had a chance to say goodbye to her . . . not that

she would have ever approved of us leaving with Mamá. But she was still my grandmother and she'd always been part of my life.

I glanced at Mamá. I hoped she was right about the U.S. because sometimes dreams don't match reality.

Which made me think of Yasmin. I had liked her more when I didn't know her.

During our first night at El Mosquito, Rodrigo told us he'd seen Yasmin and her whole family walking to the buses that would take them to Mariel. They'd been huddled near some jagged rocks near the water's edge and had crossed paths with him when he went to bathe in the ocean. They were some of the lucky ones whose wait had lasted only a few hours.

The rumbling of my stomach interrupted my thoughts. I had already gone from hungry to starving, since our only food was the occasional bits of burned rice and green scrambled eggs that the guards gave out.

I leaned my head against the edge of the cot's metal frame and stared at the feet of the old woman who had taken the bed next to us. She had arrived late last night and her family was sitting on the floor around her.

"Atención . . ."

Everyone's ears perked up as a new list of boats was read.

"*Ponti Pride, General Grayson, Alex's Song, Delta Queen* . . ."

I jumped up, not paying attention to the remaining names.

"That's us!" I exclaimed, excitement masking the hunger pangs in my stomach.

Mamá grabbed her big purse and smiled as Rodrigo stood up.

We were going to get out of El Mosquito . . . finally.

Just as soon as we stepped away from the cot, another family ran over to claim it as their own.

I didn't care. I was focused on getting on the bus and being allowed on our boat.

We lined up at the exit gate, and we could see several buses parked on the other side of the barbed-wire fence. We were one of the first families in line this time, and a couple of guards on either side of the gate were checking people off their lists and directing them to the different buses. Then a large group of about fifty men approached, escorted by soldiers on either side.

I couldn't help but stare at them, with their sullen eyes and skinny bodies. They were wearing street clothes, but you could tell the clothing wasn't their own.

"Gusanos for the *Delta Queen*," one of the soldiers declared as he stepped in front of us. "From el Combinado del Este."

Rodrigo and I exchanged looks.

Combinado del Este was the harshest prison in Havana. Some of the worst criminals were sent there, and now all these men were being put on our boat. Then again, maybe we were the ones being put on their boat.

"Primera guagua," the guard responded, pointing to the first bus.

As the men passed by us, I noticed that most of them kept their heads down, but a few were looking around with tears in their eyes. It was as if their spirits had been crushed a long time ago.

The guard on the left of the gate motioned for us to approach him.

"¿Nombre?" he asked Mamá as the three of us got closer.

"Ivette Marina Fulgeira," she replied. "And my sons, Rod—"

"No." The guard rolled his eyes. "Boat name."

"Oh, *Delta Queen*," she clarified as a couple of people began arguing with the other guard about not being on his list.

"And you said your name is Ivette Marina?" His finger hovered over the list in his hand. "Ah yes, here, bus one." He turned his head to look at the other guard as the shouting became more intense. "¿Necesitas ayuda?" he called out to the guard, his hand on his rifle.

"Yes. Come here." The other guard waved him over. "They aren't on my list. See if yours is different."

Our guard began comparing the two lists when he noticed that we were still standing by the gate, waiting for further instruction. "What are you still doing there? Go," he ordered. "Bus number one."

We quickly went through the gate and headed to the first bus, which was filled with the prisoners and a couple of guards.

As we boarded, all eyes went to Mamá.

Rodrigo and I instinctively shielded her, acting as makeshift bodyguards.

I scanned the bus and spotted a family with four kids sitting about ten rows back. The mother was wearing all-white clothes, including a white scarf around her hair, and she signaled for us to take the seats next to them.

As we made our way toward her, she smiled, showing a large gap between her front teeth. "Un poquito más and we'll soon be there," she said as I scooted closer to the window to make room for Rodrigo and Mamá.

I gave her a slight nod, refusing to believe we had made it until I saw the boat for myself.

The next several minutes seemed to take forever. After a few more men and two soldiers boarded the bus, the driver was finally given the go-ahead to close the door.

I held my breath as the bus lurched forward and pulled away from the camp.

I'd expected another mob outside ready to torment us for leaving, but the entire ride was quiet. Within minutes, we pulled up alongside a pier at the port of Mariel. I now had a closeup view of the hundreds of boats, of all different sizes, scattered throughout the bay. Some were tiny and others looked huge. Some looked like they could barely stay afloat while others looked to be fishing charters that could take on the roughest of seas. The one thing they all had in common was that they were each anchored right offshore, waiting to pick up passengers fleeing Cuba.

Then there were the boats that were already docked and overloaded with people. I could see men, women, and children standing shoulder to shoulder aboard each vessel. Each boat looked like it might sink with all the extra weight.

By now, everyone on the bus was searching for our boat. "There!" One of the men in the back pointed to a sturdy-looking fishing charter close to the end of the pier. *"Delta Queen!"*

I adjusted my glasses and strained to read the name on the back of the boat. All that I could see from my vantage point was the word *Queen* . . . but that was enough to make my heart flutter.

The foul-smelling bus immediately erupted with conversations. The air was filled with anticipation and excitement, much to the annoyance of the soldiers that were keeping an eye on all of us.

"Enough!" The tallest soldier banged his hand against the top panel of the bus to capture everyone's attention.

"¡Cállense!" another soldier ordered. "Not another word!"

I hadn't said anything, but there was a deep thrill in my bones that wanted to come out. I felt like shouting with joy at having made it. Mamá gave my hand a little squeeze as she tried to hide the smile on her face.

We knew we had to remain calm and quiet so as not to provoke the soldiers, but some of the men on the bus didn't seem to care. They kept talking, some even growing louder.

"That's it!" One of the soldiers grabbed a random man and pulled him to the front of the bus, a gun to his head.

Everyone froze.

It became so quiet that I could hear the boats outside sloshing against the seawall.

"Tranquilo, Mario." A female soldier tried to calm things down. "These gusanos aren't worth the bullet." She gently put a hand on his arm. "Let the escoria drown in the sea."

Mario glared at all of us before opening the bus door and pushing the man down the steps. "All that came from el Combinado del Este . . . get out!"

As the men filed out of the bus and were led to the boat at the end of the pier, we stayed behind with the other family.

I watched as the *Delta Queen* quickly sank lower and lower in the water with each person that boarded. It wasn't meant to carry so many people, and there were still nine of us on the bus.

Once the last of the prisoners was on the boat, the female soldier turned her attention to the rest of us. "All right, now all of you go. . . ."

"Sonia, wait!" A man in army fatigues trotted up the bus steps and whispered something in the female soldier's ear.

She gave him a nod. "Which one of you is Ivette Marina Fulgeira?" she asked, staring at my mother and the other woman.

Mamá slowly raised her hand as the man in fatigues approached.

This wasn't good.

"You and your sons have to wait. Everyone else, follow me." The female soldier stepped off the bus.

"Buena suerte," the woman dressed in all white told us as she walked by.

She was wishing us luck, as if we wouldn't be joining her on the boat.

No. I refused to let myself think that way. I wasn't going to lose hope now . . . not when we were so close.

"I'm not sure how you were allowed on this bus," the soldier said. "But you need to come with me."

"Is there a problem?" I asked.

"Outside," he instructed without answering my question.

The three of us followed him off the bus. Our only option was to comply and hope that whatever was wrong was something we could fix.

"I have our approvals. . . ." Mamá took out her folder. "Everything is stamped and—"

He raised his hand to shut her up. "These are your sons?" he asked. "Both of them?"

"Yes." She opened the folder and rifled through the papers. "I have all their information here. They—"

"So . . ." He took our approved exit visas and studied each one. "There are three of you, correct?"

"Yes." Mamá's voice quivered.

He gave her back the paperwork and smirked. "That's a problem because only two of you can leave."

"What?" I exclaimed.

"But our papers . . . ," Mamá insisted. "They're approved."

The soldier shrugged. "Not my problem. The boat is about to leave and you need to decide which son goes with you."

"I . . . I . . ." Mamá was beginning to panic.

"Sir . . ." I glanced at the overcrowded *Delta Queen*, which had now started its engines. "Can we get on another boat?" I adjusted my glasses. "We can wait at El Mosquito again if we have to. We just don't want to get split up."

The soldier laughed. "This isn't about space." He bent down a little to where his eyes were right in front of my own and I could smell his breath. "This is about your mother having to choose which one of you gusanos she loves more."

My stomach dropped. He was forcing us to separate.

"The boys will go," Mamá declared. "I'll stay."

"No!" Rodrigo protested. "We're not leaving you."

Mamá faced the two of us. "I'll figure something out. If you two are safe with your father, then I'll be fine."

The soldier sucked on his teeth and then spit on the ground. "Not an option. At least one of the boys has to remain. Delegada Fulgeira left instructions that she will gladly accept whichever boy you don't want. She'll ensure he becomes a good revolutionary."

I could barely breathe. Abuela was behind this? She was forcing either Rodrigo or me to stay? How could she . . . ?

"Hurry up!" the captain from the *Delta Queen* shouted.

The soldier shrugged. "Or all three of you can stay in Cuba. . . . I really don't care."

"I should have known," Mamá muttered. "She always finds a way to win."

I focused on Mamá, who looked like she was about to break down crying. I had to think things through like one of my chess games. Consider several moves ahead. Use every ounce of logical thinking that I possessed.

"Abuela doesn't have to win," I said. "Rodrigo can go on the boat."

"Absolutely not." Rodrigo shook his head. "I'm the oldest, so I should stay. You two go."

I ignored him. "Think things through, Mamá. Look what happened to Paco. This might be Rodrigo's only chance to get out. I have more time."

She ran her hand through her hair. "I'm not handing you over to your grandmother."

"I know," I said. "You'd have to stay here with me. We'd have to find some other way out. But we have to be logical about this. Rodrigo is in the most danger and he should go. If he's in the U.S. with Papá, then they can both work to get us out."

Mamá's bottom lip quivered. "You're right."

"No! I'm not leaving the two of you," Rodrigo said as the captain shouted from the boat.

"Tick-tock." The soldier tapped his wristwatch.

"Fuerza," I mouthed to Rodrigo. A reminder that we had to be strong. "You know this is the right decision."

Rodrigo glanced back at the boat, unsure of what to do.

"All right, that's it. If no one is going . . ." The soldier waved at the captain to go. "You can walk back to whatever place you call home."

My eyes locked with Rodrigo's as Mamá began to sob. "Go," I said forcefully. "Please. For us."

Rodrigo nodded. "I'm going," he announced.

"Better make it quick." The soldier smirked as the rope holding the boat to the pier was untied.

There was no time to say anything else. Rodrigo took off running.

The boat to our future in the U.S. was so close, only about a hundred feet away, but I'd never get to it.

"Love you, Rodrigo!" Mamá shouted as Rodrigo jumped onto the boat as it pulled away.

Rodrigo spun around and waved. "Take care of Mamá!" he called out.

I nodded, a lump having formed in my throat.

The soldier wasn't going to allow us to have any type of long goodbye. He pushed Mamá and me away from the pier and toward a row of buses that had just arrived. "Get out of here, escoria," he said, giving me an extra shove. "And I hope you've learned your lesson, boy," he sneered. "The revolution always triumphs."

27

I **GRIPPED MAMÁ'S** hand as we looked out toward the water where Rodrigo's boat had now become a small speck on the horizon. The *Delta Queen* had left, and our small family of three had now become a tiny pairing of two.

The idea of Rodrigo being gone was just starting to settle in. A part of me still couldn't believe that Abuela had been so cruel to break up our family, but I wasn't going to let her get away with it. This separation would only be temporary. We'd be together again . . . someday.

But for now, it would have to just be Mamá and me.

The two of us walked around the buses that were bringing in a steady stream of people from El Mosquito. I noticed how everyone looked disheveled, tired, and dirty. I doubted any of them had started that way. They had probably chosen their clothes carefully like we had . . . everyone wanting to make a good first impression.

"We can go to Cuqui's house first," Mamá said. "Get my wedding ring back. Maybe she'll have an idea of where we can go. Some place in the countryside where your abuela won't find us."

"What about Teo and Isabel's grandparents?" I suggested. "They moved to the countryside. Isabel can tell me where they live and—"

"No, we can't do that," Mamá said. "Not after everything that's happened."

"You mean because they hate us for what happened to Teo."

"And they should." Mamá bit her lip. "I wasn't going to tell you anything, but . . ." She took a deep breath and stopped walking.

We were next to an empty bus, but I could still feel the heat coming from its engine. A trickle of sweat rolled down the side of my chest as I waited for her to keep talking.

"Your abuela ordered the acto de repudio against us . . . the one where Teo got killed. She wanted to scare us into submission." Mamá sighed. "Teo's parents suspected it was her, and I got confirmation of it the other day. I didn't want to tell you." She scoffed and shook her head in disbelief. "For some stupid reason I wanted you to still have good memories of your grandmother. But you need to know—we will not be safe with her."

It felt like someone had punched me in the stomach. I knew Abuela could be stubborn and demanding, but I hadn't understood the lengths to which she would go to get what she wanted. She would stop at nothing . . . no matter who she hurt.

Before I could fully process what Mamá had just revealed, I heard a familiar voice call out my name.

I turned around and spotted Isabel running toward me. She had left her parents and Nani standing in line in front of a large shrimp boat.

It was almost too much to absorb.

They were here at Mariel getting ready to leave . . . just like we had been a few minutes earlier.

I hurried over to meet her halfway as a crowd of people began walking by, headed to their own boat-side check-ins.

"I can't believe you're here!" I exclaimed as she got closer. "When did you . . . ? How . . . ?"

"It all happened superfast this morning. They just knocked on our door and—"

"ISA!" her mother called out.

We both looked over at Isabel's mother motioning for Isabel to come back.

"You have to get back in line with your parents," I said, noticing that a cool breeze was blowing in from the ocean and the temperature had suddenly dropped. "It's going to start raining and—"

"I will, I will." She nodded. "I just needed to give you this before you got on your boat." She pulled out Teo's Roberto

Clemente baseball card from her pocket. "He'd want you to have it."

It was Teo's prized possession.

A lump formed in my throat. "Thanks, but you keep it." I pushed her hand away. "I'm not getting on a boat."

"ISABEL!" her mother shouted again.

"What do you mean?" Her eyebrows scrunched together. "You're not leaving?"

I shook my head. "It's a long story, but basically, my mother and I are stuck in Cuba. Rodrigo already left."

"But where will you go?"

I shrugged and glanced back at Mamá, who gave Isabel a slight wave.

Even though Mamá didn't want me to ask Isabel's family for help, it might be our only hope at surviving in Cuba.

"Listen, I have a big favor to ask," I said. "Do you know where your grandparents live? I mean, I know it's in the countryside somewhere."

"It's near Colón, I think. Why?"

"Do you think we could go stay with them . . . just for a couple of days? It's a lot to ask . . . I know, but—"

"Isabel!" Her mother was rushing toward us. "Right now. It's almost our turn."

"Let me talk to my parents," she said, turning around and racing over to her mother. "Stay there!"

Mamá approached me from behind and put a hand on my

shoulder. "I'm glad you were able to say goodbye to Isabel. You'll always treasure that friendship."

"I told her what happened and asked about her grandparents. They're near Colón," I blurted out. "She's asking her parents about it right now."

"Oh, Héctor." She looked over at Isabel talking to both her parents as they got closer and closer to the front of their line. "You shouldn't have put them in such a difficult spot. It's not right to unload our problems on them. They have enough to deal with."

"But, look." Isabel's family was now letting other people skip ahead of them in line. "Teo's dad is taking something out of that big envelope. The address maybe?"

A sense of accomplishment washed over me. I'd found a way to keep us safe while we figured out our next steps. I was taking care of Mamá just like Rodrigo had said.

"Teo!" Isabel's father shouted, staring right at us while holding something up in the air. "We're waiting for you!"

Teo? Was Isabel's father hallucinating? Had the stress made him start acting like Nani?

Even though I knew it was impossible, I still looked behind me as if Teo might magically appear from behind the bus. But of course, he didn't.

Mamá was the only person standing behind me and she was transfixed . . . completely focused on Isabel's father. She slowly gave him a small nod and then pushed me forward. "Go with them," she whispered as another new busload of people began crowding around us and making their way to the dock. "I love you."

"What?" I looked into her eyes as she fought back tears. "What are you talking about? I can't just go with them."

"¡Hermano!" Isabel shouted, causing me to whirl around and look at her. "Papi has your passport here! The boat is waiting for us."

It suddenly dawned on me. They were going to try to pass me off as Teo to get me on their boat.

But that meant leaving Mamá.

Which I wouldn't do.

I couldn't do.

"No, Mamá," I said forcefully. "I'm not . . ." I looked back and realized that she was gone. "Mamá?" I spun around. "Mamá!" I ran behind the parked bus looking for her, but she had disappeared.

A hand grabbed me by the arm.

It was Isabel's mother.

"Vamos, mijo," she said softly. "It's time to go."

"But my mother . . ."

"She wants you to come with us." She pulled me along. "You must come now."

I planted my feet. "No, you don't understand. I can't leave her."

"She's already gone." Isabel's mother gently pulled off my

glasses and handed them to me. "You have to pretend to be Teo. You two have always looked alike and they're only checking names anyway. His name is still on the captain's list because we made our plans before . . ."

She didn't finish the sentence. She didn't have to.

I felt like throwing up. This wasn't how things were supposed to be. Teo was the one who always wanted to travel and see the world. He should be here, not me.

Plus, I was supposed to be taking care of my mother. Protecting her.

"Mami! Teo!" Isabel shouted. Her family had become the last people in line, with only a few people ahead of them. "Let's go."

"Do it for your mother," Isabel's mom whispered. "Do it for Teo."

It didn't feel like I had much choice. Mamá had mentioned going to see her friend Cuqui, but I had no idea where Cuqui lived. How would I ever find her again when her plan was to disappear?

"Héctor?" Isabel's mom prodded me to say or do something.

I nodded and we hurried back to where Isabel, her father, and Nani were all waiting for us. They were risking everything in order to get me out.

I did a quick mental run-through of everything I might be asked. Teo's birthday, address, parents' information . . . I knew it all. Teo and I even looked alike in some of our pictures except for my height, weight, and glasses.

I put the frames I was holding in my back pocket. There wasn't much I could do about our difference in size, but hopefully it wouldn't come to that. Plus, my whole life Mamá had us pretending to be someone different in public. This would be another fake existence.

"They're right here," Isabel's dad said. "My wife, Sara, and our son, Teo."

The soldier gave us a quick nod and then glanced over his shoulder at the overcrowded charter boat behind him. "Go ahead," he said.

"But that's not Teo," Nani suddenly declared. "That's Teo's friend Héctor. Why is he here?"

We all froze.

It was the worst possible moment for Nani to become lucid.

"No, Nani." Isabel smiled and patted Nani's hand. "You're just confused—that's Teo."

"I'm not confused," she insisted, becoming slightly belligerent as her white hair whipped around in the wind. "Héctor lives across the street. He used to catch lizards and call them dragons. I remember." She stared at all the boats and the lines of people climbing aboard each one. "And you all said we were going on a trip, but none of this feels right. Who are all those people on the boat? I don't know any of them."

"You're leaving Cuba along with all the other scum," the soldier told Nani. "Don't you know that? You'll get to ride with some metralla released from the jails."

"What?" She looked at Isabel's parents for answers. "Why are we leaving with prisoners? Where are we going?"

Isabel's father put an arm around the old woman. "We told you. We're going to Cayo Hueso and then to Miami. Susana, your daughter, lives there with her family. She's waiting for us."

"¿Y Pablo?" she questioned. "I remember that he moved to the countryside. Is he coming?"

"Not right now," Isabel's father said gently. "Maybe later."

Nani looked at all of us. "But then why is Héctor coming with us and not Pablo?"

"Something strange is going on here," the soldier said, blocking us from getting to the boat. "Do you still have your papers?"

"Yes, they said we could keep these." Isabel's father took out a large yellow envelope with everyone's paperwork. "But Nani here is old, and her thinking is sometimes muddled. You'll have to excuse her."

"She sounds pretty coherent to me." He flipped through the passports until he got to mine. He studied the picture and then me. "What's your birthday?"

"July 11, 1969." I could feel myself shaking inside as I spoke. "Same as my sister. We're twins. Two minutes apart."

"Mm-hmm." He looked at the picture again. "You don't look much like your photo."

"He was sick for a while and lost a lot of weight." Isabel's mother gently squeezed my cheeks. "He's my flaco now."

The soldier pulled out another sheet. "And why is yours the only one that isn't stamped by the officers from the Abreu Fontán?"

I looked to Isabel's father. How were we going to explain this?

A shiver ran down my spine.

"What's the delay?" A strong voice called out from farther down the pier. "Get those boats moving! Don't you see that a storm is coming?"

"Ernesto is still with the last family, Capitán," replied the soldier standing between a big, overcrowded shrimp boat and the charter boat that was waiting for us.

I peered around Isabel's father and, even without my glasses, I could see the officer's red hair and knew that it had to be Mamá's friend Osvaldo Cepero. I quickly turned my back to him.

If he saw me, he'd know I wasn't Teo.

"Ernesto," the soldier by the shrimp boat called out. "Are they coming or not? I'm releasing the big boat."

Ernesto raised his hand. "Give me a minute."

The soldier unmoored the shrimp boat as its engines rattled to life.

We didn't have much time.

"The missing stamp is probably just an oversight," Isabel's father replied, pretending not to be concerned. "A simple mistake."

"An oversight?" Ernesto, the man who held our fate in his hands, raised an eyebrow. "I doubt that." He studied me a little more. "And your son doesn't look as clean as the rest of—"

"Wrap it up, soldier!" A familiar voice behind me ordered. "Why are you taking so long?"

I froze, knowing that I was about to be discovered by Mamá's old friend. I weighed all my options, but it didn't seem like I had too many. My fate, and that of Isabel's family, would come down to an old childhood friendship.

"Something with this family doesn't add up, Capitán Cepero." Ernesto handed Teo's passport over to him.

"Then deny—"

"Sir, please," I interrupted him, turning so he could see my face.

Our eyes locked and I could tell he recognized me.

"My paper wasn't stamped, sir," I explained as he looked down at my documents. "My mother followed all the rules, but something happened. It wasn't our fault."

I was trying to speak in code so that he'd understand why I was with Isabel's family. If he was really Mamá's friend, he'd help us.

If he wasn't . . .

"I see," Captain Cepero muttered as the large shrimp boat

pulled away from the dock, leaving behind the smaller charter boat.

"They're claiming him to be Teo, but the old woman says his name is actually Héctor," Ernesto added.

"But I am Teo," I insisted. "And our boat is about to leave. Please," I begged.

"The dragons!" Nani suddenly yelled, crouching down and covering her head with her arms. "They're attacking! Help! Help!"

"What's she doing?" Captain Cepero took a step back as Nani began flailing her arms as if she was trying to shoo something away.

"She's not well," Isabel said as Nani continued yelling and acting even more unusual than ever. "We told him."

"Let them go," Captain Cepero said, walking away from us. "We don't need any more locura in Cuba. The Yankee imperialists can deal with them."

"Yes, sir." Ernesto waved to the soldier by the overcrowded charter boat. "Put them on the *Pura Vida* and let it go," he shouted. "They're the last ones."

Nani looked at me and gave me a little wink.

She had done it on purpose. Maybe she wasn't as out of it as we all thought.

The five of us hurried over to the boat as the captain started the motor. I put on my glasses and read the name scrolled along the back . . . *Pura Vida*. Pure life.

Maybe this was a good omen even though the boat was

crowded and already sitting low in the water. Isabel's family climbed aboard, squeezing between the men standing shoulder to shoulder on the deck. I was about to join them when someone called out my name.

Or rather, Teo's name.

I turned to see Captain Cepero marching toward us.

"Get on the boat," Isabel said. "Hurry!"

I jumped onto the crowded back deck as if being on the boat would give me some sort of protection.

"*Pura Vida* . . . wait!" Captain Cepero ordered.

The boat captain, an older man with sunburned skin, shook his head. "No, no, no! There's no way my boat can hold any more people!" he shouted. "I came for eight and you've already added over twenty more. We'll sink out there!"

"You're not getting any more people," Captain Cepero replied as he bypassed the soldier untying the boat from the dock. "The boy forgot his passport." He motioned for me to come back to the dock to get it.

"Dale," Isabel's dad encouraged. "We won't leave you behind."

I scrambled out of the boat to retrieve Teo's passport and rushed over to Captain Cepero.

"Take it, gusano." He thrust it against my chest. "It's the last bit of Cuba you'll ever have."

As I took the passport, Captain Cepero grabbed the collar of my shirt and jerked me toward him. "I wrote a phone number in there," he whispered in my ear. "When your mother contacts you in the U.S., have her call that person. He'll know how to reach me and I'll try to help her."

I nodded, but he was already pushing me away.

"And that's what we do to scum like you!" he said, laughing out loud and looking over at the soldier holding the rope. "Get them out of here."

I turned around and hopped back onto the boat, tightly clutching the small bit of hope that Mamá would one day be able to join us in Miami.

"Everything okay?" Isabel asked as the boat pulled away, both of us standing against the back railing.

"I think so," I said, slipping the passport into my back pocket as my heartbeat settled down. "He's actually friends with my mother. He was pretending to be a jerk, but I think he wants to help her escape."

"That's good." She stared out at the hundreds of boats still in the port. "Mariel looks pretty from out here, don't you think?"

"I guess." I gazed out at the scene and inhaled my last bits of Cuban air. It was sweet with the smell of the ocean, but carried an undercurrent of human waste.

It was like most things in Cuba—there were always complicated, competing identities.

From a distance the view could look beautiful, but it was

ugly when you got up close and realized how people were living. Or a rude soldier could actually be a friend. And your own abuela could turn out to be your worst enemy.

Nothing was ever what it seemed.

Nothing.

There was the illusion and the reality.

Even when it came to yourself.

28

I STRETCHED MY arm over the edge of the boat and felt the ocean spray. The Cuban coastline was no longer visible and we'd soon be in the open waters of the Caribbean. The sky had grown darker over the last hour and there was an uptick in the wind and waves. I had done some calculations at home based on average boat speeds and distance, and figured that the trip would likely take about eight hours . . . so even if the seas got a little rough, every minute that passed was one minute closer to getting there.

Unfortunately, I hadn't factored in that this boat would be going slower than average with all the extra weight. We'd already seen five of the larger boats pass by us, even though each was filled beyond capacity with what seemed to be over a hundred people. I wondered how many more were crossing the dangerous straits between Cuba and Florida every day. In our boat I had counted seventeen men sitting on the back deck with us plus a family of eight inside the little wheelhouse with the captain. Most of us had claimed spots to ride out the increasingly bumpy boat ride, with Nani and Isabel's mom sheltering under a small overhang while Isabel and I chose to be closer to the railing.

"Wind is really picking up," Isabel said a little louder than normal, to be heard over the waves crashing against the boat.

"Yep." I wiped my glasses and pointed to the dark storm clouds in the distance. "And I think things might get worse. Look over there. There were some lightning flashes, too."

"Hopefully, it'll blow by before we get to it," Isabel said, taking a seat on the floor.

I tried to gauge the wind's direction and looked back out at the storm. I wondered if Rodrigo had been caught in it.

"Calculating the percentages?" Isabel teased.

"No . . ." I sat down next to her. "Sort of. The wind is coming from the west and the storm is northeast of us, so we could miss it. Might just get the tail end."

The boat suddenly lurched forward, knocking a few people off balance, and Isabel clutched her stomach.

Around us a few people were already seasick, but so far, I felt fine. I glanced back and saw Nani sleeping with her head resting against the wall and Isabel's mom next to her looking a little green.

"Can't believe Nani is out like that," I said in amazement.

"My mom gave her un calmante when we boarded. It usually knocks her out." She took a deep breath and held her stomach again as the boat continued bouncing up and down. "Let's talk about something else. Tell me about that captain at the port. How's he going to help your mom?"

"Oh, yeah. You're not going to believe it, but we happened to run into him at the Fontán. My mother says they were best friends when they were young . . . kinda like us." I pulled out the passport from my back pocket and flipped it open, looking for Osvaldo Cepero's message. "He said he wrote a number in here somewhere for her to call and he would . . ."

Teo's photograph stared back at me.

He wasn't smiling in the picture, but somehow, I could hear his voice and his laugh in my head.

A wave of guilt, larger than any real wave out in the ocean, washed over me.

Teo should've been here, not me.

I glanced over at Isabel's dad leaning against the railing a few feet away from us, talking to one of the other men. He hadn't said much to me since leaving Cuba and I could only imagine how much he hated the idea of saving someone that he blamed for his son's death.

"Héctor?" Isabel touched my knee as I put the passport back in my pocket.

"I shouldn't have come," I mumbled. "I should've stayed in Cuba with my mom."

Isabel scoffed. "Well, that's a nice thank-you after we risked everything to bring you with us."

"No . . . I mean . . . I appreciate what you did. Convincing your parents and all." I bit my lip. "But I know how they feel about me and my family. And now I'm here and Teo's not. It's not fair."

"You're right, it's not fair," Isabel's father said, having walked up behind me. "I wish Teo could be here, too." He sighed, crouching down next to me. "But he'd be glad that at least you're here." He put a hand on my shoulder. "And I wasn't about to leave a big part of Teo's life behind . . . a part of our family behind."

"I didn't convince anyone," Isabel explained. "My dad was the one who came up with the idea of you pretending to be Teo."

I looked up at Isabel's dad. There was so much I wanted to tell him, but no words came out.

He crouched down and gave me a hug. "I know," he said as my body collapsed in his arms. "I know."

And I truly believed he did.

He knew how much I loved Teo and the whole family. He knew that my biggest wish was for Teo to be here and not me. And he knew how much I needed to be welcomed back into their family.

And now I knew that he cared enough to risk everything for me.

"All right now." He pulled away and ruffled my hair. "How about you make yourself useful and ask the captain for some water for Sara." He gazed over at Isabel's mom. "I don't think she's doing well with these swells."

I popped up, ready to be of service. "Of course. Do you need anything else?"

"Water will be fine," he said. "Just explain that it's for your mother, who is sick."

"I'll go with him," Isabel said, trying to find her balance while the boat continued to rock and bounce. "I think a little water might help me, too."

We walked over to the wheelhouse door and knocked. Through the small window, a woman motioned for us to come in.

"Eh . . . Señor Capitán . . ." I stopped talking as I stepped inside, gagging at the overwhelming odor of bile and vomit in the room. I quickly noticed two little girls who looked extremely pale resting on a small cot and an old man sitting in the corner holding a bucket in front of him. There were nine people in a space that would normally be tight for four. Several of them were obviously very seasick, just like some of the men outside.

"What is it?" The captain looked back from the helm and scowled. "I'm busy."

I couldn't speak, still trying to recover from how bad the place reeked. A couple of the windows were open, but the room was warm and stuffy. Outside we might be more exposed to the rain, but at least the wind carried away most of the smells.

"Agua," Isabel said, pinching her nose as she spoke. "We need some for our mother."

The captain kept his eyes fixed on the horizon. "Can one of you help her out?"

"Over here." A man that looked to be the father of the little girls moved over, revealing a small sink right behind him. "We're the Cabrera family from Cienfuegos. Your family is outside, right?"

"Yes, sir," I said as I took a small plastic cup from a bin by the sink.

"We're twins," Isabel added.

I glanced back at her, unsure if we had to keep pretending.

She gave me a slight shrug, but Señor Cabrera didn't seem to notice.

"That's nice," he replied, taking the cup from my hand and filling it up. "My girls are a year apart." He handed me the cup. "Do you think your mother would feel better inside?" he asked. "There's not much room but—"

"Hold on!" the captain shouted as the boat began to tilt, and I stumbled backward against Isabel. Through the front window I could see the horizon shifting as if we were riding a roller coaster, slowly going higher and higher over a huge ocean swell.

And then it all changed as the boat felt like it was free-falling down the other side.

"This is going to get rough!" the captain shouted as a few people screamed from the outside deck.

"Let the women and children inside," the old man in the corner demanded. "We don't care how crowded it gets in here or what my son paid you for."

"Agreed!" The captain pointed to me. "Bring in your family. Warn the men outside that they need to brace themselves. There's another huge swell up ahead."

I opened the door and could feel how much the wind had shifted in the last few seconds.

"Evelio!" I called out to Isabel's father, forgetting that he was supposed to be my father, too. "Get them inside!" I pointed to Isabel, who was already coaxing Nani to get up.

He nodded and helped Isabel's mom stand as the boat seemed to bounce up and down while simultaneously swaying from side to side.

"The captain says for women and children to go inside!" I yelled over the howling wind and drizzling rain. "I'll stay out here with you," I said, holding the wheelhouse door open.

"No!" he shouted back. "I need someone to take care of them."

"But . . ."

He shook his head as the rain started coming down in horizontal sheets and pelted everyone outside. "I need you to help them. I can manage out here."

"Get inside, son," Señor Cabrera said, stepping outside. "I'll help your father. You can assist the captain with as much as you can."

"Por favor," Isabel's dad said, pleading with me to go in.

Before I could respond, things went from bad to worse.

"We've lost an engine!" the captain hollered. "HANG TIGHT!"

The boat was approaching a huge wave at an awkward

angle and all the men outside were holding on to different parts of the boat to brace themselves for impact. I grabbed Isabel's father by his shirt to pull him into the wheelhouse, but instead the force of the wave knocked us both onto the deck as water slammed across the boat.

I was drenched from head to toe, but before I could stand up another huge wave crashed over the side of the boat.

I could feel myself tumbling across the deck, being swept toward the edge of the boat, when a huge arm grabbed me. A man, holding on to one of the support poles for the small overhang, had stopped me from going overboard. Before I knew it, someone else wrapped his arms around me as we all braced for the next wave.

"¡Aguántate!" the man yelled as I held on to him with all my might.

The boat continued to be slammed with wave after wave for what felt like forever, but was probably less than ten minutes.

And then the rain stopped and the clouds began to part.

"Héctor! Papi!" Isabel stood in the doorway of the wheelhouse, her face full of fear.

The boat was still swaying violently from side to side, but somehow the seas were calming. It was as if the ocean had given us its final punch and then simply given up.

I looked around as each of the men near me regained his balance and stood up.

I began to chuckle.

My laughter didn't make sense, but I couldn't help it.

We looked like wet rats, but we'd survived. My eyes found Isabel's dad standing a few feet away from me, but he didn't look relieved. He was staring at something on the deck.

I glanced down at my feet and any sense of victory over the ocean disappeared.

Water was pooling around my shoes.

The boat was sinking.

29

EVERYTHING THAT WASN'T bolted down had been tossed off the boat. We were all bailing with cups or buckets or whatever we could find. The only good thing was that the sea was now calm and the sun was trying to break through the densely clouded sky.

"This isn't enough," the captain announced, holding a bright yellow duffel. "Some of you are going to have to get off. I have a raft." He looked around at all of us on the deck working to keep the boat afloat. "It should be the heaviest men, but you can decide among yourselves. It'll hold four or five of you."

The men all started talking.

I looked over at the man who had held on to me during the storm and the worn-out faces of the others. I had no idea if they were really criminals. They might have been in prison, but that didn't mean much. My father had, too, and his only crime had been speaking out against the government and trying to leave for a better life.

"We can't abandon them out here with the sharks," I said. "They'll die."

Isabel's dad put his hand on my shoulder. "I don't think that's what he means," he said. "You'll tow the raft, right?"

Everyone waited for the captain's response.

"We'll have to go a lot slower and we'll risk running out of gas or getting caught in another storm." The captain looked over at Señor Cabrera. "But I have a long enough rope."

"We have to try," Señor Cabrera answered. "We're in this together."

The man who'd held on to me during the storm stepped forward. "I'll go. I used to be in the navy," he said. "I can handle it out there if you have to let us go."

I took a long look at him. He wasn't particularly tall, but you could tell he was strong, with biceps that pushed against the seams of the short-sleeve shirt he was wearing.

"Good. What's your name?" the captain asked.

"Aguero," the man responded.

"I'll volunteer as well," Isabel's dad said to the captain. "But my family stays with you no matter what."

"No." The captain shook his head. "You stay with your family. These men are out here by themselves. . . . It's up to them." He scanned the group. "Or Aguero will choose."

Four more men quickly volunteered, and soon the yellow raft was in the water with a long rope connecting it to our boat.

We were now plodding along again, but removing some

of the additional weight seemed to have stopped us from sinking.

For now.

What should have taken eight or nine hours was likely going to take twelve or more. At this rate we'd get to Key West after dark, but I didn't care. Once we spotted lights in the distance, we'd know we were safe.

Isabel sighed as she stared out at the horizon with the sun dipping lower in the sky.

"We'll be there soon," I said as we both leaned against the railing. "Probably a few more hours."

"Not soon enough," she replied, and then inched closer to me. "But until we get there, I think you should continue to say that you're Teo," she said in a hushed voice. "Don't forget."

"Why?" I gave her a quizzical stare, not understanding why it still mattered. "We're not in Cuba anymore."

"Yeah, but what if something happens and we get taken back?" she countered. "One of these people could rat us out. Get us all in trouble."

I swallowed the lump that had formed in my throat. It hadn't even occurred to me that after everything we'd gone through, we might still wind up where we started.

"Nah, you're wrong." I shook my head. "That can't happen."

"Really?" She struck a classic Isabel pose with her hands on her hips and her head tilted to the side. "Do you want to take that chance?"

"No," I relented. "Guess not."

"You still have his passport, right?" she asked. "You should probably give it to my parents."

Teo's passport. I had forgotten all about it.

"Oh no!" I pulled it out from my pocket, soaking wet.

A bad feeling formed in the pit of my stomach as I carefully peeled back each of the soggy pages.

On the fourth page, in the upper right corner, I saw the smudged remnants of blue ink.

"No, no!" I blew on the paper as if doing so would make the washed-out numbers reappear.

"What is it?" Isabel looked at the page. "Was that the phone number for your mother?"

I nodded, trying to angle the passport to see if I could decipher what the numbers had been.

"You didn't memorize it or anything?" she asked.

I shook my head in frustration as my stomach churned. "Does it look like I memorized the number?"

It was all too much.

I shoved the passport into Isabel's hands, leaned over the railing, and threw up.

Isabel stood silently by my side as I continued to retch. When I was done, I sat on the deck floor . . . exhausted.

Isabel knelt next to me. "Can I—"

"No," I cut her off. There was nothing anyone could do. I'd let our family down. I wrapped my arms around my knees and pulled them close to my chest. I wanted to be alone, but I couldn't on this crowded boat. So I stared out at the sea, trying to think of ways Mamá could still reach out to her friend.

About an hour later the sound of the engine sputtering tore me away from my thoughts.

"Something's happening," Isabel said, having sat silently next to me the whole time.

The wheelhouse door opened and the captain stepped outside.

"Well, that's it," he announced. "We're out of gas."

"¿Y ahora?" one of the men asked. "What do we do?"

The captain shrugged. "We wait. I already sent out a distress call, and hopefully somebody . . . anybody . . . will come across us soon and give us a tow." He looked out toward the raft. "We should pull those men closer to the boat. Let them know what's going on."

"How far are we from Key West?" Isabel's dad asked.

"About halfway there," the captain replied. "So, it might be a long night. Let's hope for good weather."

"Halfway?" I was stunned. "That's it?"

"This isn't good," Isabel whispered.

"I know," I answered, realizing that being halfway there meant that it was possible that a Cuban ship might get to us first. Would they tow us back to Mariel?

We drifted for hours over the dark ocean waters. Bobbing back and forth, with the raft tied close enough that we could still see it even though passing clouds covered the moon.

Most people on board were either sleeping or quietly staring out at the darkness that surrounded us. The only noise that cracked the stillness of the night was snoring or the occasional sound of someone being sick over the side of the boat.

Isabel and I silently stared up at the sky, searching the constellations for a shooting star to make a wish on.

My biggest wish was to have my family and Teo with us right now. But that was an impossibility. A more practical wish would be that we simply make it to the U.S. without any more problems.

I thought about Rodrigo and hoped he had made it through the storm okay. I imagined him lying on the deck of his boat, floating on these same dark waters, and looking up at these same twinkling stars. Then again, he might already be in Key West and thinking that I'm somewhere in Cuba taking care of Mamá.

Mamá.

I wondered what she was doing right now. Had she made it back to Cuqui's house? There was no guarantee that Cuqui would even help her. Plus, that was my job. I was supposed to help her and, instead, she was now alone.

I was alone.

Rodrigo was alone.

Our family of three had been broken down into single components. We were each on our own.

"Gives you a new perspective, doesn't it?" Isabel's dad joined us in our stargazing. "A reminder of how small we really are in this big universe."

"Like a speck of sand on the beach," Isabel replied, continuing to scan the heavens.

"Mm-hmm." Isabel's dad leaned back on his elbows. "See those three stars right there in a line?" He pointed up at the sky. "That's Orion the Hunter's belt, but it now reminds me of the three of you. My three kids."

I sighed.

The three of us . . . except now there were only two. Another group that had been broken.

"Teo would've loved to be here," I said wistfully.

Isabel chuckled. "He would've thought this was one big adventure. He wouldn't be worried about being stranded in the middle of the ocean."

"Eso es verdad," Isabel's dad agreed. "That boy had a traveler's heart. He wanted to see the world."

For the first time the thought of Teo brought a smile to my face instead of a tear. "You know, he'd probably want to go through that storm just to come out here and see if there were more stars than back home."

"Yep, and once he saw them, he'd say he now needed to compare the stars over Switzerland or New York or somewhere else to these," Isabel added. "He was always talking to me about going to far-off places."

"Me too," I said, thinking back to our conversation about searching for the bluest sky. It was now up to me to find it. The one thing I knew was that I no longer found Cuba's sky as perfect as I once had. After everything that happened, my perspective had changed. Isabel's dad had been right; experiences can shape how you see and remember things.

"Do you two know that all these stars and constellations have classic Greek stories behind them?" Isabel's dad sat up. "Why don't I tell you a few to pass the time? There's one about Gemini, the twins, and—"

"Papi," Isabel whined. "Do we really need a literature lesson now?"

"There's always time for a good story, don't you think, Héctor?" he asked, giving me a little nudge.

"Oh sure." Isabel rolled her eyes. "Ask the one who loves school if he wants to hear a lecture on Greek mythology."

"I'd love to hear a story," I said with a smirk. "In fact, I'd like to hear several, because it's not like we're going—"

"¡Un bote! ¡Un bote!" someone shouted, pointing to the horizon on the other side of the boat.

I jumped up as everyone crowded around to see if it was true. Squeezing between people, I could see a couple of lights in the distance.

Everyone on board began to yell and wave their arms . . . not that anyone would see or hear us from so far away.

The captain came running out of the wheelhouse. In his hand he had a white flare gun that he pointed up at the pitch-black sky.

Isabel's father put his arms around me and Isabel as the

bright orange flame from the flare rocketed up toward the stars.

"¡Qué bello!" Nani gasped as she and Isabel's mother joined us.

The captain then rushed back to the wheelhouse and sounded the horn.

We all held our breath for a few seconds.

Then came the reply.

In the distance the other ship responded with a blast of its own.

Everyone on board cheered.

We were being rescued, but now the question was . . . rescued by who?

Isabel reached over and held my hand. I could feel her trembling.

Then her father clasped my other hand.

"Here we go," he whispered as Isabel's mother and Nani clasped hands, too.

The five of us now stood together facing the darkness and the approaching lights.

As a family.

30

THE BRIGHT SEARCHLIGHT reflected off the water. In its glow I could see the white ship with a red stripe approaching and the words U.S. COAST GUARD written along its hull.

A sense of relief washed over me and I wanted to dance with joy.

Isabel must have felt the same, as she was bouncing on her toes, a huge smile on her face.

"Gracias, Dios mío," Isabel's mom said as several of the men around us whooped and hollered with excitement.

As the Coast Guard cutter drew closer, our captain announced that he had radioed the vessel and formulated a plan. The Americans would pick up the men in the raft, fill our boat with gas, and then escort us to Key West to make sure we didn't have any other issues.

Isabel's dad gave his wife a slight nod and quickly made the sign of the cross. Their prayers had been answered. Our rescuers would be taking us to Key West. To safety. To a new life.

Within minutes, there were two Americans wearing all-white uniforms inspecting the engine, filling the gas tank, and preparing our boat for the rest of the journey.

Once the captain restarted the engine, the Americans returned to their ship and we were on our way again.

Except now it was like traveling under the protection of a watchful giant.

We felt like nothing could harm us, and so Isabel and I fell asleep leaning against each other out on the deck.

Excited voices woke me up just as the sun broke the horizon. Before even opening my eyes, I knew what it was.

Land.

We had made it to Key West.

We had made it to freedom.

"¡Despiértate! ¡Despiértate!" I shook Isabel's arm, causing her to stir. "We're here!"

She rubbed her eyes and sat up.

I took in the view, but it wasn't very impressive. There was nothing big or magnificent about what I saw. I knew we weren't going to Miami directly, that would come later, but I'd still expected more. From what I could see, there were only a few buildings near the port, and it just reminded me of a smaller Mariel, with the same horde of boats surrounding it.

But as we got closer, I started to feel butterflies in my stomach.

I realized that the physical size of the port didn't matter as much as what it represented. It was the doorway into the

United States. Everything I had ever heard about the country, the good and the bad, lay just beyond.

Everyone except the captain was now outside with us. Several of the men had even climbed on the roof of the wheelhouse to get a better view of our new country.

It was early in the morning, with the sky still slightly overcast, but I could see soldiers in fatigues patrolling the area and directing people where to go. Isabel's mother had pulled a hairbrush from her purse and was trying to braid Isabel's hair. I had tucked in my shirt and tried to make myself look as presentable as possible, but none of us looked good at this point and we smelled even worse. No matter what, we wouldn't be making a good first impression.

The Coast Guard cutter that had escorted us to shore pulled up to the dock first, letting all of its rescued passengers disembark. I watched as about thirty people, probably from other boats that had sunk on the journey, took their first steps in the U.S.

Then the five from our boat got out.

A few of them looked exhausted and bedraggled, but not Aguero.

After taking a few steps onto the dock, he raised his arms over his head and spun around. "¡Libertad!" he proclaimed, pumping his fists in the air. "Freedom!"

People along the docks and in the surrounding boats cheered.

"Guess he's happy not to be in jail anymore," I said, smiling.

"He was never in jail," Isabel's father replied. "He's gay. That's why they kicked him out of the country. Now he's free to be who he is."

"Oh." I took another look at Aguero, who was walking toward a small tent at the end of the pier. Again, things weren't what they seemed.

"We're up next," Isabel said as our boat pulled forward, closer to the port.

A soldier wearing camouflage gear helped tie the boat to the dock and then raised his hands to get our attention. "Primero, familias," the soldier instructed, pointing to the Cabrera family and us. "Everyone else follows them."

As the Cabrera family lined up, a woman with short brown hair and big glasses joined the soldier and stepped aboard the boat. She had a clipboard and was filling out papers and giving one to each adult in the family. One by one, as they received their documents, they were let off the boat.

"Héctor." Isabel's mother took my hand in hers. "We won't leave you. You keep telling them that you're Teo and—"

"I can't," I replied. "Not here."

"He's right," Isabel's father replied. "It's best to be honest with them."

"Are you two crazy?" Isabel threw up her hands. "Or am I the only one who has any chispa in this family? You can't be honest with government officials, no matter what country they're with." She shook her head. "We'll get in trouble for lying, and then what?"

"No one needs to know how I got on board," I explained. "I'll just say they put me on here at the last minute."

"Exactly." Isabel's father nodded in agreement. "We'll say that we're extended family and have agreed to be responsible for you."

Isabel shook her head. "And if they don't care and take him away?"

Isabel's dad looked at me. He couldn't guarantee that wouldn't happen.

I bit my lip. I might have to be by myself in a foreign country for a while, but eventually my mother would get word to Rodrigo or my father and they'd come looking for me. It was the only way.

"I've always pretended to be someone else out in public. . . . I don't want to do that anymore. I want to be Héctor. . . ." I glanced at Isabel. "Teo and Isabel's best friend."

"Then it's settled," Isabel's dad said, ushering us forward to the dock, where the woman with the clipboard was finishing up with the last of the Cabrera family. "We say the truth . . . mostly."

"Bienvenidos a los Estados Unidos . . . el país de la libertad," the woman said, speaking to us in perfect Cuban Spanish. By the way she was dressed and her attitude, I guessed that she'd been in the U.S. for a while. "I'm María, a volunteer with the Red Cross, and I'm here to help you get your papers ready to be processed. You are all one family, correct?"

"Extended family," Isabel's dad said. He then pointed to each of us, stating our relationship. "This is Sara . . . my wife;

Nani . . . Sara's grandmother; Isabel . . . our daughter; and Héctor . . . who is like a son to us."

María looked at me. "Like a son . . . but not blood-related?"

"No," I answered. "I came alone because my brother was put on another boat and our father already lives in Miami."

"I see." She wrote something down on the paper.

Isabel's mother grabbed my hand as if María were going to try to forcefully take me away.

María looked up and handed me a small card. "That's happening more and more often," she said, giving me a small smile. "Thousands of families have been arriving on different boats. We'll try to keep you all together until your family turns up. Now, go wait on the dock."

I nodded and stepped out of the boat. I felt my legs wobble for a moment as they got used to being on dry land.

It was official.

I had arrived in the United States . . . while others I loved . . .

I glanced up at the clouds.

"He's here, you know," Isabel said, stepping onto the dock next to me. "With us. Watching from above."

I looked at her as she stared up at the sky and took a deep breath. She knew exactly what I'd been thinking.

"Héctor!" Isabel's father called out. "Help us with Nani."

I turned and extended my hand as Isabel's parents helped guide Nani off the boat. Then the two of them joined us on the dock.

"Go to the front, where there is a line for the buses." María motioned toward a large, empty parking lot. "You'll be taken to the arrival center, where you can shower and get some food. They'll finish the interviews there. . . . Just don't lose those cards," she said, turning her attention to the group of men on board.

We did as we were told and walked slowly with Nani in tow. At the base of the pier, another soldier was directing people from some of the other boats to different waiting areas. He raised a hand to stop us and checked the cards we were holding. He smiled, ordered a nearby soldier to do something, then pointed to Isabel and me, asking us a question.

We stared at him with blank looks on our faces, not understanding a word he had said.

Then he pretended to be drinking something and uttered the magic words understood in any language . . . *Coca-Cola*.

Our eyes widened, unsure if he was actually offering us the drink. It was something I'd always heard about but had never actually tasted. In Cuba it was a luxury that few people could afford, and Abuela always said it was the poisoned drink of Yankee imperialism.

Isabel's father knew a little English and answered the soldier, who pointed to a nearby line as a much younger soldier brought over a wheelchair for Nani.

"¡Yo no soy una inválida!" Nani protested, pushing away the chair. "Yo no soy tan vieja que no puedo caminar."

"It's not because you're old or you can't walk," Isabel's mother explained. "They're just being nice."

"Hmph!" She clicked her tongue in disgust. "Una silla de ruedas."

"No, Nani." I spun the chair around. "It's not a wheelchair, it's a throne for the queen of dragons."

Her eyes narrowed as she stared at the chair. "¿Un trono para la reina de los dragones?"

Isabel nodded.

Nani smiled. "Está bien," she said, agreeing to sit in the chair. "Por ti."

"The other soldier . . ." I looked around, noticing that the soldier who had been talking to us had disappeared. "Didn't he say something about Coca-Colas?"

"He said we need to go wait over there." Isabel's father pushed Nani toward the last line as we followed behind them.

About fifty yards away I could see a chain-link fence that separated the parking lot from the outside world. There was a small crowd on the other side waving American and Cuban flags and cheering for us. The complete opposite of the angry mobs we'd seen when leaving Cuba.

"But . . ." Isabel looked somewhat disappointed. "I thought the soldier was telling us something about Coca-Colas."

"He was." Her father smiled. "You'll see."

Within a minute the soldier was hurrying back to us with two red cans with a white logo on the side. Even from a distance, I knew what it was.

He handed one to Isabel and one to me, before rushing over to direct another large group of men who were coming off a huge shrimp boat.

I felt the coldness of the can in my hand and listened to the hiss as I popped it open. Isabel had already pulled back the metal ring and was about to take her first sip. I quickly did the same and closed my eyes as the bubbles carried the sweet, syrupy taste of the soda down my throat.

It was the best thing I'd ever had.

Isabel giggled as she took a second large gulp and clenched her chest as the strong fizz seemed to surprise her. "I love it!" she said to me. "America is wonderful."

"Two lines, please. The buses will be here soon." A man in green army fatigues tapped Isabel's father on the shoulder. "Dos líneas." He motioned for us to go start a new line, where more people would filter in behind us.

As we pushed Nani to the front, I noticed a man in the small crowd jumping up and down by the chain-link fence.

I pushed back my glasses and strained my eyes.

"HÉCTOR!" he shouted. "HÉCTOR!"

Isabel gave me a little nudge. "Is that your—"

"Father," I said, recognizing him from the pictures.

A flood of mixed emotions hit me all at once. I was glad that he'd found me, but at the same time I didn't really know him. Isabel's dad was more of a father to me growing up than the man on the other side of the fence. I wasn't sure what to do.

Isabel's father waved at my dad and then turned to me.

"Héctor, run over there and let him know that they're taking us to a nearby center where they're processing everyone. Tell him to meet us there."

I handed Isabel my can of Coca-Cola and walked toward my father. I had so many thoughts running through my head. He hadn't seen me in years and was still able to spot me in a crowd . . . and I wasn't even looking like my normal self. That had to be a good sign.

"IVETTE!" My father waved his arm again. "IVETTE!"

He was calling for my mother.

My heart fell.

He must think she is somewhere in line with Isabel and her family. I'd have to tell him that I'd left her back in Cuba and that I'd even lost the phone number of the person who might be able to get her out. He was going to be so upset and disappointed. How could he—

"HURRY!" My father was now looking back at the parking lot behind him.

I picked up my pace, thinking that the buses must be about to arrive and that I had to get to him quickly.

Then I froze when I saw who was racing toward him.

I couldn't believe my eyes.

I broke into a full-fledged sprint, racing toward Mamá.

"Héctor! Oh, Héctor!" She thrust her fingers through the chain-link face as I collided against it. Our fingers interlocked.

"H-h-how . . . ?" I couldn't even get the words out. "You were there . . . and now you're here."

She had tears streaming down her cheeks as she kissed my fingertips. My father had an arm around her shoulder.

"Osvaldo," she answered. "He saw me watching your boat leave and was able to get me on one of the large shrimp boats." She squeezed my hand through the fence. "I was so worried when we hit the rough weather, and then when your boat didn't show up . . . I thought the worst."

"What about Rodrigo?" I asked.

"He's here, too. He's waiting for you by the airplane hangar, where they take everyone . . . in case you showed up there."

He'd made it. We'd all made it. My family was whole. . . .

"Héctor!" Isabel called me as the buses arrived. "Come back!"

I glanced over to where everyone was standing in line.

"Go," Mamá said. "Stay with them until we can get you out. It shouldn't be long."

I nodded and ran back toward Isabel and the others. As I got closer to them, I could see that Isabel had the biggest smile and her parents were waving at Mamá and Papá.

It was all too much.

My chest swelled with emotion and I had to pause to catch my breath.

I suddenly realized that I now had two families and two countries. The ones I'd been born into and the ones I'd chosen for myself.

My thoughts immediately turned to Teo, and I looked up to the heavens wishing he could be here, but feeling like he already was. It was then that I noticed that there was no longer a cloud in the sky.

Teo had said a limitless sky meant limitless possibilities.

A smile slipped across my face.

It might have simply been a matter of perspective, but, at least for that single moment, I felt sure I'd found the bluest sky of all.

ACKNOWLEDGMENTS

First and foremost, I'd like to thank God for blessing me with an amazing family and a group of friends who have become part of my family. One of the themes of this book is how the bonds of friendship and family are often intertwined, and that is the case in my own life. I was fortunate enough to be born into an incredible family, but I only need to look at my parents' lifelong friends (many whose names appear in this book) and my own friends to know that family is more than those who share a bloodline. A family is also crafted from those with whom you share the big and small moments that touch your heart. I am eternally grateful to all of you for your love and support!

A book requires a team effort, and I am so very fortunate to have a multitude of talented people in my corner. Thank you isn't enough for my amazing agent, Jen Rofé, who champions my work like no one else. For dear friends and early readers Danielle Joseph, Meg Medina, Jennifer Nielsen, Jenny Torres Sanchez, Victor Triay, and Erich de la Fuente, thank you all for your valuable feedback and advice. Mil gracias to my extraordinary editor, Nancy Siscoe, who enhances each character and storyline by providing the very best guidance on how to make the story better. Many thanks to the copy editors, designers, publicists, sales and marketing teams, and everyone at Knopf who has helped get this book into the best shape possible. My deepest admiration and thanks to the teachers, librarians, and booksellers whose tireless efforts place books into the hands of young readers.

Finally, thank you to all those who shared with me their experiences of fleeing Cuba through Mariel. May this book honor your stories and those of all immigrants who seek their own bluest sky.

SOME SPANISH WORDS AND PHRASES USED IN *THE BLUEST SKY*

abuela: grandmother
abuelo: grandfather
acto de repudio: act of repudiation
adiós: goodbye
¿adónde se metió ese hombre?: where did that man go?
agua: water
aguántate: hold on
ahora estoy sala'o: (slang) now I'm jinxed
alabao: an expression of surprise, like "oh my!"
apagón: blackout
apúrate: hurry up
aquí: here
arroz con pollo: a traditional dish of chicken and rice
asere: (slang) bro
atención: attention
¡ay, qué gruñón!: what a grouch!
ayer: yesterday
ayúdanos: help us
basta: enough
basura: garbage
bienvenidos: welcome
bienvenidos a los Estados Unidos . . . el país de la libertad: welcome to the United States . . . the land of liberty
buen sabor: good flavor
buena suerte: good luck
buenos días: good morning
cada loco con su tema: an idiom similar to "to each his own"; the direct translation is "each crazed person has his own theme"
café con leche: coffee with milk
calabaza: pumpkin
¡cállense!: be quiet!
¡cálmense!: calm down!
chispa: spark; spunk
cierra la puerta: close the door
claro: of course
¡claro que me lo dijo!: of course he/she told me!
¿cómo te fue el día hoy?: how did your day go today?
compañero: comrade; companion
con toda mi alma: with all my heart
creo que es tu hijo . . . apúrate: I think it's your son . . . hurry up
cuando tú vas, ya yo vengo: an idiom similar to "I am one step ahead of you"; the direct translation is "when you go, I am already coming"
cuidado: careful
dale: go ahead
¿de qué son estas?: what are these?
de verdad: really
déjalo: leave it/him alone
delegada: delegate
descarado: shameless
¡despiértate!: wake up!
dime: tell me
¡Dios mío!: oh my God!
disculpa la interrupción: excuse the interruption

dormilón: sleepyhead
dormiste: slept
dos líneas: two lines
dos minutos: two minutes
echada pa'lante: (slang) pushy
El Canal de Todos: The Channel
  for All
el partido: the party (referring to a
  political party)
el tiempo se va volando: time flies
¿en serio?: seriously?
entienden: they understand
entren: come in
es todo por la izquierda: (slang)
  under the table or illegal; the direct
  translation is "it's all to the left"
escoria: scum
¿ese?: that one?
eso es verdad: that is true
eso se cae de la mata: an idiom
  meaning that something is
  obvious; the direct translation is
  "that falls from the bush"
¿esos son tus hijos?: are those your
  sons?
espérate: wait
está bien: it's fine
está en el horno: it's in the oven
estás loco / ¿estás loca?: you are
  crazy / are you crazy?
estás tarde: you are late
flaco: skinny
gracias: thank you
grande por gusto: big for nothing
guayabera: a type of men's shirt
gusano: worm
hacía las mejores croquetas de
  bacalao: made the best cod
  croquettes
hermano: brother
hola: hello
idiota: idiot
inspección de varones: inspection of
  boys

la Asamblea Nacional: the National
  Assembly
las cosas están cambiando: things
  are changing
le ronca: a shortened form of the
  idiom le ronca el mango, meaning
  that something is extreme; the
  direct translation is "it snores"
¡levántate!: get up!
¡libertad!: freedom!
lo mismo que siempre: the same as
  always
lo siento tanto: I'm so sorry
locura: craziness
los pobres: poor people
malcriado: spoiled; a brat
más nunca: never again
metralla: (slang) trash
mi amor: my love
mi familión: (slang) my big family
mi hijo / mijo: my son
mira, no empieces con eso: look,
  don't start with that
mira a quién nos encontramos: look
  who we found
mis estimados pasajeros: my
  esteemed passengers
nada: nothing
nadie: no one
nadie nos está engañando, mijo: no
  one is tricking us, my son
¿necesitas ayuda?: need help?
ni lo piense: don't even think about it
niños: boys; children
no me meto: I'm not getting involved
no sé: I don't know
no seas mal educado: don't be so
  impolite
no te pongas malcriado: don't act
  spoiled/bratty
no te preocupes: don't worry
no te sorprendas: don't be surprised
no va a dar su brazo a torcer: an
  idiom meaning "he is not going

to budge"; the direct translation is "he will not allow his arm to be twisted"

nombre: name

noviecita: little girlfriend

oye: listen

¡paren!: stop!

¿pasó algo?: something happen?

perdón: pardon me

perdona la demora: pardon the delay

permiso: excuse me

pero espérate un minuto: but wait a minute

pero qué haces aquí: but what are you doing here?

pero tú sí: but you did?

perro que ladra no muerde: an idiom meaning "barking dogs don't bite"

pesada: (slang) unlikable

plátano: plantain

por favor: please

por fin: at last

por supuesto: of course

por ti: for you

primera guagua: first bus

primero, familias: first, families

primos: cousins

¿qué?: what?

qué abandono: what abandonment

qué bello: how beautiful

qué honor: what an honor

qué olor tan sabroso: what a tasty smell

¿qué pasa?: what's up?

¡qué peste!: how stinky!

qué rico: how tasty

que se vayan: let them leave

qué sed tenía: how thirsty I was

qué silencio: how silent

que somos buenos comunistas: that we are good Communists

¿qué tú haces?: what are you doing?

¿qué tú miras?: what are you looking at?

que viva la revolución: long live the revolution

¿quién habla?: who's speaking?

¿quieres una empanada?: do you want an empanada?

quizás para ti: maybe for you

ratones: mice

representando la patria: representing the homeland

saca los gusanos: get rid of the worms

salgan de los rincones: get out of the corners

sálvese quien pueda: save yourself

se lo comieron todo: did you eat it all?

siéntate: sit down

siento mucho lo de Teo: I'm so sorry about Teo

silencio: silence

sin ningún problema: no problem

solitario: solitaire

soy Isabel: I am Isabel

soy la campeona: I am the champion

¿te caíste?: you fell?

te lo dije: I told you

telenovela: soap opera

ten cuidado: be careful

tía: aunt

tienes toda la razón: you are totally correct

tíos: uncles

¿todo bien? / todo está bien: everything okay? / everything is okay

tonterías: silly stuff

¿trajiste los limones?: did you bring the lemons?

tramposos: cheaters

tranquila, compañera: relax, comrade

tranquilo: relax

trompazo: a huge punch (usually in the nose)

tu otra mitad: your other half

tu papá es un gusano: your father is a worm

tú también: you too

un bote: a boat

un calmante: a sedative

un flechazo: (slang) an arrow, such as one delivered by Cupid; a sudden romantic crush.

un trono para la reina de los dragones: a throne for the queen of dragons

una niña tonta: a silly or dumb girl

una silla de ruedas: a wheelchair

uña y carne: an idiom meaning "joined at the hip"; the direct translation is "nail and flesh"

vámonos: let's go

vamos: we go

vete de aquí: get out of here

¿viste la luna?: did you see the moon?

y ahora: and now

y cuidado con cómo me hablas: and be careful how you speak to me

¿y dónde está Teo?: and where is Teo?

y es un asco adentro: and it's gross inside

y tú: and you

yo: me

yo lo sé: I know

yo no soy tan vieja que no puedo caminar: I'm not so old that I can't walk

yo no soy una inválida: I'm not an invalid

yo no te estoy amenazando, querida: I'm not threatening you, my dear

yo quiero: I want

yo te quiero también: I love you too